what we once believed

Caitlin Press Inc.
8100 Alderwood Road,
Halfmoon Bay, BC V0N 1Y1
www.caitlin-press.com

Text and cover design by Vici Johnstone.
Cover image sourced from Unsplash. Photo Azrul Aziz.
Edited by John Gould.
Printed in Canada

Caitlin Press Inc. acknowledges financial support from the Government of Canada and the Canada Council for the Arts, and the Province of British Columbia through the British Columbia Arts Council and the Book Publisher's Tax Credit.

Library and Archives Canada Cataloguing in Publication

MacPherson, Andrea, author
      What we once believed / Andrea MacPherson.

ISBN 978-1-987915-32-7 (softcover)

      I. Title.
PS8575.P465W43 2017   C813'.6   C2016-907710-1

what
we once
believed

andrea
macpherson

CAITLIN PRESS

previously published books by Andrea MacPherson

Ellipses (Signature Editions, 2014)
Away (Signature Editions, 2008)
Beyond the Blue (Random House, 2007)
Natural Disasters (Palimpsest Press, 2007)
When She Was Electric (Raincoast, 2003)

for Nora
to the moon and back, always.

and in memory of my grandfather, Tom Rowbottom,
the original storyteller.

Chorus
by Catherine Barnett

So who mothers the mothers
who tend the hallways of mothers,
the spill of mothers, the smell of mothers,
who mend the eyes of mothers,
the lies of mothers scared
to turn on lights in basements
filled with mothers called by mothers in the dark,
the kin of mothers, the gin of mothers,
mothers out on bail,
who mothers the hail-mary mothers
asleep in their stockings
while the crows sing heigh ho carrion crow,
fol de riddle, lol de riddle,
carry on, carry on—

from *The Game of Boxes* (Graywolf Press)

"What would happen if one woman told the truth about her life?
The world would split open."
—Muriel Rukeyser

contents

No one knew where the fire had started. By the time they saw it, it had eaten away most of the house, where the kitchen and sitting room had once been, and there was only a great, gaping maw of black. Charred edges. Black meeting black meeting black, as far as they could see. Some said, Electrical, faulty wiring, these old houses, you know. Others wondered at an element left on; it would be easy to do. No one thought, Matches.

The summer had been so dry, barely a drop of rain, and the house had gone up like kindling. Gone, the rose-patterned wallpaper. Gone, the small kitchen table where countless cups of tea had been poured. Gone, the worn-down hexagonal tiles. Gone.

They put the fire out, and lamented the loss. There had been so many losses already, it seemed cruel for there to be even one more. They looked up at the house, remembering, perhaps, all the time they had spent there, gathering up their memories while the house cooled and smoked. They didn't yet notice the girl at the ocean's edge, watching the flames. They didn't yet ask her what she knew.

the beginning

The story went like this: on a rainy spring afternoon in 1960, Camille went into labour while watching *The Twilight Zone*. The image of Maple Street flashed across the screen, and the narrator said, "Maple Street, USA. Late summer. A tree-lined little world of front porch gliders, barbecues, the laughter of children and the bell of an ice cream vendor. At the sound of the roar and the flash of light, it will be precisely 6:43 p.m. on Maple Street. This is Maple Street on a late Saturday afternoon. Maple Street—in the last calm and reflective moment—before the monsters came." She didn't complain or cry out, but went through labour quietly, as if this were a penance. She was not devout, but she was aware of the number of things she'd done wrong, including becoming pregnant at seventeen and refusing to tell anyone who the father was. She had wanted that secret for herself. The baby was born quickly, on the cusp of dusk, the in-between hours of the day. She named the baby Maybe. In the hospital, she said it was the only word that crossed her mind when she looked at the tiny, mewling, pink bundle. Maybe. Her daughter. The nurses had looked at her strangely before marking the name on the birth certificate, next to the blank spot where there should have been a father's name. "Maybe?" they asked. "Are you sure?" But Camille had looked at her and thought, Maybe. Maybe I can do this. Maybe I am supposed to be her mother. She unwrapped her feet and counted ten tiny, lovely toes. Maybe.

At least, this was what Maybe had been told by her grandmother. It was one of the only stories about Camille that Maybe knew, one of the only ones she had not pieced together herself like a jigsaw puzzle, reimagined. It was a strange story to tell, the image of her mother considering her, as if she hadn't already had nine months to do exactly that. But, at least Camille hadn't looked at her and thought, No. At least she had considered being her mother. Maybe held on to that scrap.

Maybe had repeated the story to her friends at school, when she was asked about her mother's absence. Maybe said that her mother was nomadic, travelling across the continent in a dedicated way. She said her mother craved adventure, that Oak Bay was too small for her. Because how could you decide on just one part of the world, when there was so much more to see? She'd held her finger to the spinning globe and imagined Camille in any of those places; the world was so big, each pastel geometric shape offering more and more. Maybe told a different story each time she was asked; the never-ending story of her mother had so many varieties, a choose your own adventure. Maybe had notebooks she'd filled with these stories about Camille, each one turning a new corner, each one taking place in a new part of the world. At first, she'd imagined Camille in Vancouver, living in a tiny apartment on a busy street, walking each morning to a bakery where she would make cookies and tiny cakes all day. She would smell like sugar.

But Maybe had never lived anywhere but Oak Bay, an island temperate rain forest, with her grandmother. She grew up listening to rain on the roof, the lap of the ocean. She'd taken the ferry to the mainland, had walked through Gastown in Vancouver, stood beside the steam clock as it went off—and had been thrilled by the busyness of the city with its tall buildings, all the pedestrians going somewhere, everywhere, quickly. She'd scanned the streets, imagining she'd get at least a glimpse of Camille. But, those trips were few; her grandmother, Gigi, thought the city was too chaotic, all the sounds competing for your attention, each face anonymous. And so, Maybe lived on Lear Street, in sleepy Oak Bay, where nothing seemed to happen other than the huge hemlocks growing a little bit taller. Maybe waited for something to happen. She was impatient. And, Lear Street, with its white split-rail fences and tidy, thoughtful gardens, continued on as it always had been while the world around it had other plans.

It was 1971, and Maybe was thrilled and amazed by the things she saw when she turned on the TV—after Gigi relented, finally, and they bought a colour one. Their neighbour Walter Keane carried it awkwardly into the living room, and Maybe flicked it on, turned the dial, the picture springing to life. The War on Drugs. Women's Liberation. Mary Tyler Moore throwing her hat in the air. The Manson trial. Apollo 14. Evel Knievel jumping nineteen cars. The Kingston Penitentiary riot. Maybe was awestruck when she saw the streets of the capital in Washington swollen with people— women and men in flared pants, wide-brimmed hats, tasselled vests, holding their fingers up in peace signs—protesting the Vietnam War. She moved closer to the television until the picture turned grainy, indistinguishable, and Gigi said, "Scoot back," still uncomfortable with the TV and its clicking channels, endless images, endless loops of information. And in each of these images, in varying forms, Maybe imagined Camille. Protesting all the injustice. An activist, making the world a better place. Part of the revolution. It was easy to create stories about her. Maybe hadn't actually spoken to her or seen her for nine years, but sometimes, she imagined what a conversation with Camille would sound like: would she ask her about the women's movement, all the speeches and stories Maybe had read with rapt awe? Or would she ask her only about her life since she left Lear Street, how she had spent those long years? Or would she be too shy to ask her anything, later embarrassed by her own stunned silence? Maybe didn't know.

They heard all about these protests—for women's rights, for aboriginal groups, the anti-nuclear protests, and always, continually, the war—and while it seemed something was happening everywhere else, it remained distant to Lear Street. The only way to imagine these protests in any context to her own existence was for Maybe to place Camille in these scenes. Maybe squinted at the photos in the newspapers, trying to imagine the streets of Oak Bay blossoming with bodies in the same way, imagining her blond-haired mother in the left-hand corner, only her elbow left in the frame. She imagined her tucked in between the protesters, holding up one of the signs that said, "End the War in Vietnam NOW!" or "Women's Liberation" with its hand-drawn fist. Maybe's brain swirled, her dreams were full of these images. She tried to talk to Gigi about it—nudged her shoulder as they read over the paper together, pointed out the young, fashionable women with their unapologetic gazes—but Gigi just sighed and turned the page to read about the local news, a new restaurant, a sandcastle competition.

"Nothing to do with us," she said. Gigi, who had been on her own for so long, who had always been self-sufficient. "Isn't that the whole point of this *movement*? Ask me, women have been doing things for themselves for a long time." She had seen enough of wars to be weary of them, and to also know they'd continue on, with or without her approval. Maybe cut away at the papers and pasted photos and articles into her journal. The Berrigans, those "radical priests" and their protests. The beautiful, tragic face of Sharon Tate. Karen Carpenter in her pale yellow dress. The October Crisis and the long, solemn rows of armed soldiers. She wrote stories where Camille appeared in these places: Camille in the relentless sunshine of California and its high deserts; Camille in a thick, hooded parka, climbing over a snowbank in the Yukon. Her mother's life sprawled out, while her own shrunk: Vancouver Island, Oak Bay, Lear Street. Gigi's cottage. Her room, with its creamy walls, the window that overlooked the back garden and its riot of flowers. All these things suddenly smaller. Bob Dylan sang, "The times, they are a-changin'," and Maybe felt a deep ache for just that.

Maybe was eleven that summer, no longer a little girl, but not yet an adult, caught on a fine precipice. She leaned toward adulthood, and she felt things expanding in immeasurable and embarrassing ways. She held her hands over her new breasts, surprised by their hardness, the dull pain below. She read the articles in *Life* about contraception and reproduction and the appeal to abortion laws, and she understood that this would all affect her one day, but it still felt so much beyond her reach. She pasted the black-and-white photos into her journal and tried to imagine herself in the foreground in her future life. Blurry, but just visible. Other times, she placed Camille there, among the throngs of women and men, her pale hair cascading down her back. Camille, who had named her, held her, and then, two years later, had packed a suitcase and stepped out into the early morning of Lear Street. There would have been dew on the grass, making her shoes damp. Camille holds her suitcase and walks, away from Gigi and the cottage and the sea. Her footsteps are the only sound on the quiet street, too early yet for the birds. The shushing sound of the sea ahead, a lullaby. She walks without turning around, looking at the cottage where she'd spent all of her nineteen years, where she'd last seen her father, where she'd first brought her daughter. Walks away from Maybe. Maybe had asked why Camille left, but Gigi claimed she didn't know. "Camille," she said, "was always a mystery."

Her hands stretch out. The strands of her hair, golden, come forward, and behind her the sky, cloudless, a sheer blue. The image came to Maybe at surprising moments: a memory, in the hazy unformed way of memories. A glowing, golden blur, how her two-year-old mind might have recollected her mother—the softness of her arms, the sensation of lifting, being lifted, and the warmth of Camille against her. Gigi said, "You were too young to have memories," but Maybe knew it to be true. Yet nothing about the memory was particularly solid. It could be a laundry detergent ad, instead.

"If they have any decent tomato, we can do a nice fresh salad. The one you like with the olives. And maybe peaches for dessert." They were walking home from school, Gigi rattling off her list of things they'd need at the market.

Even though it was only the two of them in the cottage now, Gigi still made elaborate meals. She made things like quiche and beef Wellington and trifle. Holdovers from the days when she had had a full house, Sunday dinners. These were things she loved; she loved all the ingredients, and so she still made them at home, for her and Maybe. At the small café where Gigi worked now, people didn't want beef Wellington; they wanted grilled cheese sandwiches and cups of creamy mushroom soup. So Maybe had lamb sandwiches in her lunch kit, smoked salmon on rye bread, while the other kids in her class had bologna or plain cheese and thick layers of margarine that Maybe eyed longingly.

They took the long way home, skirting the harbour, so that they could stop at the market. "Can we have pears instead?" Maybe asked.

"Grilled pears, then. And that delicious vanilla bean ice cream."

There were boats on the water, and the ocean was a deep, reflective blue. It was only spring, but the air felt warmer, as if even the seasons were rushing ahead.

The market was busy, women and children moving between stalls of leeks, tomato, sugar peas and fat, thick blueberries. Gigi navigated the stalls easily, while Maybe trailed behind her, absently running her hands over the rinds of fruit. Everyone knew Gigi at the market. They had known Gigi's husband, who died long before Maybe was born, and had also known Camille; everyone was careful to avoid mentioning their names. The Collins family was blighted, cursed by absence. George Collins had drowned and been pulled to shore by some of the men in town years before. Gigi didn't talk about George, other than to say it hadn't surprised her, the way he died. A lush, Gigi had said, and Maybe had looked up the word in her thumbed dictionary, learned to discover for herself those dark and surprising corners within the adult world.

She watched Gigi as she moved through the market, and let herself trail farther and farther behind. It was an old habit, and sometimes she let Gigi get far enough away that she seemed like only a smudge on the horizon. Then, if she squinted, she could almost believe Gigi had disappeared into the crowd, and Maybe was left completely alone. If it really happened, she thought she'd take a bus, maybe even hitchhike like she'd seen teenagers do on the Island Highway. She could travel all the way up to Port Hardy where the wind would be stronger, whipping against her as she stood at the very edge of the sea, the tiny outer islands lurking in the pale, blue mist.

"Pick up the pace, Miss Maybe," Gigi called from a table heaving with fruit, stacks of peaches and apricots and nectarines, every shade of yellow and orange. Gigi didn't need to turn around, but somehow simply knew instinctively where Maybe was. Gigi handed the woman behind the table folded bills and then tucked four pears into her canvas bag. "Chop chop, madam."

Now, Maybe looked out again to the sea, to ships pulling out, the constant motion familiar and predictable. Looked at the boats and envisioned another life, the world opening like a morning yawn.

All those years ago, Camille would have taken a ferry to the mainland. On the ferry, Camille takes a seat near the bow, where she can watch all the other, even more remote islands slide by. Eventually, they give way to just the wide expanse of the Strait of Georgia. She is too anxious to sleep, as many of the other passengers do; she is aware that she's made an irreversible decision. You cannot leave your child asleep in her crib and expect to simply return when you change your mind. Some things are permanent.

Once the ferry docks at Horseshoe Bay, Camille collects her small suitcase and follows the other foot passengers off. The terminal is surrounded by ancient trees, a row of shops, and then houses beyond. Camille turns her collar up at the cold, and steps down the metal walkway into a life she does not yet recognize.

Maybe could see her as clearly as she saw Gigi in early mornings, still drowsy with sleep. Camille's life a silent movie constantly playing in Maybe's head. Camille on a busy street, her shoes loud on the sidewalk. Walking farther away.

Gigi was at the edge of the market, talking to Robin Hollis. The Hollises lived just across the street from them; Phoebe Hollis was Maybe's best friend, and they often wandered back and forth to each other's houses on rainy Saturdays, had sleepovers, biked down Lear Street to the beach. Robin Hollis was lovely with her dark hair and tanned skin, younger and prettier than other mothers Maybe knew. And she insisted that Maybe call her Robin, not Mrs. Hollis—*Mrs. Hollis makes me feel old, love. Mrs. Hollis is someone else.*

Robin held a book out to Gigi. She said, "It's brilliant. You should read it." The cover was deep red, the title *Power Politics* in crisp script. Maybe willed Gigi to take it, tuck it into her bag, so that Maybe might read it later, even though she knew Gigi would only toss it in a corner, saying, Who has the time to read a book?

Gigi smiled. "Only thing I have time to read are the damned depressing articles about the sinkhole."

"Wasn't it horrible? Imagine, the ground just opening up like that?" Robin shivered as she slid the book back into her purse. She and Gigi talked about the sinkhole in Quebec, the thirty-one people who'd died, each of them making the low, murmuring sounds of sympathy. The image of the world disappearing under your feet, how something so solid could just simply disappear. They didn't know anyone in Quebec, but they imagined the loss, then congratulated themselves on having escaped it.

"We should be off." Gigi lifted her bag full of fruit and vegetables. "Dinner doesn't seem to want to cook itself."

Robin laughed lightly, a pretty, clear sound. She tucked a strand of dark hair behind her ear and waved as Maybe and Gigi continued again on their way. The afternoon seemed so normal—high sun, breeze from the ocean, the pears in Gigi's bag, Robin's laugh—so like every other afternoon she'd ever known, that it seemed impossible that somewhere, people were joining hands and marching, protesting, demanding change. The world was spinning wildly. Thrillingly.

❖

Maybe watched from the front yard as Mary Quinn arrived in the spring of 1971, her car full of boxes and rolls of canvas. She watched as Mary tugged the canvases out, cradling them in her arms as she went into the house. They would later find out that she was a painter from the mainland—successful and well known, it seemed, for a series of paintings of doors in various states of rot—who had, for some unknown reason, bought a house close to the sea. Maybe watched Mary Quinn with a particular, clear devotion. She came and went alone, her car windows rolled down so that Maybe could hear the Doors or the Jackson 5 trailing behind her.

Maybe and Phoebe tried, many times, to accidentally meet her. They had paused on their bikes outside Mary's house, feigning loose chains, waiting for her to come out; they had waited at the side of the road for her car pulling out of the gravel drive; they had walked with beach towels over their shoulders, meandering down the road. But it never worked. They only ever saw Mary Quinn in the distance, carrying in cans of paint or awkward wooden easels. She was the exotic, the first new resident on Lear Street in a decade; she was the first artist Maybe had ever known—even the word *artist* sounding breathless and impossible, magic.

Lear Street had remained the same as many of the streets in Oak Bay, full of old, large homes and tall, leafy trees, shady yards and short strolls to the sea. It was the impeccable reproduction of suburbia: quiet, safe, idyllic. Most streets were carefully and habitually kept by the same families, owners passing the stately homes down to sons, daughters, grandchildren, favourite nieces. The four houses on the right side of Lear Street had always belonged to the same people who owned them now.

Gigi's tiny white bungalow was between Walter Keane's house and old Mrs. Eames's Tudor home. Gigi said it was too small, too old, too decrepit for them, but Oak Bay was expensive, and Maybe knew Gigi loved the big, sprawling garden out back. Besides, the house was too full of the past for Gigi to ever move—George had lived there, and Camille too, and all those memories were impossible to box up and re-create somewhere else—and so they stayed in the small house with the overgrown roses and the shaggy lilac trees, the small stone figures of bunnies and gnomes and the ironic Virgin Mary statues filling the garden. Gigi said the only miracles she believed in were the roses that grew up the back arbour; miracles began and ended in the dirt.

Walter Keane was closest to the sea on the right side, with his tidy, tended gardens and deep blue shutters. He had been friends with Gigi for so long, he was the only one who knew all her secrets. He appeared, sometimes, in Gigi's back garden on a particularly hot day and sat with her in the shade, drinking tall, cool glasses of lemonade. She'd laugh at things he said. He was soft, benign, with his white hair and easy smile.

Mrs. Eames had lived in her house longer than anyone, widowed at a young age in 1928. She still lived alone, and had groceries delivered, a young girl in to clean the echoing house. Walter walked down to trim back the roses and hydrangeas, sprinkle fertilizer.

Gigi had always called this side of the street—*her* side—the old side. The other side, the new side, had changed in the last few years as the old homes had been bought up or taken over by young, enthusiastic relatives. Houses were painted, pools put in backyards, wall-to-wall carpets added. Out with the old, and all of that.

The house across from the old Eames place had been bought by the Hollises years ago, before Maybe or Phoebe had started school. Phoebe's father was a professor at the university, teaching English literature. He said the reason they'd bought the house on Lear Street was because *King Lear* was his favourite Shakespearean tragedy. "The weight of this sad time we must obey; Speak what we feel, not what we ought to say,'" he quoted in his deep voice, and Phoebe rolled her eyes. Phoebe had a pool in her backyard and a mother who let them turn the radio up as loud as they wanted.

Two down from the Hollises was the tall, grey house that belonged to the Lalonde family. They had two boys: Danny and Charlie. The Lalondes were always getting in and out of the car, shuffling Charlie and Danny in and out. Maybe was used to the sound of their Volvo on Lear Street, early enough on the weekends that only the very old or the very young were awake.

Closest to the sea on the new side was Mary Quinn's house. She had renovated shortly after she moved in, but instead of simply repainting or adding window boxes, she turned it into something else entirely—a completely modern reinterpretation of the old house, all smooth lines and glassy angles. Gigi said it was because Mary was a painter, and she had a modern aesthetic. Gigi and Walter disliked the renovation; they thought she'd ruined everything charming and unique about the place. But Maybe loved it. She imagined Mary's house full of paintings in various stages of completion, of the whitecaps, of the waves, of the driftwood left abandoned. The ocean would creep into her work, living so close to the tumbling waves, the same way the ocean crept into Maybe's dreams. Seagulls cawed and swooped above the houses, their wings open wide as they came down to rest on the sandy shore. They circled, doubled back, alighted on rooftops. Mary Quinn had once painted rotten doors and urban landscapes, but now, surely, her work would be changed by this place.

The new side, Gigi would snort. All those young ones on the new side.

The house on the other side of the Hollises belonged to Aidan Felles, the most recent addition to Lear Street. Maybe and Phoebe snuck from Phoebe's backyard into Aidan Felles's through the gate in the fence. They stood behind the huge cedars, waiting to see him through the back sliding glass door. He had arrived and quickly repainted the house, a cheery, warm yellow. He'd set teak benches along the front walk, cut the grass every Saturday. Gigi said he was too young to be there all alone. She was suspicious of single men who wanted more space than a room in an apartment building.

The sea was what really drew everyone to Lear Street. It stretched, pulling in and out in rhythmic waves, the scent of salt all around them. Willows Beach became cluttered with people as the months got warmer. Maybe and Phoebe loved the particulars of the beach and wandered aimlessly, unhurried. They collected pieces of shell, leftover pieces of driftwood, small stones polished smooth so they rested comfortably in their hands. Sometimes they dove into the roiling waves with abandon, and other times they walked close to the water's edge, leaving uneven footprints behind.

Each time she came to the beach, Maybe had that memory of Camille with her hair fanning out and light all around her, and was startled by it. She almost expected to see Camille coming toward her, coming back, a sun hat perched on her head, her face in shadow. The beach a ribbon of sand spooling out behind her. Of course, she never did. Maybe watched other mothers along the sandy beach, impatient and tired, small children with sticky hands and demanding cries.

Still, the memory stuck, despite Gigi's assurance that this was only something she wished had happened, something she wished she remembered. But Maybe knew it, just as she knew the sound of Gigi walking down the hall late at night, the sound of the Lalondes' Volvo in the early morning: Camille had brought her here, held her high, laughed and laughed. She'd been loved by her mother once, however fleetingly.

By mid-May it was warm in the way of early coastal summers—the days curled moistly around you, making the back of your neck damp, but the nights were still cool. Cool enough to cause a chill, reminding you that the sea was just there, and brought with it the temperamental sea air. The smell of salt. The brine caught in your hair—another layer, another way that the sea became a part of daily life.

The heat continued and showed no signs of disappearing. It wore on and on, until the novelty of the heat waned, and by mid-June everyone was complaining it was too hot, there was no breeze, it was too hot. It was too hot.

In the classroom, Maybe and her classmates withered from the heat and the impending end of the school year. Soon, there would be the glorious two months of summer break spread out before them—two months of freedom that would quickly, quickly turn to monotony, to the sheer expanse of boredom. Maybe might dive into the Hollises' pool and skim her fingers on the bottom. She might go into Victoria with Gigi and visit the wax museum, or watch the boats effortlessly pull into harbour. White sails against the sky, the water too blue, the parliament buildings stoic behind.

But now, when Maybe woke, summer was still ahead, out of reach. The morning was already hot, and the yawning day ahead seemed endless.

The sun filtered in through the open window, strong and sure of itself. She could hear, already, the birds in the garden and the creaking floorboard in the kitchen where Gigi would be making breakfast, starting coffee, taking plates from the cupboards. Maybe was tired, thick with sleep. Gigi had always said she was an old soul—"Wise beyond your years," with a wink—and that was exactly how she felt this Saturday morning: old.

Maybe sat up and brushed her hands over the bed sheets, giving them a perfunctory smooth. The floorboards were still cool under her feet as she made her way across to her small desk, where she kept her pens and books and journals. The journals were stacked chronologically, bulging. Articles from newspapers. Photos. Postcards. Her own stories. And one photo of Camille— sitting in the back garden, slightly blurred, the lines indefinite, out of focus. She had on a white sundress with embroidery across the chest. Maybe was not in the picture, but she imagined that Camille had been watching her sit on the grass, watching her pick at the blades or a newly bloomed flower. Camille was absent from the photos on the walls in the cottage, and the albums all contained shots of Maybe, growing year by year when you flipped through. One afternoon, Maybe had asked why there were no photos of Camille, and Gigi had shrugged, chopped up a leek and said, "I have a good memory." Maybe examined the single photo of Camille most mornings, to remind herself what she looked like. She'd been gone for so long, Maybe was afraid she would forget. Her pale hair, strands at her chin. Her long neck. The way she held her hands in her lap. Maybe convinced herself that this was the Camille from her memory, and not the other way around.

Postcards arrived sometimes, messages hurriedly scrawled and signed only with a large, curled C. A loop and sigh. Not Mother. Not Camille. Just C. One arrived from New York the year before, and Camille had written, *Women's Strike for Equality!* on the back, and Gigi had said, "Women's lib. Bunch of noise." A few weeks later, Gigi's *Time* magazine arrived and Maybe pored over it, reading about Kate Millett and Gloria Steinem. She had read every article in the papers that could tell her more about their stories, and finally found a picture of the strike, women with long hair and heavy placards, some smiling, others with furrowed brows and deep frowns, yelling at the cameras, calling to one another in an unending chorus.

Maybe ran her hands over the glossy pictures of the postcards she'd glued into her journal. The last one had mentioned a trip Camille planned to take, somewhere in Northern California. She was hoping to get to San Francisco, was excited by the literary scene there. Gigi said Camille was working as a journalist of some sort, her descriptions vague enough that Maybe had to fill in the blanks. Gigi changed the subject when Maybe asked anything more.

When Maybe went into the kitchen, Gigi had already started the coffee and was busy frying eggs. She delivered them with a slick slide onto a plate next to stacked slices of toast and a handful of brilliant red strawberries. "Eggs up," she said. Gigi wore her purple robe, her hair tied up in a messy bun. She pushed a few loose strands of greying blond hair back from her face. "You slept late."

"Tired, I guess."

"Well, thank you, Miss Obvious." Gigi leaned against the counter, sipping her coffee. "Hot day already."

Maybe scooped up some of the eggs. The yolks burst and filled her mouth like sunshine.

"Robin says they're having some kind of pool party today. Says of course they'd love to have you."

"Okay." Maybe ate a strawberry. It was perfect, juicy in the way that only summer strawberries could be.

"Or you can stay and putter with me. Cut back some of the roses. Thrilling stuff."

It was Saturday, so Maybe knew Walter would wander over and he and Gigi would sit in the leafy shade, laughing at one of his jokes, or arguing over the best way to get rid of black spot on the roses.

Gigi had lost her husband years before, and, many years before that, Walter had lost his young wife and infant son. He'd never remarried, rarely spoke of their deaths. Walter seemed to have been able to come out the other side of it, understood the tragedy and his very real, very clear loss. But he had survived. He had been the one to live and continued to live, long after his young, pretty wife and tiny son had not. He'd grown tomatoes, worked his years at the high school. Ate fresh mussels. Found the joy in things, in bees in roses, in tall glasses with clinking ice cubes, in Gigi's strange, hard humour. He had survived the worst thing he could imagine. Someone had to remember them, see the things they never would.

Maybe said, "I'd like to swim. It's so hot already."

She ate more egg. Tore strips of toast and dunked them in the yolks. Wondered if she'd remembered to wash out her swimsuit after the last time she'd gone swimming, or if it would still hold the high, sharp smell of chlorine.

There was a small pile of mail on the table. A hydro bill, and a pamphlet from the local nursery on top. There were dahlias, big-headed and showy, on the cover. Maybe flicked through the mail with one finger until she revealed an envelope with Camille's name in the space for return addresses. She picked it up, delicately, while Gigi had her back to her, scrubbing at the frying pan in the deep sink. Maybe turned it over in her hands.

Pale cream, smooth, smelling the way all mail smelled. No other marks, nothing to reveal anything. Not a postcard this time, a letter. Still sealed. She tore the edge open, desperate to see Camille's words.

At the sound of the paper ripping, Gigi turned from the sink. "Maybe! Put that down. Does it have your name on it?" She gave her soapy hands a perfunctory wipe on her pants, then snatched the envelope from Maybe's hands. "Mind your own beeswax."

"But it's a letter! From Camille!"

Gigi tucked the envelope in her pants pocket. "And it's addressed to me, Nosy Parker." She went back to the sink, and Maybe waited for her to say something more, to change her mind and sit at the table so that they could read the letter together. But she didn't. She scrubbed the pot. Maybe's stomach lurched; she felt her cheeks burn.

Gigi finally said, "I made some pecan tarts you can take over to the Hollises." As if the letter were not there, as if Maybe hadn't just had it in her hand, as if it had never arrived at all.

the party

The Hollises' backyard was full of sunlight, brightly coloured bathing suits, clinking glasses and the thick scent of suntan lotion, coconut brilliance.

Professor Hollis stood at the grill, talking to Guy Lalonde and Aidan Felles, and Maybe couldn't see Robin anywhere. All she saw were children and parents, stretched over every inch of the lawn. The Lalonde boys were already in the pool, tossing a striped beach ball back and forth between them. Phoebe sat at the long picnic table, eating a huge slice of watermelon. Maybe shifted from one foot to the other, her arms achy and heavy with the ceramic tray piled with pecan tarts. She wasn't sure if she should go straight to Phoebe, or find someplace to leave the fragrant tarts.

"Maybe, honey, let me take that." Robin appeared at Maybe's side and, in one swift movement, took the tray from Maybe and encircled her with her free arm. "Phoebe will be pleased as punch that you are here." Robin manoeuvred her through the yard, placed the tray on the patio table and brought Maybe to Phoebe and the huge slices of watermelon. Tiny black seeds surrounded Phoebe.

"Take a break," Robin said, nudging Phoebe. "You're going to explode." She turned on her heel—leaving the coconut sweet scent of suntan oil, her dark ponytail swishing—and disappeared into the party. More people arrived at the back gate, swarmed and buzzed and laughed.

"There's so many people," Maybe said as she slid in next to Phoebe. The wood of the picnic table bit into the back of her legs. "I thought it would be just, you know, us."

"My mum likes parties." Phoebe shrugged as she wiped her mouth with the back of her hand. "Today she's *entertaining*," Phoebe said as she rolled her eyes.

The Hollises had had parties before, but they had mostly been people from the neighbourhood, the Lalonde boys playing soccer or croquet or bocce, while Mrs. Lalonde looked wilted in the sun. Gigi and Walter came sometimes as well, sitting in the shade, helping Mrs. Eames into a padded lawn chair. At the Canada Day party, she'd worn red lipstick and had three martinis and laughed like she was a teenage girl again. This party was different, bigger and more sprawling and, somehow, more noisy and less joyous. There were neighbours and colleagues, all held apart from one another. Adults laughed, sipped from their glasses, blended together until they were one large mass of heads and hands.

"What's this party for, anyhow?"

"Dad got tenure. It's a big deal."

"Gigi said she'd come with Walter later, after it wasn't so hot."

"You mean after everyone leaves."

"Probably."

The girls sat in silence for a while, watching bowls of potato chips and raw vegetables appear, glasses being refilled, women rubbing suntan lotion on children's faces and husbands' shoulders. Maybe watched Aidan Felles as he moved between the small groups. She had only seen him when he was painting his house or leaning over his fence to talk to Professor Hollis, but something about him was compelling; people gravitated toward him. Now, Maybe watched him cross the patio to stand beside Robin, who held a tray of bottled beers. He leaned toward her and she laughed, tilting her head back, and Aidan then touched the small of her back, the spot where her wrap skirt met her spine.

"The pool. The boys are finally out. Let's go in." Phoebe went ahead, striding toward the water in her bright blue suit. Maybe pulled her sundress over her head and tossed it on the grass. Her suit was red and white, small flowers, her first two-piece. She had begged Gigi for it, promising she'd never ask for another thing again. It suddenly felt too small, she was too exposed, so she ran to the pool's edge and dove in.

The water was crisp and chilled, exactly the way a long, rectangular pool should be in the beginning of summer. Calm, quick, cool, deep. Maybe stayed below the surface, watching Phoebe's feet as she treaded water. They were suspended, weightless, hovering. Maybe came up, breathless, and pushed the hair from her eyes. Her lungs ached from holding her breath.

They spent the afternoon racing the length of the pool, doing somersaults, practising handstands. Maybe held her breath, touched the bottom of the deep end. She went under again and again, pushing herself longer and longer. Phoebe dove, her form perfect. They floated on their backs, looking at the sun high in the sky.

By the time they got out—fingers wrinkled, ridges swollen and prominent and strange—Robin had piled the long side table with hamburgers and hot dogs and potatoes in tinfoil and salads. Gigi and Walter sat in folding chairs, each holding a tall glass with limes floating near the top. Many of the guests had already left, but a dozen or so remained in a semicircle on the stone patio, balancing paper plates on their laps. The sun had moved, edging west.

Maybe and Phoebe filled their paper plates, aware they'd never be able to eat it all, but so hungry that they could not choose. They sat at Gigi's feet on the patio, the stones warming their bare legs.

"It's the word *confessional* I object to," one of Professor Hollis's colleagues was saying. "There are no priests here. The label is misguided. It's memoir, plain and simple."

"Autobiography," another said, and Maybe concentrated momentarily on the difference between autobiography and biography. They seemed slippery, too closely entwined, conjoined twins. She imagined the two words wrapped around one another, indistinguishable.

"No. Memoir. Not a whole life, just something. That moment." A woman with a tall pile of chestnut hair, sunglasses that eclipsed her face, waved her hand in the air, cutting off the man who sat beside her. "It's provocative, by the way. The new one about the mother."

Maybe saw Gigi roll her eyes, whisper something to Walter. She'd think the serious, earnest woman with the large glasses ridiculous; she was being neighbourly, crisply polite by still listening. The academics, she would later say. So serious about everything.

"Which one is that?" Professor Hollis had arrived with a beer in his hand. The golden liquid sloshed to the side, threatening to tip over the lip of the glass. He leaned casually on the back of Gigi's chair. Walter turned to smile at him, raising his own glass in thanks.

"Oh, the one. You know, the one everyone is talking about. The mother. The mother of the girl."

"Haven't read it," Professor Hollis said.

Maybe took a bite of her hamburger and watched Gigi shift in her chair, bored by the conversation. She'd be counting the minutes until she could leave, taking Walter with her. He drank his cool drink, munched on a carrot stick, watched the Lalonde boys play croquet on the abandoned lawn.

"Carl, you know the one I mean," the woman with the sunglasses said to the man beside her, grabbing his arm. "That *one*."

The man—Carl, it seemed—shut his eyes, deep in concentration. After a moment, he opened them. He smiled at Maybe and she saw he was pleased with himself, too pleased; the kind of man to often be too pleased with himself. "*The Other Mother*. Collins. Somebody Collins."

Gigi stiffened. Walter looked up. Professor Hollis touched Gigi's arm, his voice wide and deep and joking when he said, "A Collins, Gigi. Know her?"

Carl snapped his fingers. "Camille Collins! That's it. *The Other Mother* by Camille Collins. Quite the book. Quite the stir."

Maybe let her plate drop to the grass. Camille Collins. Her mother. She said, "Gigi?"

The air shifted in the moment when Maybe realized they were talking about Camille, her mother, and a book. Gigi said nothing. A book. Her mother had written a book.

Professor Hollis registered the connection a fraction more slowly; his expression changed from interest to regret, mouth set straight. He said, "Gigi, I'm sorry, I didn't know."

"Neither did I," Gigi said quietly.

"Oh, how wonderful," Carl said, oblivious to the quicksand they had all been sucked into. "You know the author? She's caused quite a stir with the women's movement. Autonomy and family, all that."

Gigi did not answer. She placed her glass and plate on the stone beside her. She got up from the chair, straightened slowly and deliberately. "Maybe, dear, we need to go."

Maybe watched Walter say the goodbyes for them. Phoebe took a step toward Maybe, but Robin touched her shoulder lightly to halt her and Phoebe froze.

Maybe followed Gigi and Walter, their bodies leaned close together, their voices low. She watched her feet on the trim grass of the Hollises' lawn, realized she'd left her sandals behind, but all she could think about was the strange title, the book that her mother had apparently written. There was a book out there that she had never heard of, and Maybe's fingers itched, wanting to hold it in her hands.

the other mother

It wasn't that Robin Hollis was unhappy, exactly. That was not the word she'd use. Unsettled. Untethered. Uncertain. There was something she could not quite put her finger on, something she felt when she wiped another sticky counter, folded another fraying towel. She thought, There was supposed to be more. All those years ago—thirteen years? Could that be right?—she had expected so much more.

Robin (then, of course, she had been Robin Sweet, a name that both suited and embarrassed her) met Alan Hollis while they were both students at the University of British Columbia. It had been an accident, as these things tended to be, Robin going to a party with a friend and Alan sitting in the corner, drinking gin. It had been predictable, the shape and inevitability of the courtship. In the daytime, she attended classes and learned about injections, dosages, broken bones, and felt her life had order to it, a clean, crisp line: she'd study and graduate and become a nurse, the course delineated down to the month. She liked the precision of it all—the tip of the needle, her words on a chart, even the way she imagined her uniform would fit: taut, creaseless.

Alan was a couple of years ahead of her, and proposed on the night he graduated. She was in a long, cream dress dotted with pearls at the bust, and somehow the dress made it seem that she had already said yes, before she had. Alan got into a graduate program at the University of Toronto, and so it became inevitable that Robin would quit nursing school—just for now—and earn some money working at a respite home while he finished his master's degree.

"Then," he said, "you can go back to school and I'll teach." It was simple, practical, and Robin agreed, still smugly proud of her handsome, smart husband and the life they were building together. Other girls she knew rented apartments and ate sad meals of tuna on crackers when they'd finished a twelve-hour shift. Robin would have so much more than that, her impeccable uniform, her clever husband.

Six months before Alan graduated for the second time, Robin sat in her doctor's office and listened as the doctor informed her that she was two months pregnant. She'd already known, of course, but had managed to pretend otherwise. Then, there was no pretending.

They'd agreed—she thought; it all seemed hazy and unreliable now—that Alan would take a job and Robin would stay home with the baby. The words *for a while* might have been said, but now they seemed tinny to Robin. There had been those early years with Phoebe, all plump and creamy and yawning with pleasure. And now, here they were, Alan teaching literature at the University of Victoria, coming home happy and tired and energized by the students and their hunger for knowledge, and Phoebe was eleven, on the cusp of teen years, still smiling and gentle but edging toward something else, and Robin was still at home.

Robin felt like she'd agreed to something she'd never really understood, like buying a station wagon when you wanted a sports car. She knew she'd agreed—happily, at the time, all those years she wouldn't want to give up—but she also knew that there was no end date to the agreement. It went on, languishing into the future. When Phoebe had started school, she'd suggested that maybe now was the time to finish her nursing degree. It had only been five and a half years; she could still remember all the things she'd been taught, was still craving lecture halls and textbooks and the thrill of blank exam forms.

Alan had looked at her quizzically. "Sure, if that's what you want. I just thought you'd want to be here for Phoebe. You know, it's a big change for her."

His words clicked, pierced her as any criticism—intended or not—about Phoebe did. The guilt swelled. Of course, she wanted to be there for Phoebe. She had been, every minute of every day for over five years. She wanted to say, Why is it just me? Why can't you be here for Phoebe, too?

Alan was a good father—kind, generous, attentive—and Phoebe adored him. But when Alan was home, he had marking to do, or reading to catch up on, or a paper to write for a conference. Or, he needed just a few minutes to himself. Then, Robin wanted to scream, When do I have time for myself? Alan had no problem putting his needs first—before the laundry, the groceries, the school projects, the gardening, the play dates, the vacuuming, the lunches, the cooking, the parties, the bills, the dusting, the bed making, the bathing. It seemed easy for him to leave all these things to her, to assume his wants took priority, that somehow it would simply all get done. That she would do it all, because she always had, and so had the other women before her.

And Robin did it. She did it well, but angrily, resentfully. It was easy for him to shrug these things off, as if it was his right. And this thoughtlessness, this presumption of entitlement, made Robin pull away from him at night, keep her body separate in a small action of rebellion.

When Alan suggested another baby, Robin bristled, found reasons not to have sex, found reasons to argue. She hated to admit it, but she did not want another baby. She loved Phoebe fiercely—in that deep, draining way that she'd scoffed at, that she'd never believed before Phoebe arrived—but she also believed that she'd barely survived it. She felt torn apart, shredded by motherhood, wifedom. She would not do it again. It would be tempting fate. So, she went to the doctor and got a prescription for the pill, washed clothes, wiped counters, read books, held barbecues, made lunches and all the while tried to understand how she'd gotten there—so far away from what she'd imagined.

And so that was how Robin (Sweet) Hollis found herself in a slippery, unknown place. It felt like a buzzing just beneath the surface of her skin, a vibration. She had somehow become an extension of Alan—she was now Alan's wife, never just Robin. She had become flattened out, colourless. And the worst part was, she had no idea how to change it.

✥

Silence filled Gigi's house in the days after the Hollises' pool party, after the discussion of Camille and the book. Maybe hovered near Gigi, who busied herself with everything else. Anything else. The house sparkled, every surface shone, the air was pure lemon.

"Have you heard any more about the book?" Maybe asked.

"Nope." Gigi moved around the living room, rubbing a cloth over the coffee table, the mantle.

"We should get it. We should know what it's about. I'm sure Professor Hollis—"

"Maybe. No." Gigi's voice was sharp, prickling Maybe's skin. *No.* She had continued to dust the room, as if that were more important than what Maybe was asking of her. That had been days ago, and they had not discussed the book since.

Now Maybe stood looking at all her own books lining the bookcase. She'd read every one of them, careful to keep the spines unbroken and perfect, turned the pages greedily. It seemed incredible to her, improbable that Camille had written a whole book, and had never so much as mentioned it to them. Gigi had said that Camille was a journalist of some sort, but instead of newspaper articles in papers that Maybe would never see, she had written a book. A book.

The Other Mother.

The words sticky, heavy. They felt like dangerous words.

Maybe glanced at the clock on her bedside table: 9:33. She did not hear the floorboards creaking. She did not smell coffee brewing, or toast toasting. The days since the Hollises' party had been strange. Maybe had heard Gigi on the phone a few times, speaking quietly so that Maybe might not hear. Maybe had stood halfway down the hallway, in the spot where the floor did not cry out, and listened. She couldn't make out everything Gigi said, but she heard her hiss, "Camille!" into the receiver. Maybe knew she was asking about the book and what it meant.

Maybe pulled on a clean pair of shorts and a white T-shirt before leaving her room. The hall was dim with the bedroom doors all closed tight. She passed the photos on the right—Gigi and George

Collins's wedding photo, a small photo of Gigi holding a tiny, indistinguishable bundle that Maybe had been told was her as a baby. She passed by them quickly, stepping into the warm yellow light of the kitchen.

There was an empty glass on the small table, its bottom stained amber; Gigi had been up at some point during the night. Maybe put the glass in the sink and took a piece of Gigi's famous homemade bread from the breadbasket on the counter. She grabbed a slice to eat plain; she wanted to leave the house before Gigi woke. She left a short note on the countertop for Gigi. If she pushed against the back door as she opened it, it would give way easily, allowing Maybe to slip out of the house silently. This old house, she knew its tricks.

Her bike was where she'd left it, leaning against the shed at the back of the yard. Green, even though she had wanted red. "Honestly, Maybe," Gigi had said, "it's just a colour. I promise they pedal the same." Maybe had taken the green bicycle, and Gigi was right, it pedalled just the same, but that hadn't stopped Maybe from watching red bicycles with sheer longing whenever one passed her.

Maybe righted the bike. The morning was quiet and particularly still. Weekends gaped and stretched, leaned and yawned, spread out long and wide and aimless. Most weekends, Maybe felt this way as well. But today, this morning in late June, Maybe's day had a distinct shape to it—purpose and determination wrapped up tidily together. Maybe hopped onto her bike, angling herself quickly out of Gigi's yard and toward the library.

❖

Maybe did not find the book. She'd searched cautiously, carefully, her finger on the spines of the books. Billy Collins jumped quickly to Frank Collins. No spot for Camille. She'd even asked the librarian, who knew Maybe well after all her visits, the armloads of books she left with, and after searching through the index cards, furrowed her brow and shook her head. They simply did not have the book.

She had imagined, briefly, asking Gigi to take her to Munro's in Victoria, but knew it would not happen. Gigi would scoff, wipe her hands on her thighs and shake her head. For what? Gigi would ask.

What would you need that book for?

Maybe had never told Gigi about all the lives she'd imagined for Camille. She didn't tell her that was why she was greedy for newspapers, both for the knowledge of the vast world beyond their picket fences, and for the possibility of seeing Camille there. Gigi didn't know that all of Maybe's stories were about Camille. Maybe saw the way that even the sound of Camille's name caused Gigi's brow to tighten, just so slightly, pained. She understood enough to keep her own thoughts quiet.

Maybe had asked Gigi, years ago, where her mother was. Everyone else at school had a mother; no one else she knew lived with their grandmother, eating crab cakes and tarte Tatin. Maybe had become quietly aware of her difference. Gigi had been washing dishes, a bright yellow salad bowl, and she had placed it quietly on the drying rack, wiped her hands on the blue-and-white striped tea towel, and turned to look at Maybe. "Sometimes," she'd said, and then faltered. She put her hand to her mouth briefly, as if she could hold the words back, keep them swallowed down low where Maybe could not hear them. After a moment, she continued, "Sometimes people aren't sure what they want. Sometimes people need space to think. Sometimes, people make bad decisions, darling."

"Was I a bad decision?"

Gigi's eyes turned damp and threatened to spill, her mouth puckering a little as if Maybe's words were simply too sour to stand. Gigi crossed the room and put her arms around Maybe, pulling her against her chest.

"No," Gigi said as Maybe breathed in her scent, dish soap, her perfume, the dryness of her skin, the leftovers of Jergens hand cream. "You were not a bad decision. I didn't say it right. What I should have said is that sometimes people are just plain selfish."

They remained like that for a while, Maybe pressed so close to her that she could feel the rhythmic beat of Gigi's heart against her cheek, until Walter appeared at the open back kitchen door, holding a bag of fresh oranges. They ate the quartered oranges in the back garden, and that smell, the thickly sweet, hotly orange citrus scent,

what we once believed

became what Maybe thought of when she thought of Camille's departure. The word *selfish* and the tang of oranges.

Maybe knew what Gigi was trying to say about Camille, but the words left her unsatisfied. *Some people are selfish.* Camille was selfish, but surely there were plenty of people who were selfish and still stayed with their children. So she imagined endless possibilities to the story of Camille's life, another life entirely, a life where she was happy and smiling and present. She might even have other, happy children. Camille in a warm kitchen, boiling milk for hot cocoa, three tiny children circling her feet. A lodge on a mountain, skis propped against the outside walls. She would pick the children up if they fell, hold them tight to her chest until they stopped crying. Touch their pink cheeks.

Just thinking this made Maybe feel dizzy and sick all at once. She looked down, concentrated on her feet on the bicycle pedals. She pushed harder, feeling the bike surge ahead, feeling the wind come at her in whips, feeling everything whiz by her at a shocking pace until everything blurred: rubber on cement, wind in her hair, all the words in her head melted and merged and then were nothing at all.

28 ❖

under a canopy of trees

Robin had been there when Aidan Felles moved in, had watched the strangely sad stream of tidy boxes going into the house. Sad, because there were so few and they seemed so light in Aidan's arms. She watched him systematically bend, lift, disappear into the house, only to do it all again. She was surprised by the smoothness of his shaved head, tanned and perfectly shaped, by the casual strength when he moved. They'd always hired movers.

Over the next weeks, month, Robin saw Aidan Felles cutting back the dead branches, painting the house trim, installing shutters. She did not see anyone else come or go; Aidan seemed quietly, confidently solitary, at home in the shady yard, an axe or a hammer in his hands. He was her age, younger than Alan, but reminded her of her father and uncles, the men who did not—would not—hire others to re-roof the house or build a bookcase; he was different than Alan, rougher, stronger.

Finally, Robin stopped watching Aidan from the window and carried a plate of oatmeal cookies over to his house. She'd read *The Female Eunuch* the year before, and *The Feminine Mystique* before that, and she felt sinkingly guilty, crossing the manicured lawns with her arms full of warm cookies, the dutiful, welcoming housewife. She thought, briefly, she should have brought a bottle of whisky, cold beer; instead, her white-and-blue china plate (so he'd have to return it?) full of cookies in her practical hands. She touched her hair, tugged at her skirt, as she waited for him to answer the door.

"Hello?" He was lean, tall, tan. She saw the edge of paler skin at his T-shirt collar, forced herself to look away. When he smiled, easily, his eyes wrinkled slightly in the corners.

"I'm from next door. Robin Hollis. I guess we're neighbours now." She held the plate out, her predictable, too-plain offering. "Oatmeal," she said.

"I'm Aidan," he said with a smile. "Aidan Felles." He took the plate, lifting it lightly from her hands. "Thank you."

They stood quietly for a moment, neither talking, each waiting for the other. Robin tried to think of something to say—should she ask him where he was from? Invite him to their house for a drink one night?—and was surprised when he spoke first.

"It's quiet here. You're the first neighbour I've met."

Robin said, "I'm the bored housewife. Nothing else to do." She regretted it the moment she said it, feeling tidy in her denim skirt and white cotton blouse, carrying cookies and admitting her deepest, most awful fear: I'm a bored housewife, that's all.

Aidan looked at her evenly with his warm brown eyes, frowning a little, and then nodded. "Okay," he said. "Still my only visitor."

Aidan had moved from the interior of British Columbia, where he had been a firefighter. He'd gotten a small inheritance, and decided to move to the island. He loved the water; he'd wanted to live on the coast since he'd first seen the ocean. Robin asked him about firefighting, if he missed it, but he only shrugged. She understood that he didn't want to talk about it, that there must have been a reason why he decided to leave, why his life had changed so suddenly. She imagined a woman, some love story gone wrong. And then she hated herself for assuming something so predictable. He didn't say what he planned to do now, if he planned anything at all, and Robin didn't ask. And then Aidan asked about her—what did she do? What was she interested in? He did not ask about Alan, or Phoebe, when she finally (guiltily?) mentioned them. He asked why she hadn't finished her nursing degree, said he was sure she would have made a great nurse. She flushed. She felt colour spill back into her when he said her name.

She suggested a drink one night when Alan would be there, and Aidan smiled a slow smile, looking straight into her eyes, and nodded. Robin went home, feeling off balance, and was unable to get him out of her mind for days after.

He came for drinks, laughed with Alan and praised their home, invited them over to see the changes he'd made to his own house. Robin watched Alan talk to Aidan, watched him become animated in the presence of another man his age. There was a certain ease between them, the ease that seemed to only come between youngish men in backyards, cold drinks in their hands. But every so often, Robin caught Aidan watching her for a moment too long, found his eyes trailing over her unhurriedly. He didn't look away when Robin caught his eyes; he didn't seem embarrassed or apologetic. His gaze was plain, open, and Robin felt herself flush again, quick and true. It was the first time in years that she had been aware of another man's gaze, his obvious interest in her. And the first time she had felt so thoroughly powerful because of it. His gaze made her brave.

One hazy, grey spring evening, Aidan invited Robin and Alan over for a drink. "You go," Robin said. "I'm not feeling up for it."

"Come on, be social."

"I have a headache," Robin lied.

Alan raised his eyebrows, and Robin knew she'd go: it seemed begging off for a headache was too obvious. Surely, Alan would wonder why she was suddenly cautious, when she had always been happy to see Aidan. Later, she'd say it was something like intuition, maybe premonition, the dark pit she carried in her stomach as she and Alan crossed the dusky lawn to Aidan's house. Dusk, and Robin felt the first suggestion of dew on her shoulders, the way the evening turned into itself. Alan carried a bottle of wine, held her hand during the short walk.

They talked, laughed, and music soared and then turned bluesy when Aidan changed the record. Robin drank more than she usually would, and Aidan politely refilled her glass when it was empty. His hand touched hers—only briefly, so momentary it could have been accidental, but she knew it was not, could not be—and she looked up sharply at him. He watched her evenly, his eyes crinkling in the corners, and she did not look away. She looked back, sure that he could see what she meant. Something thrilled in her chest.

Alan told a joke, poured himself a glass of scotch and laughed at his own cleverness, and then started to talk about the conference he planned to go to, and Aidan watched Robin in her measured responses: a nodding of her head, murmurs of support. She was aware she was playing a role, was doing exactly what Alan would expect her to do, and that Aidan was seeing something else entirely, the artifice behind it, the real her remaining cool and indifferent below. The room felt too hot, too close, and when Alan offered to run next door and get another bottle of wine, Robin said she'd just step outside to get some air.

The yard was dim, dark, crowded with tall trees and limbs heavy with needles and leaves. The moon was high, a crisp silver blue, and it lit her path as she moved away from the house and into the privacy that the trees afforded.

Alan had had most of the trees taken down in their own back-yard, claiming the needles clogged up the pool filters. Their yard was open, bare, full of sunshine all day long. But here, in Aidan's yard, there were shadows and swaying tree branches, something that felt magical.

Under the trees, partially hidden from view, Robin felt her head clear. She took a sip of her wine, and the warmth trailed down her throat. She looked up to the sky, the stars bright and the clouds whisper thin, and wrapped her arm around herself.

"Cold?" Aidan's voice, low and clear, came from her right. She turned, slowly, and smiled at him.

"Just a chill, that's all."

They stood in silence, Robin still looking up at the sky and Aidan—Robin knew, could feel it—looking at her. Music drifted back from the open sliding glass door, and Robin took another sip of wine. It seemed like the minutes dragged on, painfully slowly— where was Alan?—while they waited. Waited because Robin knew what was about to happen, just not how exactly. But she felt the heat of his skin against her arm, smelled his warmth, the undercurrent of soap and skin. There was no question about what would happen between them.

The boughs shivered, the shadows shimmied. Aidan touched her arm lightly. She turned to him, and he was shadowed. She wanted to put her hand on his chest, but did not. She breathed the cool air in, looked up at him. Aidan smiled a slow smile, and then she moved forward, kissed him hard and deep under the boughs.

She loosened, her body quavering, and she concentrated on his mouth, his hand warm on her back, how lean and hard his body was against hers. She thought of Alan in a distant way—what would he see if he came out into the yard now, wine bottle in hand, wondering where Robin and Aidan had gone?—but then abandoned the thought and pressed against Aidan, his kiss deepening as she demanded more of him. They stumbled backward until Robin was against the wide trunk of a tree, bark against her skin. The bite of the bark seemed right. There was something different about this kiss—pure need, desire so clear it strained. She'd never experienced this before. She moved against Aidan, feeling the dark ache in her pelvis, the hot spread until they were interlocking, thigh against thigh, hands on backs, breasts, chest. Robin sighed, slackened, as Aidan's mouth moved down her neck and she dropped her wineglass; it landed with a dull thud.

"Robin?" Alan called from somewhere within Aidan's house. It was distant, indistinct, and Robin pulled away from Aidan, more slowly—grievously—than she might have expected. As if there was some part of her that wanted to be caught. Aidan stepped easily into the moonlight, and Robin touched her lips, bruised and plump. She looked at Aidan, smiled apologetically—for what, for pulling him against her, and into the wreck of her life?—and he called toward the house, "Out here, Alan."

Robin straightened her blouse, bent to pick up the wineglass, watched Aidan wave Alan out to the yard. Robin touched her hair and then turned brightly to where she knew Alan would be emerging. It had been so easy—she had kissed him, confident in his response to her. So assured. She had wanted to kiss him, wanted to feel his body thrumming against her, knew that touching him would make her actually feel something, and so she had done it. Her heartbeat pulsed.

"I was just admiring all the trees," she said. "I wish we'd kept ours."

Alan had an easy, unsuspecting smile, and an open bottle of wine in his hand. He took Robin's glass and refilled it. "Too much work," he said. "I like things simple."

Robin took a long drink of wine, and listened half-heartedly as Alan and Aidan debated the merits of trees, of hours of maintenance, of nature. Aidan told Alan all about the wildfires he'd seen in the interior, and Alan listened, filling his own wineglass. Still, his words remained in Robin's mind: I like things simple. For some reason, she was sure he was talking about more than yardwork; he was talking about her. Simple. He saw only the surface of her, the parts of her he already knew, and she realized she'd always known this, somewhere deep and secret within her. It explained her dulled unhappiness, her feeling of being flattened out, airless.

Alan was talking about something—Robin couldn't hold the threads of the conversation, his words blurred and merged—and she looked away, up to the stars between the treetops, and she knew why she had been so reluctant to pull away from Aidan: this would be the only time she felt that way, the hard edge of real want. She'd go home with Alan and all her days would continue as they had, unending and static. Grey.

I like things simple.

When she turned to look at Alan—trying to concentrate on what he was saying, trying to make some sort of decision—it was Aidan who was looking at her. Even though Alan might see, if he paid attention. Had anyone ever looked at her so plainly? Recognizing her in a pure way? His smile reminding her of what they had just done, how she'd ached for him. She touched her tingling lips. All she had risked. Willingly. Her cheeks burned, and she was glad for the dark, glad for Alan drinking his wine and talking, oblivious.

It was that moment when Robin knew she'd let this happen again, this and more, and that she was many things but simple was not one of them.

❖

School ended and summer began in earnest. Summer meant that Maybe slept later, was prodded awake by Gigi, rolling over in her bed to cover her eyes and pull the pillow firmly over her head. Nine o'clock seemed early, unnecessary, where seven o'clock had so recently been normal. And it had been harder and harder for Maybe to sleep since the Hollises' pool party; she spent the night tossing and turning, her bed suddenly too small, claustrophobic, sleep impossible. Images of Camille raced through her head; she imagined endless versions of Camille's book. Morning was edging itself into Maybe's room by the time she finally fell asleep. When she woke, she was exhausted, as if she hadn't slept at all.

Gigi worked four days a week at the café; there had been money after George's death, and she had been careful. On those four days—Tuesday through Friday, thanks to seniority—Maybe was shuffled between the Hollises, Walter and Mrs. Eames. The summer before, Maybe had spent the fourth day with the Lalondes; but, now, as Danny and Charlie got older, schedules became more complicated, life more complex. Now, Maybe tried to argue that she was old enough to stay home alone. The idea of all those hours alone, all those hours where she would try to piece together Camille's life, seemed like a perfect gift. But Gigi scoffed at the idea. "You're only eleven," she said as she touched Maybe's arm. Maybe heard it in her voice: only a child. She bristled, but knew she would not win this argument. And so, for the first time, Maybe would spend one day a week with Mary Quinn. This both thrilled and terrified Maybe.

Mary had offered quickly and certainly, surprising everyone. Robin had said, "We'd love to have her, all four days, even," as she squeezed Maybe's shoulder, and even after Mary's offer, it had seemed that this was what would happen. Even though Mary and Gigi had become quite friendly, Gigi said dropping Maybe off at Mary Quinn's house every Wednesday morning would be intrusive, too much to ask, too familiar. Politeness and boundaries were not lost on Gigi. But Mary Quinn insisted, said she'd like to have the company, and so Gigi had finally agreed.

"It's just one day," Gigi assured Maybe, and Maybe suppressed the cautious excitement within her. So, instead, she said what Gigi expected: "It will be okay. I'll make do."

The day with Mary would be different from the rest—it wouldn't be swimming pools or silver garden shears or stacks of old books and too-sweet iced tea. Maybe imagined that Mary might talk about her life before she'd come to the island, the other places she'd been, things she'd seen. The thought alone made her swoon. The potential of it was almost enough to assuage the insult of Gigi calling her *only a child.*

"Listen to Miss Quinn," Gigi said as they crossed the street and passed by Aidan Felles's quiet house. "Eat whatever she serves you. Don't be difficult."

"Never am," Maybe said. She was busy staring at Mary Quinn's house, as if it might tell her something more about her. She'd never known anyone like Mary—successful, unmarried, no children to run after, to flatten her out. Maybe wanted to know everything about her.

Gigi tapped her on the head. "Listen, listen."

Maybe nodded, smiling at Gigi as they turned up Mary Quinn's driveway, the crushed gravel announcing their arrival. Big, showy white hydrangeas lined the drive, and the house sat back from the road, partially hidden by leafy trees. She'd painted the house grey, so on a misty day it blended in with the horizon and the rolling sea beyond. A large copper pot sat at the front door, spilling over with hot-pink geraniums. Everything was very orderly, nothing out of its place.

Gigi rapped quickly on the door and they waited, standing in the shade. Gigi peered in the window beside the door.

"Do you think she forgot?" Maybe asked quietly.

"No, no. I'm sure she's here." Gigi knocked again, this time harder, and Mary appeared, pulling the dark door wide open.

Her coppery hair was twisted up on top of her head, a few stray strands coming down around her face. She wore a ripped pair of jeans and an oversized, white, men's button-down. There were paint splatters on the shirt, shades of blue and a long, lone streak of yellow.

"Sorry," Mary said, and her voice was lower, more melodic than Maybe remembered. She sounded like honey, warm and deep and amber. "Time got away from me." Mary had a streak of yellow on her cheek. It was high up, and Maybe wanted to wipe it away. Instead, she put her hand to her own face, as if there were a streak of paint there as well.

"Come in, come in," Mary said, holding the door wide and stepping back. "Lost my manners along with the time. My mind's next." She winked at Maybe, but it was Gigi who laughed, an awkward, clipped laugh.

"Thanks again," Gigi finally said. "Are you sure it won't be..." She trailed off but Maybe knew what she meant: a bother, too much, too difficult. But Mary only laughed and shook her head, smiled her warm smile at Maybe.

"We'll be grand," Mary said. "Honestly, I'm happy to help out."

It was the way she said it, earnest and a little desperate, that made Maybe realize that Mary Quinn was nervous, too. She was used to being solitary, but on Lear Street she was meant to be a part of it all. A part of them. Maybe smiled back at her, hoping to reassure her even a little.

"I should be back around four," Gigi said. "Before the big supper rush, but long enough to wear me out."

Mary smiled, was careful in her responses as if she had practised. She was new to these strange, forced play dates. The geniality of leafy suburban streets.

"She has her bag. She'll eat anything but liver or Brussels sprouts. If she gets bored, a book or notepad will keep her busy."

Gigi gave Mary Quinn her number at the diner and reminded her that Walter could always help, that Robin was home today as well, before she kissed the top of Maybe's head and said sternly, "Be good."

Maybe watched Gigi leave (turning back once halfway down the driveway, squinting at the house) and then she disappeared onto Lear Street and Maybe and Mary Quinn were left alone standing at the open front door. Maybe suddenly felt very self-conscious. She tugged at her T-shirt.

"Well," Mary said as she wiped her hands on her jeans. "We could have some breakfast in the backyard. How does that sound?"

Maybe nodded and followed silently behind Mary through the house. It was all warm wood and white walls, large turquoise bowls, tall yellow vases and huge, stretched canvases that took up most of the wall space. They moved through the living room with its long, deep sofas and shaggy carpets, and then through the kitchen, the windows unadorned and open to the early sunshine. Glass doors led to the backyard, where there was a long teak table and chairs. Everything in the house was nicer, newer than what Maybe and Gigi had. Mary ducked her head into the refrigerator and told Maybe to head outside. "I'll bring the feast," she said.

Outside, the breeze came in through the trees, and the stone patio and lawn were dotted with patches of sunlight. The air was warm already, and promising to get warmer. Maybe could see the sea between the tree trunks, a still, certain blue, the edges of driftwood.

"Here we are." Mary appeared with a tray piled high with toasted rye bread, a tub of cream cheese, a plate of smoked salmon, tiny capers and one tall glass of orange juice next to a wide red mug of coffee. Mary put it down with a flourish, bowing slightly as she said, "Voila."

Mary handed her a plate and Maybe went about spreading cream cheese on her toast, careful to cover it just so. They ate in silence, only the sounds of the sea and the birds around them. Maybe shifted in her chair, drank her orange juice too quickly. Everything she did seemed wrong.

Finally, Mary said, "Frances—Gigi—has told me all about you. She said you like to read."

Maybe swallowed a bite of her toast. It felt dry, sticking in her throat. "I do."

"I don't read a lot. I'm more visual." She laughed when she said this, as if she were letting Maybe in on a joke.

Maybe nodded, trying to figure out a way to ask Mary all the questions she had—about Mary Quinn's art, her life before she came to Lear Street. She was trying to formulate a question that wouldn't make her sound like just another kid, when she heard herself say, "Why did you come here?"

Mary tilted her head to the side when she looked at Maybe. "Don't lots of people want to live near the ocean?"

Maybe heard the lie in her answer, knew that there was some other reason, a reason Mary did not want to talk about, for why she was here. Maybe smiled as if she believed her, nodded, and Mary busied herself with cleaning up the breakfast dishes while Maybe sat outside, wondering if this would be how they would spend the next hours, moving cautiously around one another. The hours stretched, loomed.

Mary went into the house and Maybe could hear the gentle tinkling of dishes under water. She walked toward the treeline that bordered the sandy beach, and the ocean beyond. The trees were thicker there, clustered closer together, keeping Mary's yard private from anyone who wandered the beach. Along the treeline, Mary had planted some bright purple flowers that hovered low to the ground; tucked into the foliage was a wooden carving of a face, the profile smooth and oiled. Maybe looked at the face, wondered, what it meant, why Mary wanted it here in her garden. It was a sad face, eyes downturned and mouth set, nothing hopeful or triumphant in it, and this, more than anything, made Maybe curious all over again about Mary.

Maybe only knew that Mary Quinn was successful, that her paintings had sold quickly and for a lot of money, and that she lived alone. Had visitors once in a while, cars pulling in and out of her driveway. Gigi said Mary Quinn just needed a change, would not say any more, though Maybe was convinced she knew more about her. And now there was this strange, sad face staring up at Maybe from the garden. It felt like a clue to Mary Quinn's past.

"I did read your mother's book." Mary appeared silently from the house, her bare feet quiet on the grass.

"You—read it?" Maybe could tell by Mary's face that she had thought this would be something they would have in common.

Mary nodded. "It was good. I mean, for what it was. What she had to say."

What she had to say. There was an edge behind Mary's words, but Maybe could not interpret what she meant. So she nodded, but realized too late that Mary had expected her to have a response, too. Her silence only confirmed things. She'd given herself away.

"You haven't—oh, never mind. Never mind." Mary turned away to look at the carved face in the greenery, obviously embarrassed by her misstep.

Mary kept looking at the face, and Maybe couldn't say anything. She felt the moment when she might have confessed that she hadn't read it but longed to pass, flit away into nothingness. It felt childish to admit that she had not been allowed to read it. "I don't remember anything about her."

"About your mother?"

"I was really little when she left. I mean, I have this one kind of memory, of her reaching down to pick me up. At the beach, I think, but that's it."

Mary turned away from the face in the garden to look at Maybe. "That's hard," she said. "It's been a long time."

Maybe nodded, and felt her eyes filling with tears. She could not—would not—cry in front of Mary Quinn. She bit the inside of her cheek, hard. The quiet stretched and ached, until Maybe could bear it no more. She finally said, "I wonder—I mean, would you want to show me how to paint?" She saw Mary's shoulders ease, her face relax, and her honeyed smile return.

"Yes. Sure. That's a great idea. We'll need some things," she said as she disappeared back into the house. Maybe waited, looking at the carved face and wondering where Mary Quinn might keep Camille's book. *It was good...for what it was.*

For the rest of the afternoon, Mary taught Maybe about painting, giving her her own long canvas to streak paint across. Maybe ran her brush across it, back again, unsure of what she should be trying to paint. Mary turned the radio on loud, and from the house "Brown Sugar" and "Maggie May" called out to them. There was finally a pulse and a rhythm to the day. Things turned easier, comfortable. Maybe painted in reds and soft corals. Mary used blue.

Mary told Maybe that she was painting a series based on the saints—on *women* saints—and how she had suddenly found herself concerned with the colour of their robes. She mixed and remixed the paints. Painted over sections. "Silly, isn't it?" Mary said. "Their robes were probably all brown."

Maybe meant to say something about the woman on Mary's canvas, how beautiful she was, the way she'd made the eyes perfectly reflect light, but hesitated. It wasn't exactly what she wanted to say. What she needed to say. Instead she asked, "Can you tell me about the book?"

Mary Quinn looked surprised. But then her eyes turned sad. Maybe hated the feeling of pity washing over her. Mary said, "I don't know what to say about it, really. I've never had any children. I don't know what it's like."

Maybe turned back to her canvas, trying to hide her disappointment, trying to understand what Mary meant about children, and her cheeks reddened. She did not mention the book again. She knew the words, her desperation, hung between them like the lick of salt air.

Gigi found them painting in the open air of Mary's backyard. She cocked her head at Maybe's odd painting—she'd only managed streaks of paint, colours bleeding together, her mind too busy with Mary's words, *I've never had any children. I don't know what it's like*—but didn't say anything. The long streaks of yellow across coral. She thanked Mary, who insisted Maybe could come back any time. Not just on Wednesdays. She winked at Maybe, and Maybe felt the thrilling rush of acceptance pulse through her.

"I told you it would be fine," Gigi said as they crossed Lear Street toward the cottage.

"She's nice," Maybe said, thankful that Mary Quinn hadn't said anything to Gigi about the book. The embarrassment of her own desperation for information still hummed within her.

"Halibut for dinner?" Gigi asked as they passed into the yard and through to the back door. "Fresh," she said as she put her key in the lock and pushed. Maybe followed close behind her, close enough that she found herself crushing into Gigi's back when she stopped short just inside the kitchen. The bag of halibut fell to the floor with a wet thud.

"Gigi—" Maybe said, but stopped when she stepped to the side and saw what Gigi saw.

The blurred face from her memory. The golden hair. Camille sat at the kitchen table with a glass of wine. She calmly said, "Hello."

redemption

In the spring of 1971, Prime Minister Trudeau married twenty-two-year-old Margaret Sinclair. Everyone pored over newspaper clippings and segments on TV; Margaret was so beautiful, so young, and it all seemed desperately romantic. Maybe said Mrs. Trudeau reminded her of Robin. Phoebe snorted, unwilling to see her mother as that glamorous, ever that young. Still, the two girls stared hard at the photos until they became a mass of dots only, nothing more than shadow.

Gigi called Prime Minister Trudeau charming, but she said it in a way that Maybe knew she meant something else entirely. Maybe squinted at the photos of him and tried to see what Margaret Sinclair saw. Kind eyes, maybe. A quick sparkling smile. But he was so much older.

Maybe and Phoebe memorized the photos of Prime Minister Trudeau and his new wife. They took note of Margaret's shoes, the way she combed her hair, the corners of her smile. Everyone was fascinated with the Trudeaus. They watched, they listened, they imagined—just for a moment—that they, too, could have this fairy-tale ending one day.

And they all lived happily ever after.

Maybe didn't like to admit that even when they looked at the articles, all those simple, smiling pictures, she didn't really believe in happily ever after. When she read a book where everyone turned out happy, content, blissful, she felt cheated. The endings of the old fairy tales—the young girl eaten by the wolf, the Queen dancing in red-hot iron shoes, the stepsisters' eyes pecked out—seemed more realistic. But Maybe was cautious to acknowledge that black, hard part of herself. She didn't know what happily ever after looked like, really. Couldn't imagine it.

And so when Maybe and Gigi walked into the house to see Camille sitting at the kitchen table, Maybe thought that perhaps this was happily ever after. Her mother had come home. It was the kind of ending she had been meant to believe was happy. Camille at the chipped table, a glass of wine at her elbow, a long strand of turquoise beads at her neck. No longer just a possibility in smudged newsprint, no longer a character in Maybe's notebook. As if Maybe had willed her into appearing. Camille hadn't stood, but ran her finger lightly around the lip of her glass, making it whine. She'd said, "Hello."

They had an awkward dinner. Camille spoke cautiously to Maybe over their forkfuls of halibut and roasted potato. "Do you like school? What's your favourite subject?" Camille tilted her head toward Maybe, but something in the flatness of her eyes made Maybe wonder if she'd been listening at all.

Maybe fumbled with her words—she'd said something about liking language arts—and then Camille settled back into her chair, as if her questions had created a buffer between them. Maybe was quiet the rest of dinner, instead watched Camille toy with her fork, turning it over and over in her hand.

Gigi said, "Why didn't you call?"

Camille shrugged. "I thought it would be a good surprise. Isn't it?"

She looked directly at Gigi, her gaze asking for something. Gigi did not answer.

They talked about the weather, the ferry, the halibut that Gigi cooked. They didn't talk about Camille's return. They didn't ask where she had been. Maybe wanted to ask her about the protests, about being in New York with the other women in miniskirts and holding placards, but she felt small, smaller than she ever had before.

Camille touched the gold dangling earring at her earlobe. She blotted her mouth too many times with her napkin. She was so polished and perfect in her billowing skirt and sheer top, her armfuls of bangles; she'd seen more than just Oak Bay, more even than Victoria, and now everything about her felt too big for the small cottage. Maybe tried to imagine Camille putting the water glasses away, pinning towels on the clothesline, closing her bedroom door quietly late at night. But the images were never quite right; they faltered, lost focus.

And then Gigi had clapped her hands and sent Maybe to have a shower and go straight to bed.

"No dawdling," Gigi said. Camille hadn't protested, had only looked at Maybe, watched her walk down the hallway. Maybe turned the shower on and then stood at the bathroom door with her ear pressed up against it, straining to hear what they were saying. She knew Gigi would be asking all the questions she had now that Maybe was not at the table. Her voice would be tense; her words clipped. But everything was too distant, too faint. So instead she waited for the shower to steam up, and wrote Camille's name with her fingertip on the stall door before rubbing it away.

After, Gigi came down the hall to say good night ("To bed for you! Sleep. Close your eyes and close your ears.") and pulled the door shut with a decisive click. Camille stayed in the kitchen.

Maybe looked up at her ceiling, her hands folded behind her head. Camille was just down the hall in the kitchen, and she was here staring at her plain white ceiling. All she wanted to do was rush down the hall and ask, *Where were you? Why did you leave? Why are you back?* But even now, as Maybe stared blankly up, she knew she wouldn't ask Camille; the words were too raw, too frightening, acidic in her mouth.

Camille would stay in the spare room—the room Camille had grown up in but now they called the spare room, as if Camille had never been there at all.

Where were you?
Why did you leave?
Why are you back?

They jumbled, incoherent and chaotic in her mind.

revelations

The morning was the kind that stays in sharp focus in your mind, hyperdeveloped, the colours and edges crisp. The sunlight was deep and heavy, already a full yellow, the sky a long, lean, cloudless blue. She wasn't sure what time she'd fallen asleep; after a while, Camille and Gigi's voices had become even quieter, and she had felt herself drifting before she'd fully realized it. It had been deeply dark when she'd finally given in and let herself sleep a thick, dreamless sleep.

The house was quiet—there were only the small sounds of Gigi, already out in the back garden—and Maybe slipped silently into the bathroom, looking at herself in the mirror. Her hair was flattened on one side, her face still creased red from the sheets. She brushed her teeth, smoothed her hair into a ponytail and then washed her hands before she padded down the hallway toward the kitchen.

Camille's bedroom door was closed. No sign that she had woken yet. No sure signs that she was still there. No sign that she had ever been there at all. Maybe wondered briefly if she had imagined her.

Outside, Gigi held a garden hose to the beds, rhythmically moving it back and forth. The shushing sound was the sound of every summer, of summer moving past them. The light spray from the hose caught the sunlight and shattered, making the garden smell damply earthy, as if everything was growing as they stood there, watching.

"Morning." Gigi didn't turn to look at Maybe, but continued on her route around the yard. Her pale purple robe was thinned by wear, almost white in the sun. "I haven't put breakfast on yet."

Maybe stepped onto the damp grass, pushed her toe at the blades. She wanted to ask if Camille was still there, but she didn't. She couldn't bear the idea that she'd been allowed only those few, slim hours with Camille, still not knowing anything about her. And that she'd squandered them, staring up at her ceiling, instead of going back down the hall to yell, or cry, or demand answers.

Gigi turned the spray of the hose down low and looked at Maybe. "Did you sleep well?"

Maybe shrugged. "Sort of."

"Were you up late, spying?"

"Couldn't hear anything." Maybe said it before she'd meant to. She tilted her head and looked at Gigi, a smile crossing her face. Gigi shook her head, but Maybe knew she was amused, that she'd expected exactly this of her.

"What are we having?" Maybe asked. Gigi turned the hose back on full force and moved on to the sloping willow trees near the back of the yard. Maybe watched her tug the hose behind her. When she raised her arm, stretching the hose out, the elbows of her robe were worn nearly translucent.

"Eggs. Poached maybe. Or I could do Benedict."

"I hate hollandaise." Camille appeared in the kitchen doorway, stretching her arms high above her head. She wore a short, white, sleeveless nightgown, her tanned legs long and slim beneath it. Camille looked softer than she had the night before, her hair twisted up, her face bare, her nightgown short like a child's. Maybe was startled: this could be the mother she remembered from the beach. The sun behind her, her hair buttery. As if no time had passed at all.

"We could have omelettes," Maybe said quickly.

"Maybe likes Benedict," Gigi said without turning around. "Since when do you hate hollandaise?"

"Since forever." Camille came out into the yard and sat at the small wrought-iron patio set, tucking her legs beneath her.

Forever. The word pulled and stretched, snapped back. Forever was longer than Maybe knew. She couldn't stop looking at Camille's toes, perfectly red, peeking out. She looked down at her own feet, unpainted, unadorned, the tan lines from her sandals. She put one foot over the other.

"Forever is an awfully long time," Gigi said over her shoulder. "I seem to remember you eating Benedicts in this very garden."

Camille rested her chin in her hand, looked both bored and deeply tired. She said quietly, "Isn't it too early for this, Mum?"

Mum. A word that had been noticeably absent in their house until now. Mum. Gigi didn't answer Camille, didn't even acknowledge that she had spoken. There were a few minutes of deep quiet before Camille got up from the small table and said, "Coffee?"

Gigi made eggs, hollandaise on the side, and cooked the bacon. Maybe buttered the toasted English muffins. Camille drank her coffee and, eventually, brought plates and cutlery out into the garden. The knives clanged against the iron table.

They unfurled napkins on their laps. Maybe cut her eggs up smaller than she would have any other day. Camille cleared her throat a few times as if she was going to speak, but only took a long drink of water, ice tinkling in her glass.

"So," Gigi finally said, touching her blue napkin to her mouth. "What are your plans?"

Camille shrugged. "Hadn't made any, really. Maybe go to the beach later, I've missed swimming—"

"No." Gigi glanced at Maybe, and Maybe caught the question in her eyes. She was asking when Camille would leave.

"Oh." Camille smiled slightly. "Oh, I assumed, I mean…I'm going to stay."

"For how long?"

"No, Mum." Camille leaned forward. "I'm *staying*." She paused, looking at Maybe, then back at Gigi. "Well, who knows? We can sort things out."

A warm flush spread quickly over Maybe. Camille's words were light, hopeful.

Gigi said evenly, "You can stay as long as you like."

There was a flash of something between them, then—Camille shifted, softened, pleased that her mother had relented. Pleased,

Maybe thought, that Gigi also wanted her to stay. It was more difficult to say what Gigi wanted, but Maybe saw her look at Camille from the corner of her eye, with something like pleasure, or the moment before pleasure.

"That would be great. Thanks, then."

"They might be hiring at the museum."

"Oh, no." Camille laughed, a clear, quick laugh. "I have a job, Mum. I'm working on a new project. Another book. I *have* a job."

Gigi pushed her chair back. She stacked up the plates, balancing them carefully to take into the kitchen as Maybe had seen her do so many times before at the café. It was what Gigi did when she wanted to avoid whatever was happening around her: she moved, she cleaned, she stacked, she busied herself.

"My editor is very excited about it," Camille said quickly. She smiled at Maybe, as if she wanted Maybe to be excited too, and Maybe smiled tentatively back at her. "He's been such a big champion of my work."

Gigi took the plates in, then returned to collect the glasses. She put them on a long, white tray silently.

"That's great," Maybe said. She didn't know if she was supposed to ask about the book, if she was supposed to pretend she knew what it would be about. So she didn't say anything. The silence was awkward, splayed between them so casually. Camille smiled at her again, but only briefly, quickly turned back to Gigi.

"Mum? I sent you a copy of the first book. Did you get it? Did you read it?" Camille seemed suddenly so young, in her white nightgown, sitting in the sunshine, knees jutting out. Maybe could see the teenager in her, the girl she'd been so recently. She was looking up at Gigi, and Maybe knew that she was hopeful—she wanted Gigi to have read it. She wanted her to be proud. Gigi had never mentioned the book, and Maybe knew if she had read it, she would have told her. Of course, they would have looked at the book together, marvelling at Camille's name on the spine. Maybe was sorry for the disappointment Camille would feel when Gigi told her she'd never received the book, hadn't read it.

Gigi picked up a water glass and paused, the glass in mid-air, as if she was considering whether to place it on the tray or let it drop. Then she moved again, purposefully, cleaning up the forks and smudged napkins, and it was just an ordinary moment again.

"Yes," Gigi said quietly. "I read it."

Maybe felt the wind knocked out of her. For a moment she thought Gigi was lying to spare Camille's feelings, but when she looked up at Gigi's face, she knew it was the truth. She had read the book, and let Maybe find out about it in the Hollises' backyard, surrounded by strangers.

Camille said, "So, my editor, he's very excited about this new one." She smiled up at Gigi, relieved and pleased that she had read the first book. Proud. "I mean, after the first one and all. It's become a bestseller. I'm a little bit famous now." She smiled awkwardly and then paused, picked momentarily at her nails, before saying in a perfectly practised, casual manner, "What did you think of it?"

Gigi still would not look at Maybe. She waited for Gigi to say something, but didn't know what those words would sound like. Not, I'm sorry. Not, I meant to tell you. It was something bigger and more complicated Maybe wanted. She wanted Gigi not to have read the book. To have never opened its cover, fanned the first pages, read every single word Camille wrote. But now Gigi and Camille were complicit in something, and Maybe was left outside it all. She suddenly felt very small and very invisible.

Finally, a bird trilled in one of the trees and Gigi dropped the cutlery onto the long white tray. Her disappointment was palpable. She sighed and looked directly at Camille, exasperation clear on her face. "Oh, for God's sake, Camille. What do you expect me to say?"

"The truth," Camille said, but it came out quiet, wavering.

"Fine. Not much. I didn't think much of it at all."

Camille got up with such force that she nearly knocked the chair over. It wobbled, hesitated, then righted itself. Maybe touched its arm lightly, holding it to the ground, willing it to stay put.

"I knew you wouldn't be happy for me. Couldn't be! You

wouldn't be able to grasp what I accomplished—" Camille's voice lost its music, turned plainly angry.

"There was more that you should have accomplished here."

"You don't understand it, even after you read it. I thought maybe then—maybe!—you'd finally understand. The world is different now—"

Gigi picked up the white tray, now full of glasses and cutlery and the small blue balls of napkins, and turned her back. She didn't look at Camille, merely continued in her practised movements, but everything in her gestures revealed her frustration with the conversation. She was tired and unwilling to continue. "All I understand, Camille, is that you left. You left. And now you're back and nothing has changed."

Was it true? Had nothing changed, even with Camille's return? Camille stared at Gigi for a moment, then walked across the patio and into the cottage, slamming the door shut behind her. Maybe was left staring at Gigi's arms, full of glass and silver. She felt the panic come, hot and quick, like the moments before she would get sick. She felt it come, and wanted to push it down but didn't know how. Maybe said quietly, "She'll leave again."

"Maybe, it's not—"

Maybe walked the length of the yard to the back gate. She unlatched the gate, hopped barefoot onto her bicycle and pedalled away from the cottage, ignoring Gigi calling out after her.

visions and saints

Mary Quinn might have thought she saw an angel when she looked out her studio window that Saturday morning in July. It was a blur of the palest pink, moving fast as a moth's quick-beating wings, and, just as quickly as she had seen it, it was gone.

She pulled open the studio doors and stepped out onto the front lawn and the strangely warm morning, noticing the high blue sky, cloudless. An angel. Surely a sign, now that she was working on her saints series. This was something. It meant she was moving in the right direction, that her choices hadn't been all wrong. She was sure the apparition—the quick, hot flash of pale pink, whatever it was—had gone toward the sea, and so she went that way, too.

Mary took her shoes off when she reached the beach; she liked the feeling of sand between her toes, the very visceral notion of it, and she could move more quickly. She looked to the left and then to the right, but all she saw was shoreline, abandoned beach, and the blue, all the blue. There was no sign of the angel. She closed her eyes and deeply breathed in the salty air, relieved once again that she had come here, that she had left everything else behind and had made the journey to the island. Despite what it cost her. The smell of the ocean, the salty reminder of life in all its gritty reality, was enough. She opened her eyes slowly, and saw her, not fifteen yards down the beach, crouched beside a piece of driftwood.

Maybe Collins.

Maybe in her pale pink nightgown, barefoot, with her bicycle thrown haphazardly against the low, green bush delineating beach from forest. Maybe's bike looked old, second-hand, certainly older than Maybe: the paint was wearing thin, pulled away in places, and there were no additional decorations, no cards in the spokes, no stickers on the frame, no tassels from the handlebars, as Mary had seen on other young girls' bikes. It was simple, functional, and something about it made Mary understand Maybe in a new way.

Mary walked toward Maybe slowly, taking her time as if she had not seen her at all. She was still thinking about the day when Maybe had come to her house, when she had made the mistake of mentioning the book, and the way Maybe had looked at her, her eyes wide and waiting for Mary to say something profound, apologetic, kind. And Mary had said nothing. She didn't know how to respond to the need she saw in Maybe; she didn't realize, until too late, that Maybe's mother was as much a mystery to her as she was to everyone else.

Maybe was crouched low, her toes buried in the sand, her hair tangled from sleep. Her nightgown shivered in the slight breeze. Mary said softly, "Hey, Maybe."

Maybe looked up, and Mary had a sudden vision of her at two, five, seven—she was an accumulation of all those ages and more—those eyes, accusing, pouting, unhappy, but still with something beautifully sad behind them. Mary smiled and, to her relief, Maybe smiled back.

"Oh, it's you."

Mary understood that Maybe had expected someone else; or, rather, that she was hoping for someone else. She stepped closer to Maybe, took a seat on a piece of driftwood. They were quiet for a while, Maybe poking at the hollowed-out piece of wood and Mary watching her, unsure of what to say. Instead, she watched Maybe's clumsy attempts at gouging the bark, the way the stick bent under her weight. Gulls cried. The ocean lapped in and out again, the sound comforting. Finally, Mary said, "Come on. Let's go paint."

Maybe looked up, pushed her hair from her eyes and dropped the stick. She sighed, a sigh so heavy and weary, it almost broke Mary's heart; it was as if Maybe had the weight of the world on her slim little shoulders.

Back at Mary's house, Maybe relaxed. She ate a piece of toast, drank a watery, milky cup of tea while Mary set up two canvases (her own half-finished, a new one for Maybe) in the backyard, facing the sea. Each of Mary's strokes—green, yellow, red on the palette—felt purposeful. Her strokes were confident on the canvas. She knew exactly how Saint Agatha should look, the expression she would be wearing. She motioned for Maybe to come closer, to take her own palette and brush, and Maybe came to her side, hovering.

Maybe painted and Mary watched. Her lines were not practised, were instinctual but clear, long lines of blue and yellow and orange, not the colours she would have expected Maybe to choose, but unflinching: Maybe had a vision that she wanted to commit to the canvas. She worked silently, pausing only now and then to shift her weight from one foot to the other, rotate her angle. She wiped her hands on her nightgown, leaving a streak of blue at the hem. Mary looked more closely at the canvas, thought one corner of the painting might be an earring. There was blue, yellow. A rectangular shape.

The sound of the doorbell surprised Mary, but Maybe kept painting, moving her arm in a fluid arc across the canvas. There was no pause, no falter. Mary left Maybe in the backyard, and went to the front door, saw the outline of a woman outside before she knew who to expect.

Mary recognized Camille Collins from the picture on her book jacket, but now she appeared flustered, younger than she had seemed in the photo, her fair hair piled on top of her head. She wore a turquoise ring, a long strand of amber beads.

"I'm—well, I'm looking for Maybe. My daughter."

"Camille?"

"Yes—have we…met?" Camille's brow knitted together.

"No, I read your book. I recognize you, that's all." Mary realized she had not answered Camille, had not told her Maybe was in the back garden, painting something strange and beautiful. "Maybe's here."

Camille made her way through the house, and Mary watched the twitch of her hips. She stepped out into the back garden and was quickly shadowed.

"Maybe!"

Mary moved quickly, but did not catch the exchange between Maybe and Camille. By the time she went out into the yard, Maybe had put her brush down and was wiping her hands on her nightgown.

"I'm sorry," Camille said. "She—well, she ran off, and I saw her bike in your yard."

"It's fine," Mary said. She smiled at Maybe. "We had a nice time."

Maybe smiled up from under her lashes at Mary and brushed her shoulder as she passed her into the house.

"I'm sorry," Camille said again as she stepped forward, following Maybe back through the house. "If we bothered you, if we interrupted you, I'm sorry." Camille touched Mary's arm awkwardly, her fingers light and cool. Camille was looking at Maybe, her head tilted to the side. She let her fingers remain on Mary's arm for another moment, a moment longer than necessary.

"Really, it was fine," Mary said. "She's a great kid."

Camille smiled, and Mary was not sure if it was from pride or relief. She followed Camille back through the living room and past the kitchen, down the hallway to the front door. Following a trail of bread crumbs, back the way they'd come. Maybe was nowhere in sight, but there was light from where the front door had been left open.

"Your house is lovely," Camille said. She looked out to the front yard, where Maybe was righting her bike on the grass, and then turned to face Mary again. She touched the beads at her neck. "I remember it, from before. You've done a great job with it."

"I get the feeling most people don't share your opinion."

Camille chuckled softly. "It's the street that time forgot. They're not big on change."

Mary nodded and then said, "Come on by for coffee one day. If you like." It wasn't exactly what she had imagined she would say, but it did not surprise her either; she thought of Camille's hand on her arm, how smooth and cool her fingers had been.

"I'd like that." Camille smiled, then turned back to glance at Maybe, who was now on her bike, still barefoot.

Mary watched Maybe pedal ahead, away from Camille, her nightgown blossoming pink and full behind her just as it had before, as if she were an angel being lifted into the air. And Camille trailing behind, her legs silhouetted beneath her cream dress, firmly dedicated to the ground.

the next one

Maybe didn't speak to Camille after she had come to collect her from Mary's yard. She felt foolish, *childish*, for having run off like she had; she didn't know what to say to Camille to explain her behaviour. And she could not talk to Gigi after what had just happened, so Maybe strode into the house, passed Gigi in silence and slammed her bedroom door behind her.

She heard the sound of Camille and Gigi's voices—high and strained from the kitchen, maybe the hallway—but then they were gone, the house quiet, and Maybe thought perhaps they'd both left, disappeared to God-knows-where, and only when she peeked out her window did she see Gigi in her floppy white hat, crouched over the far garden bed.

Maybe looked at the ceiling, trying to focus on anything other than the questions circling her mind. *Why did you leave? Where did you go? Why did you come back?* She knew that Camille would not answer, or would certainly not give her the answers she wanted. Maybe wanted to determine if Camille was really trying to get to know her. Or, get to know her *again*—she must have once known everything about Maybe, held her hands as she learned to walk, changed her diapers, dressed her in footed pyjamas. But Maybe had none of those memories. If they were true, they belonged to someone else. They might belong to Camille.

When Maybe woke, she wasn't sure if she'd been asleep for minutes or hours. The room was still bright, warm, and her arm was uncomfortably twisted behind her head. She walked down the hall, each step creaking and announcing her presence. Camille's door was almost shut, only a slim sliver of light coming from inside. Maybe paused. She heard Camille shift on the bed, imagined her staring out the window and thinking about the life she'd had, the one she had relinquished to come back.

When Maybe pushed the door open, Camille sat on the bed, a notepad on her lap. Plain yellow, lined, the kind you could find in any drugstore stationery aisle. She concentrated on whatever she was writing, and Maybe watched her pen move across the page, filling it quickly with her compact black script. Camille didn't look up at Maybe, didn't seem to notice her at all; her attention was singular. Maybe thought Camille would feel her eyes on her, maybe lift her gaze to acknowledge Maybe. But she did not. She wrote. Finally, Maybe said, "Is that your new book?"

When Camille looked up, her expression was unfocussed, as if she was still attached to her words, to the place that the notepad inhabited. She smiled at Maybe slowly, and put her notepad aside. The pages were crammed with words, every inch full, Camille using each line as two, as if there were no end to her words.

"Sort of. It's just some thoughts for it. I'm feeling my way around."

Maybe leaned against the door frame and waited for Camille to say more, but she didn't. She just looked at Maybe in that strange, distant way of hers. She wondered if Camille still thought of her as the two-year-old she'd been, and was surprised that Maybe had aged at all. Was surprised that she'd grown, had had a whole life unfurling and expanding in Camille's absence. Had Gigi written to her over the years as well, including school photos, telling her about the spelling bee Maybe had won in grade three? About the time Maybe had fallen from her bike and found a spoke threaded into her thigh, needing four painful stitches? Perhaps Camille had seen her life like those flip comics, where you fanned the pages and saw the action unfold: Maybe growing up before her eyes. Perhaps she had been a silent observer of Maybe's whole life.

"What's it about?"

Camille glanced at the notepad. "It's a continuation in a way. I'm exploring what it really means to be a woman. I mean, in these times, with all these—" She waved her hands in the air as if she were searching for words that eluded her. "All these constraints. All these *expectations*."

The room was hot, overly close, despite the open windows and the scent of salt beyond. *A continuation.* She couldn't tell Camille that she hadn't read the first book—hadn't even seen it—and didn't know anything about it, other than the title. That title.

"It's about, well, navigating the world as a woman now. Asking the questions everyone is afraid to ask." Camille shook her head, pushed at stray strands of hair that had come loose. Her red nails fluttered through her hair as she repinned it. "It's about choices. It's about all the stories that women have."

"I've read some other books about that. From the library. Gigi doesn't really believe in the women's movement."

Camille laughed. "Of course she wouldn't."

"So, are you a part of it, then?"

"Maybe. That's certainly how my publishers positioned it. But I was just writing my story."

"Is that why you went to New York? To be part of it?"

"Sort of. New York was something important. But I also wanted to see other places. Places other than here."

Maybe felt her face flush hot with Camille's words. *Places other than here.* She had left Maybe, and Gigi, and the life they'd had here. It was a fresh sting for Maybe, this reminder that she had propelled herself simply away.

Camille leaned forward toward Maybe. "Oh, Maybe, I'd have died if I just stayed here. Marrying some boy from my class, cooking him pot roasts, worrying over his happiness." She paused. Maybe knew Camille was expecting some understanding, some complicit agreement. Maybe knew what Camille meant. But she also knew that these were the things women did. They were ordinary gestures. "I'm almost thirty now. Thirty. Christ." She rubbed her forehead as if the thought of thirty weakened her. "I'm getting so old."

"No, you're not," Maybe said quickly. Camille was beautiful, and she was young still, shiny and modern and smart. But Maybe

felt silly saying it, and immediately wished she'd said something—
anything—else.

"You're so sweet," Camille said. Sweet. Childish. More than
predictable. Maybe hated the word, the way it sounded coming
from Camille.

Maybe could not bear to look at her again, so instead looked
around the room. Camille's suitcase open in the corner, a blue skirt
spilling over the side. She'd left a pair of silver sandals at the foot
of the bed, a stack of bangles on the dresser. Maybe looked hard
at each of these objects, willing them to tell her something about
Camille, but they remained static. Just things. Things. Maybe knew
that she'd missed something in Camille's words, something essential
about why she'd left, but she could not bring herself to ask Camille
again. These were the things she should instinctually understand.

"Well, look at you two in here, happy as clams." Gigi's hand was
quick and light on Maybe's back.

"Phoebe's at the back gate," Gigi said, and Maybe understood
this as Gigi asking her to leave. Gigi would stay and she and Camille
would argue in low tones or say nothing at all, each of them wilfully
silent, Maybe couldn't tell which.

"She's waiting," Gigi said, and still Maybe didn't move. She was
looking at Camille, trying to decipher what she'd almost revealed.

"It's fine," Camille said softly, and Maybe moved away into the
hallway. She had instinctively obeyed Camille. A hot, primal instinct.
Her cheeks burned, and she rushed away from the room.

❖

Maybe and Phoebe rode their bikes away from Lear Street and
the beach, taking Beach Drive inland toward their school. The
playground at Willows School would be abandoned, the swings
and slides and monkey bars all free, as it would never be during
the school year. There was something a little eerie about an empty
playground, the way the play structures appeared to be waiting for
someone to occupy them, bereft in the sun.

Maybe pedalled hard, standing up to push herself further, liking
the strain in her legs, the whip of wind against her face. She wanted

to put as much distance between herself and the cottage as she could. She'd seen the disappointment in Gigi's eyes when she'd finally moved away from Camille's door. The guilt of it was hot and damp on Maybe.

For as long as she could remember, there had been the ghost of Camille around them, surrounding them, but ghosts were different than the living. Camille was, at once, exactly as Maybe had imagined, and nothing like the version she had created in her head. And then there was Gigi's obvious distrust of Camille's return, so swift and unpredictable. And the new book. The first book. There was so much she didn't know, it clouded her mind.

Maybe and Phoebe pedalled past the closed red brick school, left their bikes at the edge of the schoolyard, leaned up against the fence, and walked to the swings. For a while, they swung in tandem, in silence, before Phoebe finally said, "My mum wants to meet your mum."

"Oh yeah?"

"She read her book or something." Phoebe pumped higher, her dark hair spilling out behind her. The schoolyard was thickly hot with the sun coming down to greet the pavement and gravel, the deep red walls of the school. Heat radiated. Maybe thought she could see shimmers of it coming up from the dark grey cement. It made everything seem unhinged, carefully separate from their legs kicking high into the air.

Her book, her book, her book. Everyone was talking about it—Mary Quinn, Robin, Gigi and even Camille herself—and Maybe still hadn't even seen it. She'd looked around the cottage for it, but only found Gigi's cookbooks, a few paperbacks about gardening, two tattered murder mysteries. Yet the title *The Other Mother* made something twinge in Maybe. *Other Mother.* Maybe had had love and certainty, she'd had comfort and reliability. But not a mother. Not *her* mother. Maybe had often imagined Robin singing to Phoebe as a baby, tucking her into bed, and it pained her a little, knowing she'd never had that with Camille. The pain still surprised her; she hadn't known it was so clearly there, just below the surface.

"What did she say about the book?" Maybe asked.

"Nothing really. Just that she read it. And wanted to meet her."
Phoebe turned to look at Maybe, becoming a blur, moving forward
and up, again and again. "What's the book about?"

The words were in brilliant lights in the sky, pulsating: The
book. The book. The book. Maybe wanted to tell Phoebe that she'd
gone to the library, had tried to find the book without any luck, but
the memory of searching the shelves for her own mother's book
quieted her. Maybe finally said, "I don't know. Haven't seen it." She
hoped her voice sounded normal, but she heard the hollow twang
of it even in her own ears. "What did it look like?"

Phoebe shrugged. "A baby blanket, big letters." Maybe had
imagined any number of words within its pages. Could it be about
her? Or perhaps about Camille's own youth, about Gigi? Or something else entirely. There were nine years of events, losses, joys, that
Maybe knew nothing about. She couldn't bring herself to admit any
of this to Phoebe, who knew every detail of her mother's life. She
was jealous of the way Robin touched Phoebe's hair, smoothing it
absently. "I don't know."

Maybe pushed harder, higher, and watched the gravel of the
playground below her, the shades of grey merging and pulling away
from one another until she felt dizzy with the motion. Still, she
kept pushing. She shut her eyes and then felt only the wind in her
face, the way it fluttered through her hair, the hardness of the chain
against her hands.

"I could get it for you." Phoebe's voice seemed to come from
nowhere; the world was still darkly orange behind Maybe's closed
eyes. When she opened them, Phoebe was looking straight ahead,
no longer pushing her swing higher, faster, but drifting, slowing
next to her.

Phoebe said, "I saw it under the bed. I could get you the book."
"Really?"

"Sure." Phoebe shrugged, toeing her sneakers into the gravel.
Her swing jerked to a sudden stop. "It's too hot. Come on, let's go
back to the beach."

Maybe let her legs drop, waiting for the swing to slow, for her
feet to once again touch the ground and for everything to go back

to normal. For her head to stop spinning. To stop imagining the book in her hands.

They walked back to their bicycles in silence, the afternoon humming around them. Maybe said, "Will you? Get the book, I mean."

"Sure," Phoebe said again as she climbed on her candy-apple-red bicycle. She'd gotten it a few years ago for her birthday, brand new. Maybe had been awed by how shiny it was, how smooth and certain and solid when Phoebe pulled the ribbons off. How red.

"I'll sneak it out." Phoebe winked at her and everything shifted back into normalcy. It was just a summer afternoon with her best friend, the promise of the beach and, later, the sizzling Hollises' barbecue filled with burgers or kebabs or steaks, and Maybe wiping her mouth on a napkin printed with watermelon slices at the back-yard picnic table, while Professor Hollis smiled at Robin and Robin pretended to be annoyed.

Maybe hoisted herself onto her bike and rode beside Phoebe back the way they'd come, the smell of the sea getting stronger with each pedal of her bike.

collections

It didn't happen gradually, all sidelong glances and whispered promises. There was none of that. No hesitation, no uncertainty. That first kiss was a declaration, and everything after it inevitable. Robin didn't really remember the days between the kiss and everything else, and it didn't seem to matter: they fell quickly into a pattern, and it felt like things had always been this way. She looked out the window to Aidan's house, and imagined what he was doing—something as ordinary as making a turkey sandwich, or hanging laundry on the line—and she had an ache to be beside him, their hands touching in the dailiness of routine.

The first time they were together, Alan was at a department potluck, and Phoebe had gone to Maybe's house, excited at the prospect of making a lemon meringue pie with Gigi. Phoebe wanted to be the one to use the blowtorch on the meringue, though Gigi raised her eyebrows and said, "We'll see."

At first, Robin convinced herself that she'd spend the night reading, or taking a long, scented bath. All the things that she *should* do. Even as she thought it, she knew that it would not be the case; it would only be a matter of time before she put red lip gloss on her lips—the one she loved, but Alan thought was too bright—and left the house. She tried to convince herself she was just going for a walk, or just angling to the beach, watching the waves crash against the shore. But she left the house out the back sliding door, and crossed the yard to the gate, nowhere near the beach. She walked under the heavy-limbed trees, purposeful, and knocked on Aidan's back door.

They had wine. There was music. Aidan laughed when she told him stories about Phoebe and Maybe. Aidan sat beside her on the couch, and she kissed him. Later, she didn't remember exactly how it happened, only that it did, and they were in Aidan's bed, the sheets smelling of laundry detergent, and he smiled at her, at the sight of her below him illuminated by moonlight. The whole night seemed to be only moments, snapshots, nothing moving in chronological order. And, later, when those moments came to her at strange times during the day—her hands immersed in a sink full of soap, pulling the sheets tight on Phoebe's bed—she'd be momentarily caught, amazed that it had been she who had done those things. The tattoo on his shoulder a surprise. The lean, hard muscles of his lower back. His mouth on her stomach, her thighs. The way he seemed to instinctually know her body, understand what she wanted. It seemed like someone else had pulled his shirt over his head quickly, impatient; someone else who, after, had straddled him, his hands on her hips as she moved against him. After, she'd curled next to him, the length of their bodies aligned, as she had only ever done with Alan. She tried not to think about how different it felt, how every part of her body was alive, all bare nerve endings and impulse. How different.

She'd gone home grudgingly, after they'd made love again, his mouth everywhere, her want of him bottomless, afraid that night would be the one when Phoebe got one of her earaches, got weepy and needy, and would return to the house to find it empty. Robin went back to the quiet house (so few nights in her life had Robin been alone, really and truly alone) and spent the night sleepless, still electrified from Aidan's touch, from her own boldness. How had she never felt this before? How had she assumed the dull pleasantness with Alan was all there was?

She woke in the middle of the night, sore and disoriented until she heard Alan snoring, rolled over to see his hunched form under the blankets. And she was afraid she'd dreamed it after all.

But then, the next time Robin saw Aidan (across the flames of a neighbourhood bonfire) he held her gaze steadily, so much declaration in that gaze, Robin felt a deep ache and she knew it had happened. And would happen again.

❖

When Maybe first learned to read, she opened her books to marvel at the way the letters now co-operated with one another. And later, when she understood that the people around her had had lives before she knew them, long, spiralling histories that transformed them into new people she had not yet met, she started collecting stories. Maybe had spent her childhood surrounded by people much older than her—Mrs. Eames had introduced her to poetry, pressing a worn copy of Emily Dickinson into her hands, and Walter taught her to play cards, how to shuffle so they snapped—and her interest in their stories seemed natural. She was curious about who they had been when they were young. Maybe it was because she was, as Gigi said, an old soul, but by listening to their stories, collecting all the details, she was envisioning her own future life. Walter had survived the death of his wife and son. Mrs. Eames had salvaged herself after her husband's disappearance. Gigi had buried George Collins, and later watched her daughter walk away. If they had come through all these tragedies, Maybe could certainly survive the disappearance of Camille.

Walter had once told Maybe a story about Camille when she was young, a simple story about burned waffles and Camille scraping the char off and eating them anyway, just because Gigi offered, instead, to make crepes. It was a normal story that Maybe should have known about her mother, but she did not, and this made her cry. He put his arms around her and shushed her.

Maybe couldn't explain it to him. She didn't have any memories of Camille, and she was envious that he did. She said only, "I don't remember that," and Walter misunderstood what she meant. He said, "Of course you don't, sweetheart. It was before you were born." He didn't understand what she meant. They were at his kitchen table; Maybe's arm stuck to the plastic placemat when she raised her hand to wipe at her eyes. She was embarrassed by her tears, and embarrassed even more by the way Walter looked at her, pitiful, sorrowful. In an effort to comfort her, his stories shifted to those about Maybe as a child, or he went further back to when he was a boy himself.

Walter hadn't grown up on the island—he'd only seen the ocean when he came to Vancouver as a teenager looking for work. He'd lived in the interior all his life, on his parents' farm in a valley town. He said he'd been happy enough there as a child—they'd fished in the lakes, gone on horseback into the thick forests bordering the town, had enjoyed all the easy pleasures of childhood—but that the town was stifling for a young man considering his future. His father gave him two hundred dollars and took him to the train station, where he bought him a one-way ticket to Vancouver.

When Walter got off the train in Vancouver, he walked with his small suitcase through Chinatown and to the harbour where he stared at the ocean in wonder. It was so vast, such an unending length of blue, that he could not see any end on the horizon. It simply went on and on, pushing past the towering buildings and bobbing boats toward the mountains. Still snow-capped, even in summer. It was wondrous.

Maybe asked if Walter's father had ever visited, if he'd seen the ocean as well. Walter shook his head. His father had died shortly after Walter left; he'd never seen him again after that morning at the train station. His father shook his hand, and Walter got on the train thinking only about what lay ahead for him. He hadn't yet known he needed to remember what he was leaving behind.

When she was younger, Maybe had gone with Walter to the harbour just to watch the boats pull in and out. Walter watched the boats, and Maybe watched Walter. He looked at the ocean the same way she imagined he would have as a boy: in awe of its size, the power beneath its smooth surface. It was easy to see Walter as a man much younger, with his whole future ahead of him, watching the pull of the ocean.

The next time Maybe wandered down to the beach, she was alone. Dinner had been dismal, with the strangeness between her, Camille and Gigi lingering. Gigi watched her closely, and Maybe was careful in the way she spoke to Camille. Once the dishes were cleared, Maybe slipped out into the warm night air. The sky was that in-between colour that came before sunset, the blue all but disappeared as a glowy orange took over. It would be hot again the next day, and the day after that, until the entire summer merged into one long, relentless day. The road was lined with the dark silhouettes of trees, only giving way when Maybe reached the end, where it opened wide to the beach and the sea.

There were only a few people left farther down the sand, and their laughter floated back to Maybe. Someone had started a bonfire, the flames glowing in the new night. Maybe turned away and walked in the other direction. The water was glassy and still, calming for the night ahead. When she crouched to sit on a piece of driftwood, she noticed something in the hollow of the log. She kneeled on the sand and pushed her hand in. Her fingers found the edges of a book. She knew what it would be before she pulled it out. She tugged it slowly. And there it was: Camille Collins. *The Other Mother.*

The bonfire glowed. The night sky turned darker. Maybe slipped the book in the back of her waistband and pulled her T-shirt down over it. She watched the sun lower itself toward the sea, until the sky was a long strip of indigo, and then a deeper shade still; all evidence of the day drifted out as it had come, the sky turning blank again.

spinning

Mary Quinn was surprised when she opened her front door to Camille Collins. She hadn't seen Camille since the day Maybe went missing, and hadn't particularly expected to see her again. Camille had been cold, distanced, and Mary hadn't quite known how to respond to her. And then there was the moment when Camille touched her arm, and Mary had been taken aback, caught off guard, and she hated feeling that way. She'd had enough of uncertainty.

"Camille."

"Am I bothering you? Are you busy? Painting?"

Mary's mind went blank for a moment, thinking of the brush she'd left, wetly full of sticky blue-grey, and then she had a quick desire to be back there, painting in the back studio, the gestures of Saint Agatha almost right.

"Do you mind?" Camille asked. "Could I come in?"

Mary found herself opening the door, this routine of the suburbs, opening her door to a neighbour and saying, "Come in."

Camille looked grateful, her face bright and sunny. She moved through the house lazily—touching a lamp, the Eames chair, the stone mantel—before finding the doors that led to the backyard. Mary had had them closed while she was working in the studio, but Camille pushed them wide and disappeared as quickly as she'd arrived, as if Mary had dreamt her. Another apparition.

In the yard, Camille folded herself into one of the Adirondack chairs and sat silently. Waiting, Mary thought, for her to join her. She knew she should say something, ask Camille why she was here, what had propelled her down the road, but Camille seemed so young in the chair with her elfin blue dress that Mary Quinn found herself unable to say anything.

Mary recognized that Camille was used to having people attend to her, that she hadn't had to work particularly hard to get what she wanted. People made allowances for Camille. Catered to her. She was, after all, this bestselling author, this denizen of the women's movement. Mary Quinn looked at her more closely. Camille seemed happy to wait, as if she was used to this vague balance, the manipulation in her calm. Mary had seen many people like this, newly famous painters or writers or sculptors, who only wanted admiration, reassurance. They were only comfortable with others' eyes on them.

"So, Camille, what can I do for you?" Mary sat tentatively on the edge of the other chair, facing her.

Camille sighed deeply, leaned her head back to expose the long, golden column of her neck. She said quietly, "My mother is driving me crazy."

A flush went through Mary, hot embarrassment at Camille's confession. It was ridiculous, Camille complaining about her mother as if she were a teenaged girl and not a mother herself, an adult who had already made a long list of choices about her life. Mary could clearly see it all—the posing, the sights, the dramatic entrances: Camille was still the eighteen-year-old girl she had been, all those years ago. Despite her years away, all the things she'd said she'd seen and done, Camille was still that same uncertain girl.

"I think mothers tend to do that," Mary finally offered. She sat back in her own chair, the wood cool through her thin shirt, and folded her legs beneath her. Camille twisted her turquoise ring on her finger so it flashed silver, turquoise, silver, again and again.

"I guess I'd forgotten. I've been away—" Camille caught herself and did not finish her sentence. Mary could see the rest of the thought, just below the surface: I've been away from them for so long. Camille had left them all, had left Maybe and, it seemed, hadn't looked back for nine long years. Mary wondered how many times Camille had thought of her daughter and her mother, had imagined herself coming back.

How had she done it? Had she even recognized Maybe when she came back? Had she wanted to?

Silver, turquoise, silver. Silver, turquoise, silver.

Camille shifted, tugged on the edge of her dress, spun her ring again.

Mary had only met Camille the once, and yet here she was, sitting on Mary's Adirondack, complaining about her mother as if they were the oldest of friends. All her faults. Her judgments. Camille must be lonely; she must have returned to a life she no longer recognized, and now, she no longer recognized her place here. Mary understood that, knew something about suddenly losing your sureness. She felt a pulse of compassion. Camille was flailing. Mary knew precisely how that felt. Camille pulled her dress over her knees, only to have it inch up again. Her kneecaps were bony, tanned.

"I'm just feeling a little"—Camille looked over her shoulder at the tall pines and firs, the clusters that would give way to the beach—"out of place. You know?"

Mary smiled, shrugged. "It must be hard." She knew about feeling out of place, yet she did not have her footing with Camille, and couldn't yet gauge if she should just sigh in the appropriate places, or if she should respond, ask Camille the questions she really had. She finally said, "But you chose this, right? You left."

Camille shook her head suddenly, as if making some decision, and looked up directly at Mary. "I had to go," she said. "I felt like I was shrinking every day. Shrinking and shrinking until I'd be nothing at all." She smiled, apologetically. "Anyhow, enough of that. Tell me about you. How did you wind up here, of all places?"

"I thought it would be inspiring." It sounded lame, even to Mary herself. "So far, it's been mostly quiet."

"That's Lear Street. You didn't expect quiet?"

"I did. I do. It's just—really quiet. More quiet than I imagined."

"Tell me about it." Camille toyed with her ring as she talked, twirling it around her slim finger. "And where did you live before? It wasn't quiet?"

"Vancouver. I had a tiny studio. And now I have"—Mary waved her hands around her—"all this."

Silence settled between them then. Camille uncrossed and re-crossed her legs, and Mary watched those bony knees appear and disappear again. Mary touched her own neck and could only think of Camille's fingers last time, cool and light on her arm.

Camille smiled, leaned forward a little, and the light behind her was a hazy grey. Rain would come, surely. A brief, episodic West Coast rain. It had been so long since Mary had heard the patter of rain on her roof. Camille's face softened.

Mary looked away, but from the corner of her eye she caught it, the quick flash.

Silver, turquoise, silver. Spinning. Spinning.

❖

Camille swam. Every day, she disappeared from the cottage at some point, bathing suit underneath a thin cotton dress dotted with stars. She carried a towel in her hand, her feet bare. Sometimes she went early in the morning (Maybe wondered if she'd slept at all) and other times she waited until dusk, the only person out on Lear Street. She swam out far, until her head was only a tiny speck on the horizon. Her strokes sure, her arms strong and straight in the water. She pushed against the current, or with it, floating on her back to look up at the sky. So wide, blue.

Camille said swimming helped to clear her head; she could think only of her body aching against the current, her lungs straining when she stayed under longer, testing herself.

Camille told Maybe that she had been swimming in the ocean since she was small. She'd started when she was tiny, holding Gigi's hand when she slipped into the sea, the salty waves coming up to meet her. As she grew, she became more confident in the water, swimming out farther and then farther again. After a while, Gigi sat for hours on the beach while Camille swam, looking up sporadically to maintain sight of her. It seemed, now, to be the only thing that Camille had really missed about Lear Street; she swam with dedication. She swam alone. She swam until she was exhausted, worn down to sheer muscle. When Camille swam in the mornings, she came back to the cottage just as everyone else on Lear Street was waking up for the day, percolating coffee, slipping into cars to drive into the city for eight hours at a desk. Then, Camille would rub the sea from her hair, disappear into her room and sleep until the day was plenty past noon.

Maybe watched her slip away from the house, sometimes followed her down to the beach. Camille left her dress and her towel on a driftwood log, slipped into the sea as if it were muscle memory. Right foot, left foot, dive. She remained under the water until she was far enough out that Maybe could not see her face, could see only the pale top of her head among the waves. Each crest seemed to swallow her up.

Camille did not ask Maybe to join her, did not take her to the beach and smile down at her—hair across her face, sun behind her, that memory of Maybe's again, come alive—and Maybe bristled at this exclusion. So, when Camille suggested that she could watch Maybe on Tuesdays, Maybe was suspicious.

For nine summers, Mrs. Eames had watched Maybe on Tuesdays. Mrs. Eames left the door unlocked as she went about her Tuesday morning, making a pot of thick, dark tea and toasting two English muffins, butter for her, sweet cherry jam for Maybe. Tuesday mornings sounded like the shuffling of Mrs. Eames's slippers on her hardwood, the shush-shush-shush of them the score. "But, Mrs. Eames looks forward to our visits. It's good for her," Maybe said quietly. She knew it sounded false, tinny even to her own ears, but she felt a surge of desperation. It was petty, refusing Camille this as Camille had refused her so much more. But saying the words felt good, a sharp tang to them. "I'd feel bad, you know, not going."

Camille nodded slowly, turning back to the newspaper spread before her. "Of course," she said evenly. "You wouldn't want to disappoint Mrs. Eames." Maybe knew that Camille saw clean through Maybe's lie.

"That's true, Maybe. Evelyn does enjoy her time with you." Gigi's gaze revealed nothing, but Maybe knew she understood her actions. Maybe would not be so easy, so accommodating. She could not. It seemed that Camille had assumed that she could return and it would be like no time had passed at all. The years had been long for Maybe. And Camille still thought it would be as easy to walk back in. That Maybe would forgive her, as if forgiveness were that simple. Forgiveness was messy; forgiveness was not easily won.

Gigi went back to cleaning out the Lazy Susan in the corner, and Maybe watched her for a moment, the way she paused before kneeling down, the way her body seemed to disagree with her, and she thought, briefly: Gigi's old. Gigi was only fifty-two, not technically old but decidedly not young, but Maybe saw the beginnings of aging clearly: aching bones, a sore back, trouble sleeping, general pains attributed to "age." She couldn't imagine Gigi older, curved with pain, sick. Gigi pulled out bowls, a blender, a few large, seasonal trays, and stacked them on the floor beside her, going to work with her soapy cloth. She left a trail of lemony fragrance behind her.

Maybe gathered her things, slowly, purposefully not looking at Camille. She put a book in her bag—*The Mirror Crack'd from Side to Side*, even though she liked Poirot better than Miss Marple—and then quickly pulled Camille's book from its place tucked under her mattress. She slipped it into her bag as well, knowing that late in the afternoon, Mrs. Eames would fall asleep in her painted chair and Maybe could read in private. The book practically vibrated in her bag.

"Chop-chop, Maybe. Evelyn will be waiting."

Maybe hoisted her bag over her shoulder and followed Gigi out through the backyard. Camille was leaning against the fence in cut-off jean shorts and a yellow linen top, smoking. Maybe felt a fresh swell of guilt at the sight of her.

"We'll be back later," Gigi said as she passed by; she didn't stop.

Maybe watched Camille blow smoke into the air. She was barefoot and her hair fell around her shoulders, loose. She still looked out of place at the cottage; Maybe thought she could disappear again as easily as she'd reappeared. If she blinked, counting to thirty, Camille might be gone. Maybe paused, the weight of her bag suddenly doubled in Camille's presence, the book a secret. She said, "Okay, well, I guess I'll see you later. After."

Camille smiled as she tapped ash from her cigarette into the garden bed. She held Maybe's gaze for a moment, then a moment longer. "Sure," she said. She smiled, a small smile. "Go on," she said. "Gigi's waiting."

Gigi tapped on Mrs. Eames's door before pushing it open. "Evelyn, we're here," she called as they stepped into the house. It was dim and cool, like always, and smelled faintly sweet, like soap and wilted flowers. The scent that Maybe always associated with Mrs. Eames. Maybe dropped her bag near the front door and padded after Gigi toward the back sitting room, where Mrs. Eames would be.

Maybe had heard the story of the sitting room many times over the years. The sitting room was an addition to the original house, built by Stanley Eames himself in the early summer days of 1925. Stanley turned the radio dial until he found Al Jolson and then spent the day climbing his ladder, hammering two-by-fours into place, adding on a wide, bright space attached to the kitchen that looked out over the back garden. He said he wanted Evelyn to be able to see the apple trees when she was in the house, wanted to give her all the sunshine and brightness that the summer months could offer. He laid the new planks of wood flooring, papered the walls in the pale flowered pattern that Evelyn chose. When he was done, Stanley stood at the new, wide windows and looked out to the garden. The roses and hydrangeas and geraniums looked back. Stanley said, "I could stare at this forever."

All these years later, Mrs. Eames still favoured the back room, with its wall full of windows and light that came in all day. Mrs. Eames had a small, round table pushed up against the windows, with two small chairs covered in an apple print. The apple tree outside had withered years ago, and Walter had chopped it down, easing the roots from the ground while Mrs. Eames cried. She said Stanley loved that tree. Now, Mrs. Eames sat at the table, the early light coming in and across her hands, folded around a steaming cup of tea.

"Good morning, darling," Mrs. Eames said to Maybe, as she turned to smile her wide smile. She wore a grey cardigan and her heavy fuzzy slippers, despite the heat outside, as always.

"Hi," Maybe slid up against Mrs. Eames and gave her a one-armed embrace. She smelled how Maybe imagined age smelled:

slightly musty with a hint of baby powder and drying skin. Mrs. Eames patted her arm tenderly.

"I'll be back by four," Gigi said as she did every time she dropped Maybe off. "Don't let her get away with anything." Gigi touched Mrs. Eames's arm and kissed Maybe on the top of her head. Maybe pulled back in surprise; Gigi did not kiss goodbye, did not hug or squeeze tenderly. This was different. Then, Gigi brushed her hands efficiently, hoisted her purse, as if nothing had happened. Maybe squinted, trying to see what had changed between them, and Gigi swatted at her.

"Have a good day with Evelyn." Gigi went back out the way she'd come. She had been suddenly sentimental, and Maybe had to assume that this had something to do with Camille. She wanted Maybe to be cautious, wary of the sudden return, and Camille's new interest in her. Maybe thought of the book tucked away in her bag just near the front door, and her fingers tingled, imagining opening it and finally understanding Gigi's anger, and Robin's curiosity. What could the book possibly say? The book had to hold all the answers.

Mrs. Eames poured Maybe a small cup of tea, heavily doused with milk and sugar, and pushed it silently across the table. The cup had tiny yellow flowers, the lip of it delicately thin. Maybe took a sip.

She knew how the day would unfold: Mrs. Eames would tell her stories about her youth until she became tired, then she'd doze while Maybe read her book. Lunch and maybe a short walk around the block before Gigi returned, smelling of oil and bacon, her hands red from constant washing. When Mrs. Eames would fall asleep, Maybe could finally open Camille's book. It would reveal why she'd left, where she'd had to go. Perhaps even why she'd come back. There would be another story there, perhaps long and twisted and complicated. Maybe would finally—*finally*—understand her mother. Perhaps she would like her, feel sorry for her, empathize with the choices she'd had to make. Because she had to make that decision, right? She'd had to. She would not have left if she had any other choice. There were so many variations to one person's life. The possibilities were endless. The loop ran in Maybe's head.

The tea was warm, the room pleasant, and soon enough Mrs. Eames was talking about her first years on Lear Street, when she was young and happy and hopeful, before the crows arrived and her husband went missing.

❖

Stanley Eames worked for his father's shipping company after he came home from the war. It had long been assumed that he would take over when his father retired, a fact that neither surprised nor interested Stanley. He was the only son in their family—staunchly Irish Catholic on his father's side, "wishy-washy" Canadian on his mother's—a fact that seemed to be a general source of vague embarrassment. Stanley had three sisters, two of whom had died in childhood, the third living forever in the coddling shadow of her mother. So Stanley, of course, was the only hope to take over the business. Stanley had no passion for it, no real passion for anything, and so he'd enlisted, imagining he'd see the wide, welcoming shores of France, Ireland of course, maybe even someplace foreignly exotic like Italy. He'd never really thought about fighting, about what war, in all its messiness, meant.

Later, Stanley didn't talk about the war, other than to say that that was where he'd met Evelyn. No one said he was any different, but then no one said much about Stanley once he'd returned with a new, English bride. They settled quickly into the house on Lear Street that Stanley's father bought them as a wedding gift, and Stanley started working at his father's business. In many ways, it was an unremarkable story, exceptional only with its ordinariness. Stanley went to work, Evelyn stayed in her new home in her new country, and no one talked about the years Stanley had been away.

In the years that followed, Evelyn got used to the quiet of Lear Street and Oak Bay and Vancouver Island. She missed her mother and sisters in England, and wrote them long, sentimental letters talking about the new rain forest she lived in. Their replies came in pale blue airmail envelopes, smelling of another kind of rain. And, each month, Evelyn waited to discover she was pregnant. Each month, she was disappointed. There were no children to fill the large house, to take to the shore, to tell stories about England and Evelyn's youth.

Their lives continued in an ordinary, companionable way. People moved in to the houses around them, planted gardens, took their children to school, sold their houses and moved to the mainland. Stanley built the addition to the house, still hopeful. New neighbours appeared and stayed. Evelyn and Stanley watched, and aged.

Then, one crisp fall morning in 1928, Stanley kissed Evelyn goodbye, took his brown-paper-bag packed lunch and stepped out the door. Evelyn heard the car start, heard Stanley pull out of the driveway and thought nothing of it. She thought nothing of the flock of crows that landed on her roof while she pulled weeds in the back garden, their black bodies making a long, lean line on the pitch. She thought nothing of it when he did not return at five o'clock. She slid his plate of chicken and mashed potatoes back into the oven, keeping it warm. She only began to worry when seven o'clock and then eight o'clock came and went, when the night turned deep and dark, and still Stanley did not return.

The police looked for Stanley, but could find no trace of him. They finally found his car, parked out near the beach in Sidney, but Stanley was not there. They assumed the worst; they said he must have gone into the ocean, and never came back out.

Evelyn talked about this in a matter-of-fact way. She said Stanley wore a navy coat the last time she saw him, and kissed her tenderly. She liked to think that Stanley had gone somewhere else, that maybe he had just walked away from their life together and started another one somewhere else. He might be working on a farm in the Fraser Valley, or living in downtown Vancouver somewhere, perhaps even just at the other end of the island, in a small house with a new wife and several small children. This seemed to be a kinder thought. Disappearance, after all, was kinder than death.

❖

Only, this was not true. Maybe watched Mrs. Eames sit at her small table, looking out the window to her garden, where she must have once imagined her whole future would unfold, with children on blankets, and fruit heavy on tree limbs. But Stanley Eames had built this strange, unnecessary gift for her, and then he had simply disappeared. Now, the sitting room was a macabre testament to him, his handprints all over the structure.

After Mrs. Eames fell asleep in her large, wide chair next to the window, Maybe covered her with a light blanket and crept out of the house with her bag and her book. She remembered to be careful with the back door, knowing how it cried out if you pushed it too hard, too quickly. Maybe understood that Mrs. Eames's story about her husband was supposed to make her feel thankful that Camille had only disappeared for a short time. Somehow, though, this did not make Maybe feel any better. Death trumped absence.

Maybe stepped out of the cool, quiet house and into the backyard. There were trim hydrangeas, a low line of boxwoods, two stately Japanese maples and generous patches of shade. Everything was green and getting greener. Mrs. Eames had wooden chairs with thick flowered cushions that had been faded by too many years in the sun. Maybe took an assortment of the pillows and piled them in a shady spot, curling into them. Then she looked at her bag. It was a delicious feeling, knowing the book was so close. Gigi had kept it a secret, and this alone made Maybe believe there was something dark waiting for her in its pages. Something damning that could not be undone. But it had been days now, and Maybe hadn't yet been brave enough to open the pale yellow cover. She was not sure why. Was it worse to know, or to imagine? She had only looked at Camille's picture on the back—her blond hair piled on top of her head in a topknot, amber necklace at her throat, her expression bored or superior or both—and then flipped back to the quiet cover with the faded flowers and baby blanket. She thumbed it, touched the pages lightly, listened to the sound of the pages snapping back to their original place. But she still had not read a single word of it. Not a word.

Gigi had kept the book a secret. Robin Hollis had shoved the book under her bed. Mary Quinn called it interesting. They were all careful around Maybe, doling out considered words. There was something about Camille, and this book, that was dangerous.

Maybe lay on her back, looking up at the leaves, how they made complex puzzle pieces in the sky. She closed one eye, then the other. Blue summer sky, as if nothing had changed in the last few weeks, as if the world had not been shaken loose for her. Camille's return with her soft blond hair and heavy necklaces, her billowing skirts and long white cigarettes, with all her talk of liberation and equality and the world beyond Lear Street. Camille, who would now be leaning against the back door of the cottage, staring out at the mass of roses, the grass that needed a cut, the tiny silver bird feeders that hung from the tree branches, thinking, How quaint. Just that.

Maybe had imagined Camille's life so many times and in so many ways, she was almost certain that the actual story would disappoint her. She knew that was why she hadn't opened the book yet—once she read it, there was no way to reimagine the years Camille had been gone. The truth was strict and plain. It did not bend.

Maybe rolled onto her side in resignation and reached for her bag. She tugged the paperback out and stared. The same yellow. The same flowers and blanket. She ruffled the pages with the back of her thumb, the quick snapping of them loud in the quiet backyard. Nine years caught between the covers. Nine years of absence. Nine years of Maybe pasting together scraps of Camille's life. Nine years of Maybe imagining and reimagining this woman who was her mother. Nine years of all these stories. The words were right there. Maybe read the first line:

When I was seventeen, I became a mother, but not the kind of mother you're thinking of.

those who came before

Robin Hollis planned a party, claiming to celebrate the summer, but everyone knew it was really to finally get to know Camille. Phoebe said to Maybe, "She's, like, obsessed with your mum," and rolled her eyes. Robin had come to Maybe's house with a tray of lemon squares, another time with a sweater that Maybe had forgotten at their house. She was uncertain around Camille. Maybe watched Robin as Robin watched Camille closely, Camille regarding her coolly from the kitchen table, where she invariably sat with a steaming cup of tea or a tumbler of scotch, depending on the time of day. Robin suggested dinner, maybe a drink while the girls played in the backyard, but Camille never accepted. She said she was too busy with the new book. Maybe wanted her to want to make friends, to take interest in the neighbours and Maybe herself, but Camille never did. It was obvious that Camille was different from the other women, the ordinary housewives and homemakers and widows. She would talk about the cities she'd been to, causes she was involved with, at the drop of a hat. She called the march in New York transformative. She said, "You have to think about your place in the world. Challenge it." Maybe saw the light in Camille's eyes when she talked about these things, but something in her words sounded hollow, like Camille was saying the things she thought others expected of her. Maybe listened to her talk, trying to decide which words were true. Or, if any of them were true.

Finally, Robin stopped arriving at the front door with an excuse at hand. Then came the phone call, inviting Gigi and Maybe and, of course, Camille, to a barbecue. "We have such short summers," Robin said. "We need to take advantage of it while it's here."

Gigi told Robin they'd be there and promised to bring a dish. After she had hung up, she went back to cleaning the two large pots in the sink. Her scrub rhythmically scratched against the metal, her movements consistent and familiar for Maybe.

Maybe picked at her lunch, tearing the bread of her corned beef sandwich into tiny pieces. Gigi hated when she did this, but she was distracted now, staring hard at the suds and her gloved hands. She was always cleaning now. Always scrubbing and shining. And Camille was at the table, as she'd been for so many days, writing on her notepad. Maybe watched with fascination, still trying to discern the words spreading across the pages. Camille's writing was hard to read upside down, but Maybe was still too cautious to move next to her.

"Who will be there?" Camille asked without looking up.

"At the barbecue? Everyone from the neighbourhood, I'd imagine," Gigi said.

"She didn't say?"

"I didn't ask."

Camille paused, her pen hovering. She would still only say it was her new book; she waved her hand in the air, and said, "Oh, just the new one," as if Maybe should understand what that meant. But she didn't. She didn't understand her first book, even after reading *The Other Mother*. It felt like a jigsaw puzzle, missing too many pieces to see the picture clearly. Camille hadn't wanted to be a mother at all, or she had wanted more for herself, that she imagined something beyond motherhood and Lear Street. That it was about freedom. Her words were pretty, but bleary. There was no real shape to them, no definition. The plot incomplete. The book simply told Maybe that Camille left, and that she left for herself. That she believed this was necessary. Brave, even. Maybe had reread a section of the book over and over, feeling like there was something in her words that would explain everything to her. *Leaving was what I had to do; even at nineteen, I knew this: the most important thing was to be true to myself, to honour my need for self-determination and fulfillment. Despite how difficult it would be. I couldn't become trapped, as so many women before me had been trapped by the endless duties of households. But the male writers I admired did not become hostage to the domestic. They remained individuals. And above all else, I was committed to doing the same.*

And when Maybe searched for herself, perhaps mentions of regret or guilt, or, even love, she'd been only an endnote. The book was cluttered with details about Camille's life away from Lear Street—the first years she'd spent in Vancouver, before making her way south, into the USA, through Seattle and on to San Francisco, where she started writing. Down to Berkeley, where she got involved with various popular causes. New York. Toronto. Montreal, where she learned French. Met a man and lived for a while in Old Montreal, imagining herself in Paris. It was exotic, the kind of life Maybe had imagined for her all along. But there was barely a mention of Maybe. Only there at the beginning, when Camille walked away from Lear Street and into the misty morning, and then again at the end, a single line about wanting Maybe to have the gift of her story. She did not say she kissed Maybe goodbye, treasured the memory of her lips on her soft forehead. She did not say that she thought about Maybe, dreamed about coming back to her. She said none of the things Maybe had stupidly hoped to read. In the end, it seemed Maybe was only one thing for Camille: the reason to leave. Maybe didn't know how to respond to Camille's story: Was she supposed to admire her for abandoning her? Admiration felt wrong. The story only reflected Camille as she wanted herself to be seen. Independent, freethinking. But whose story was it, really? It wasn't complete without Maybe. Did putting the words on paper make them true? Maybe wondered if a story ever really belonged to only one person.

"Will Mary Quinn be there?"

Camille's voice was so clear. *Mary Quinn. It's always Mary Quinn.* Gigi didn't look up from the sink, but kept scrubbing. Harder.

"I don't know. Probably."

Camille tapped her pen against her notepad, rested her chin in her hand. Mary Quinn, Mary Quinn, Mary Quinn. Maybe could practically hear Camille thinking her name.

Mary was independent and moderately famous, like Camille. Another artist. She didn't really belong to Lear Street, either; Camille and Mary Quinn didn't spend their days busy with the stuff of children and husbands and kitchens. They worked. And Camille had emphasized this in her book, that she felt her work set her apart from women who were *only* mothers and who *allowed themselves to be defined by such slim, outdated parameters.* At the end, she had even said that she hoped one day her own daughter (she never named her, referred to her only as M, which was another slight, Maybe's name even lost in Camille's retelling of the past) would find something that would *fulfill and sustain her, giving her intellectual and emotional satisfaction. Ultimately allow herself to be as greedy and assured as men.* And there was that one line that Maybe couldn't ignore. It stood out to her as if it were the only line in the book at all, a hard slap: *Avoid child rearing.*

Were these the only options—Maybe could be mother or artist, mother or writer? Family or independence. Here or there. Or, or, or. Maybe wondered why this had to be *or.* Why this could not be *and.* Wasn't that the point of the women's movement, after all, to give them the possibility of *and?*

Maybe carried her plate and half-eaten sandwich to the garbage can. The sandwich slid in with a satisfying thump, and Gigi turned to raise an eyebrow. Maybe slipped her plate into the frothy water of the sink.

"I'm sure Mary Quinn will go," Maybe said. "She likes the Hollises." She didn't understand why Camille felt she couldn't do both—be Maybe's mother and continue writing books. Maybe was a good student, quiet: Gigi had called her "easy as pie." Maybe wouldn't be a bother to Camille at all. The personal is political, Camille had said, and Gigi rolled her eyes. It seemed Maybe didn't quite fit in to the life Camille imagined for herself.

Gigi looked at Camille as if she were someone new, not the daughter she had raised in this very house. Camille had reinvented herself entirely in her absence. This was someone surprising. Maybe ached to know the Camille who had slept in the small bedroom and woken late, coming into the kitchen rubbing her eyes, still bleary and smeared with sleep. The Camille that Gigi had held on her knee, braiding her hair into smooth plaits. The Camille that scraped charred waffles. And, mostly, the Camille that had held her hands to her stomach, feeling Maybe move beneath.

"Does she?" Camille asked. "I wouldn't imagine she'd have much in common with Robin."

Maybe looked at the suds in the sink, and watched her plate disappear. She put her finger to one perfect bubble and watched it pop. Pop. She popped another. She said quietly, "They're nice."

Gigi touched her shoulder with her wet, yellow glove. Just that touch and Maybe felt like all her emotions were exposed: greed for Camille, embarrassment for all that greed, and thick, inky shame at her constantly trying to defend their small, happy life. Camille had been able to leave Maybe behind, leave all of this behind like dirtied laundry. She wanted the life ahead of her, not the life behind.

But she came back.

This was the thought that kept returning to Maybe. The echo of, *She came back.* She couldn't tell if the thought was too hopeful, ridiculous. Reflex to defend her mother. The book hadn't told her anything about why Camille had returned; it stopped long before Camille had appeared at the cottage.

Maybe leaned her head on Gigi's shoulder. Gigi looked at her for a moment too long, too hard, and then went back to the scrubber in the sink. Maybe glanced at Camille at the table, hoping for—what? A sympathetic look? A glance that told Maybe that she loved her, had missed her, had dreamed about her? But Camille was looking down at her notepad. Maybe closed her eyes, and wished to be anywhere but here.

❖

Maybe balanced a platter of cherry tarts in her arms and concentrated on her feet as she crossed Lear Street toward the Hollis house. She watched her feet as they moved, and the ground moved quickly below them, hazy, the subtle shades of grey and speckles of shimmer unfurling. It felt like a hand was at her back, directing her to the house.

The sky was blue and mostly clear, only a few puffy white clouds in the distance, and the heat had settled around them comfortably. The day would be fun, she should be looking forward to it, and yet she felt anxious; she had a vaguely dark feeling about the day. And she knew why: because Camille had decided to come.

She wasn't sure how Camille would act, if she'd say something embarrassing, or if she'd ignore them all, bored by a backyard barbecue. Yet it had been Maybe who'd orchestrated her attendance. And she was already regretting it.

"Pick up the pace, Miss Maybe," Gigi said from behind her.

They stepped up onto the wide expanse of lawn, still lushly green despite the long stretch of summer. Professor Hollis had often been outside, lazing water across the lawn, setting up a spinning sprinkler, leaving the grass shining and wet. Phoebe said he was doing research, writing an article, and so he sometimes could be seen in his yard, doing something but never really doing anything, in his sandals, sometimes holding a tumbler of scotch. On especially hot afternoons, he would set up the sprinkler in the backyard, and Maybe and Phoebe would run through it, despite the pool only a few feet away, loving the crisp spray, the icy droplets on their skin.

Maybe couldn't count how many times she'd walked these same steps, on these exact eleven stepping stones, how many times she and Phoebe had chalked hopscotch onto them. Now, she listened as Camille's heeled sandals clacked on them, the sound echoing.

Gigi tugged open the side gate and said, "Hello, Hollis family. We're here."

But there was no one in the backyard; it waited, blank and desolate. Phoebe wasn't in the pool, Professor Hollis wasn't at the barbecue, Robin wasn't filling wineglasses; there was an eerie silence where there should have been groups of people, laughter, music, the sound of children squealing and cannonballing into the pool.

Maybe looked at Gigi. "Are we early?"

Gigi shook her head quickly, glanced at her wristwatch. "No. We're right on time."

Usually, there would be trays of food and cut-up fruit and colourful paper napkins. But this afternoon, Robin had put out planters of white flowers, a picnic table full of white platters and real china plates, tall, clear wineglasses, a stack of white cloth napkins and lanterns with huge candles surrounding the pool. Everything elegant and coolly calm, no hint of the children and families who would attend the party, the busyness of a neighbourhood afternoon barbecue. It was nothing like all the other parties Maybe had been to.

Maybe watched Camille absently touch the large amber beads at her throat, calmly surveying the backyard.

"Oh, you're here!" Robin stepped out from the sliding glass door, carrying a platter piled high with a variety of meats. "You're the first." She was in a flowing blue dress, her hair darkly glowing against its lightness, the intricate embroidery at the chest and hem. It reminded Maybe of something Camille would have worn.

"Everyone else is fashionably late, I suppose," Robin said. Her eyes flitted to Camille and then quickly away. Her voice was carefully bright, a false happiness to it that Maybe had not heard before. "Come and sit, please. I'll get you a drink."

While Robin got wine, and lemonade, Professor Hollis and Phoebe appeared, carrying more food, and slowly other guests trickled in. The Lalondes were first, Danny carrying a soccer ball, followed by Walter, and then Aidan Felles with a bottle of whisky in his hand. Professor Hollis put James Taylor on the record player, and then grabbed Robin and twirled her around the flagstone patio as "You've Got a Friend" filled the air. She moved with him, the edge of her pale blue dress lifting to reveal a bit more of her long, tanned legs. Many afternoons, Maybe swam the length of the pool while Robin lay on one of the loungers in her navy two-piece bathing suit, slathering herself with baby oil and sliding on oversized black sunglasses. When it got too hot for her to bear, Robin got into the pool, shivering when the cool water touched her bare stomach. The blue of her dress, now, as Professor Hollis guided her around the patio table, and her long, tanned legs made her look even younger, more like a beautiful teenage girl rather than someone's mother.

"I'm dizzy, Alan," she finally breathed, and he let her go with a flourish.

Maybe watched Robin fix her dress, turning away from Alan in what appeared to be annoyance. The adults clapped—Maybe and Phoebe watching them from afar, sitting at the edge of the pool— as Mary Quinn walked into the backyard. She wore a striped shirt and cut-off denim shorts, and carried a huge bundle of flowers in colours ranging from pink to red to purple and back again. The flowers framed her bare face, her copper hair pulled back in a low ponytail.

"Oh," she said as Robin came toward her, embraced her and took the flowers, "you already have flowers."

Robin smiled. "You can never have enough. They're beautiful."

From each of their places in the backyard—Lalonde boys on the grass, bumping the soccer ball back and forth, their parents at the table with Gigi and Walter, Professor Hollis at the grill with Aidan, Camille apart from everyone in her chair, coolly watching Robin take the flowers—Maybe watched them turn to look at Mary. Mary Quinn was still a mystery, this woman who had fled the mainland with certainty and speed. Mary shifted from one foot to another, looked uncomfortable with all the eyes on her. Maybe wanted to offer a smile or a shrug to show her she wasn't alone, but Mary did not glance toward the girls by the pool. She smiled at Gigi, and then let Robin guide her over to the other partygoers at the patio table. Mary finally took a seat next to Gigi, relief flashing across her face as the party resumed, voices rising in laughter, the soccer ball's endless bumping between the boys' feet, the music turned up louder. Robin got Mary a glass of wine and she was introduced again to the Lalondes, said hello to Walter. Camille stayed in her chair, leaning forward slightly, as Mary slipped into easy conversation with Gigi.

Phoebe jumped into the water. "Come on, Maybe!" Maybe watched Phoebe's blurry figure beneath the water, her legs kicking, her yellow suit a beacon against all the blue. Phoebe came up for a quick breath and went back under. Phoebe kicked her feet so fast that Maybe couldn't distinguish one from the other. Everything turned blurry.

The music was turned up yet again—Marvin Gaye now, the first wailing strains of "What's Going On?"—and Maybe looked up to see Mary watching her. Then Mary smiled and winked at her as if they were the only two in on a joke, and Maybe felt herself flush with pleasure.

"Maybe, come in." Phoebe had surfaced, her hair plastered to her head.

Maybe said, "I'm hungry. Let's eat." She turned away, snapped the edge of her bathing suit and made her way over to the table where Mary sat. Food crowded the table: devilled eggs, pickles, a Jell-O mould, potato chips, a whole tray of cold cuts and cheese. Maybe stood, dripping, by Walter, and helped herself to two dev-illed eggs. She liked to eat the paprika yolk first, then the whites, and it drove Gigi crazy. She popped the whole egg into her mouth instead, now, cheeks bulging.

Walter was asking Mary about her renovations to the house, and Mary was quietly talking about all the new skylights she'd installed. Camille watched intently as they chuckled, Mary Quinn touching Walter's arm affectionately. Camille crossed her legs, her high-heeled sandals jiggling.

"I think I'll give the boys a hand over there," Walter said, put-ting his hand on Mary's shoulder before crossing the patio to the barbecue where Professor Hollis and Aidan stood guard over racks of ribs and a long, lean pink salmon.

Mary leaned back in her chair and looked up at Maybe, her eyes a startling blue in the afternoon sun. Mary said, "How goes it, Maybe? Still into painting?"

The image of the canvas in Mary's yard flashed across Maybe's mind. She'd spent all her time obsessed by Camille's book, sen-tences coming back to her, stuck in her brain, unwilling to budge (*I expected motherhood to be transformative, to take away any doubts or regrets. But I only had more. I didn't recognize myself anymore, and I des-perately needed to*). This was this bestseller that everyone either had read or wanted to read, that was supposed to be a clear, smooth window into Camille's life. All the words that crowded Camille's own life—discovery, understanding, the female experience—in the end were hollow words. It was a selfish book, Maybe thought; it was as if she'd completely forgotten about Maybe. She could count all the instances where she appeared in the book on one hand.

"Good. And yes, sure," Maybe said. Mary smiled, and Maybe saw that she had relaxed a little, was starting to enjoy the party.

Behind Mary, flowers wavered in the slight sea breeze. A patio chair scraped the cement. Ribs sizzled on the grill. The sliding door whined as it was pulled open, and the soccer ball thumped against the fence. All the things Maybe associated with every backyard barbecue she'd ever been to. Drinks were refilled, people laughed, the music was loud with bass thumping behind them.

"I wondered if you'd be here."

Camille tugged her chair forward, moving up to the table, closer to Mary. She put her wineglass on the table and smiled. "I hoped you would be." Camille's voice was a golden glow. She was confident in herself, and Maybe saw the woman that Camille was outside of their house. Here was the woman who'd written that book, who was comfortable with adoration and admiration. She was transformed.

"Did you, now?" Mary asked.

"I did," Camille said. "I've wanted to talk to you about your work. Since—well, since the last time we talked. Before, even." Camille touched her necklace, crossed and recrossed her legs, put her fingertip against her wineglass. Maybe watched her gestures and saw the quick, sharp tooth of it—Camille was nervous with Mary, maybe a little in awe of her fame.

Mary didn't respond and Maybe watched how she leaned back in her chair, tilted away from Camille, how her eyes narrowed slightly, her smile subtle in its corners. Only just there, a hint. If you didn't look closely, you would not see it.

"I wasn't aware you were a fan." The words sounded like a dare, as if Mary didn't quite believe Camille.

"Refills, anyone?" Professor Hollis appeared at the table with a bottle of wine and the pitcher of lemonade. Maybe felt the air shift. He refilled both Maybe's and Phoebe's glasses without waiting for an answer, but waited until Camille nodded to pour more wine in her glass. Gigi, from her place just down the table, had turned her head toward them and now watched silently. She was always watching now.

"Of course I am. I have to think, it's so damning, isn't it? Being a woman and an artist, the judgment. I'm sure you'd agree."

Maybe had heard these words before—they were echoes of words that appeared in Camille's book. She sounded rehearsed and insincere; she was quoting her own work, her own ideas about women and men, all the unfairness and inequality. The book had revealed at least this to Maybe about Camille: she wanted something, something else that was just out of reach. Something more than being Maybe's mother here in Oak Bay. The life of an artist, but more importantly, an artist in the way she saw it applied to men. Camille thought she'd have a better chance of being accepted as a writer if she were not also a mother, that there was something about being a mother that was shameful. Maybe didn't know what that was, and she wasn't sure that Camille understood it either. Perhaps that was why she'd returned, seeking that something she had still missed.

Maybe looked out across the yard; Danny and Charlie had moved on to croquet, banging the tiny ball between them, and Phoebe stood at the edge of the lawn, watching the boys hammer the balls through their tiny arches. The pool was still, a single yellow ball floating on its surface. Maybe imagined herself under the water, looking up to the blue sky, stretching so wide. She imagined floating, floating, until she was weightless. The blue was endless. Everything had become too complicated since Camille had appeared at the kitchen table. She longed for the days when things had been simple, when Camille was a bunch of stories and a stack of postcards. Another story, another version. Her creations of Camille's life could be changed endlessly. Stories depended only on who was doing the telling. But now, Maybe was confused by Camille, and, if she was being truthful, confused by herself.

Aidan and Professor Hollis laughed about something Walter was saying. Camille continued to talk to Mary, her eyes never leaving Mary's face. The sun started its slow, smooth descent, inch by inch, shade crossing the backyard. Maybe pulled her towel tighter around her, aware of the slow drip of water down her legs, pooling on the flagstone at her feet.

Robin appeared at the patio door, a bowl of steaming potatoes in her arms. She crossed the patio in her pretty blue dress and put the bowl on the table. She smoothed her hands over the skirt, and turned to look at Camille. She shifted the bowl over an inch, then back. She put wooden spoons down beside the bowl and straightened them, her eyes still on Camille. She was nervous with Camille there.

When there was a pause in the conversation, Robin said, "I'm so pleased you could come, Camille. It seems our paths never cross." She smiled, her teeth white and straight behind her pink lips.

Camille looked up at her slowly, annoyance clear on her face. She touched the amber necklace at her throat, but remained silent. Robin pulled up the closest chair and sat next to Camille at the table. "I thought it was interesting, what you had to say about the perception of mothers. How motherhood is dismissed—"

"I was just catching up with Mary, Robin. Could you give us a minute?" Camille interrupted.

Robin touched her collarbone and her cheeks flared red beneath her tan. "Oh, no, I'm sorry. I didn't mean—"

Maybe's stomach dropped and swirled. She felt clammy in her damp suit. She looked at Robin, and the flush on her cheeks made Maybe feel queasy. She wanted to put her hand on Robin's, but couldn't.

"Please. It's nothing," Mary said, reaching out to touch Robin's hand, apologizing through her fingertips. "We can catch up any time." Mary Quinn's words were pointed, chastising Camille.

The words startled Camille. She looked quizzically at Mary and then leaned back in her chair. It was obvious that she was unused to having anyone question her, dismiss her. She was the darling, the young, beautiful woman that everyone wanted to know. She smiled at Robin, a tight smile, and then said, "I apologize. Please, go ahead."

Robin looked from Camille to Mary and back again. Maybe felt a flare of anger well up in her; she had loved Robin all these years

Camille had been gone. Robin had watched Maybe, fed and bathed her, brushed her hair out after swimming. She had tucked her into bed beside Phoebe, kissing them both good night, her lips warm and dry, the scent of lemon coming off her. Robin was everything that a mother was supposed to be. Everything that Maybe had dreamed Camille would be. And now Camille couldn't be bothered to even talk to Robin. Dismissing her. Maybe's heart contracted and beat fast.

Mary smiled at Robin and something passed between the two of them, a minute gesture of solidarity, and Robin's confidence returned. She straightened the neckline of her dress and said, "I was interested in the book. I was saying I found it interesting."

"That's very kind," Camille said. Maybe felt her heart pick up its pace, beat fast enough that she thought it might burst out of her body. Camille wanted to end the conversation, she could tell, in a rush to get back to Mary. She was looking down on Robin's admiration. Maybe was clogged by embarrassment. Robin, who had held back her hair when she vomited, rubbed her back to comfort. Maybe watched Robin toy with her bracelets, watched Camille sit silent, and then Maybe felt the burst she'd been waiting for, words coming up to her mouth before she could really articulate them.

"Stop it," she hissed at Camille. "Just stop it. She's trying to be nice to you. She's *trying* and that's more than you've ever done! You don't know her—you know nothing about her—so just stop it. Just—" Maybe's voice turned tight and high, edging into a hysterical squeal. "Stop!"

Maybe felt a hand on her shoulder and turned, expecting Gigi, but instead she looked up to Walter's face. "Maybe, honey," he said quietly, "I think that's enough."

The yard was suddenly quiet. Everyone was staring at her. She'd made a fool of herself. She was standing in a dripping bathing suit, yelling at her mother while everyone watched. Maybe flushed with hot shame. They'd say she was acting out, being childish. They'd say she was having trouble adjusting, that it was normal under the circumstances. They'd say all these things and they would be true, but also not at all. Maybe was furious, more angry than she'd realized, but she'd been able to push it down, pretend it didn't exist until this very moment. Camille had left her. Left her. And Maybe was angry in a pure, undiluted way.

Gigi was watching Maybe from across the table. She didn't smile, didn't frown, but there was something in Gigi's eyes that Maybe understood: she also had been waiting for this moment, when Maybe would finally show her hurt, all the anger and betrayal, be mean. When she would demand more of Camille. When she'd finally ask all her questions, yell her hot, pure disappointment, loud and clear and true.

Robin reached out and touched Maybe's arm. She squeezed, and in that gesture was all the love she'd ever felt for Robin. "Maybe, love, really, it's fine. I'm okay. It's fine."

Camille twirled a ring on her finger, over and over as she looked up at Maybe. "It's okay. She can say what she'd like," she said. She smiled, but the smile disappeared from her face as quickly as it had arrived. "It's good for Maybe to have her own opinions."

Robin smiled a tight smile Maybe had never seen before, a smile that was not sincere, not actually revealing happiness—and then she leaned forward, putting her elbows on the table. "I was interested in your book. But there's a lot written about the role of motherhood in the female experience. Betty Friedan, of course, and Gloria Steinem. Others. It did seem a little derivative."

Camille's expression changed, and she looked squarely at Robin in a new way, as if she'd seen something she hadn't known existed. It was something that Maybe hadn't ever seen before, either: this was a new, glowing side to Robin, when Maybe had believed she knew everything about her. Camille tipped her head slightly, watching Robin more closely, and Mary laughed loudly, tilting her head back to expose the long, lean line of her neck. And with that, the air was punctured, shifted by Mary Quinn's laugh; the afternoon sagged, tension deflated. Maybe sagged a little with relief. "Derivative," Mary Quinn repeated, laughter still in her clear voice.

the yearning that women suffer

That summer moved more slowly or suddenly lapped forward. The sun came out and then stubbornly refused to leave, the grass turning spiky and yellow beneath Maybe's feet. Even the breeze from the ocean was slight, coming only in the smallest puffs. Sometimes, it rained at night while everyone slept and then they woke to tiny pools of water on the leaves. But by noon, it had evaporated, and it was back to sun, sun, sun. Everyone was hot. Everyone was cranky. When Maybe turned on the TV, she learned that the rest of the world was cranky, too. Jim Morrison's death in that French bathtub. More British troops to Northern Ireland. Gloria Steinem's address to the women of America. She reluctantly turned the TV off, but the images continued to run through her mind.

Everyone meandered to the beach at some point during the day, in bathing suits or short pants with bare feet, standing at the edge of the ocean to feel the mist, to just look out at the long seam of blue and feel cooler. When Mary Quinn came, she brought a large umbrella and faded blanket, tucking herself into the shade. Gigi and Walter would sit on the driftwood, watching boats float by. Camille swam with her sure strokes, and then often walked the shore alone, her footprints spilling out behind her. Aidan Felles and Professor Hollis appeared only after work hours, and then sometimes sat together with a hibachi barbecue between them, each holding a sweating bottle of beer. Robin stood in the waves with Phoebe and Maybe as they watched their toes being swallowed by the sand, revealed again only when the water pulled away. It seemed to Maybe that everything that summer was being hidden and revealed.

Sometimes, Robin swam, strong in the water, her arms straight and hands cupped. Phoebe watched her mother go out farther than she would have liked, her mouth turning pinched in panic, but she never said, Don't go, she just walked more slowly, her eyes on her mother's dark head, hesitant to lose sight of her.

When Robin returned, coming out slick and dripping, she smelled salty like the sea, and her hair was loose and thick down her back. She lay on her beach towel, reading a book—now, Maybe noted, *The Bell Jar*, corners turned over from wear, another title she would look for in the library—until she was completely dry, as if she'd never been in the water at all.

Gradually, Camille began sitting with Mary on the nubby blanket after she'd walked along the shore. They spoke quietly, their voices lost in the pulse of the ocean's swells, but Maybe knew from the way Camille laughed and leaned forward, closer to Mary Quinn, that there was something uneven in their new friendship. Camille was plainly trying to win over Mary. Robin never spoke to Mary when Camille was there, but if Mary was alone, she might stop on her way back to the house. Today, Maybe watched Mary looking at Robin's long, tanned legs as she went back down Lear Street. When Mary saw Maybe watching her, she waved her hand in hello, like they were old friends.

Phoebe poked in the sand with a long, curved stick she'd found, and Maybe listened to the scratching sound of it, before she said, "I'm just going to talk to Mary Quinn for a second. Be right back."

Mary motioned for Maybe to sit once she got close enough. The blanket was warm, woolly beneath Maybe's bare legs. Her bathing suit was still wet from a morning swim in the Hollises' pool, and the high scent of chlorine clung to it.

"You're getting tan," Mary said. "I never do."

Maybe looked at Mary's bare arms, pale and freckled, dotted with paint. Maybe shrugged. "I guess so. I'm outside a lot."

"I just burn." Mary smiled, leaned back on her elbows and looked out to the sea. "I should start swimming. I used to swim all the time at the Y."

Mary often made casual references like this to her life on the mainland, and Maybe wanted to ask Mary all about living in Vancouver, how different it was from here, how busy and noisy, but found herself still shy, despite the Wednesdays they'd spent together. Maybe said, "I've never lived anywhere else. I've only swum here."

"That's lucky. It's nice here. Peaceful. Other places aren't so calm," Mary said. "Other places make your head spin."

"Is that why you moved?"

"Sort of. I just needed someplace different."

"Because of your work?"

Mary smiled. She flicked sand off her cut-off shorts. "Oh, for everything. I had a friend in Vancouver. She was sick, and it was hard."

The ocean moved and swished and rushed, and Maybe lay back on the blanket to look up at the underside of the umbrella. Blue and white stripes. "Is your friend okay now?" Everywhere there was blue: blue sky, blue umbrella, blue sea.

"No," Mary said. "She's not."

There was finality to Mary's words, and so Maybe didn't say anything else, just looked up at the wavering stripes above her. She knew Phoebe would be counting the minutes she had been gone, that she'd want to wander down to the concession farther along the beach, but Maybe didn't move, just listened to the gulls and distant voices on the beach. It was peaceful. She thought she could stay here like this with Mary Quinn all day. It was only when a shadow appeared against the umbrella that Maybe sat up, face to face with Camille.

"Oh," Camille said, "it's you." She kneeled on the blanket, and Mary moved her leg to make room. Camille sat next to her, their knees just barely touching.

Maybe smiled a small, hard smile. She had not forgiven Camille for the party, did not forgive her now for the way she said, It's you. "Yup. It's me."

No one spoke. Maybe sat for a few long moments, waiting for Camille to say something in return, before getting up, standing in the full sunshine. She was dazzled for a moment, coming from under the shaded umbrella, and held her hand up to her eyes as a visor. "Well, I'm going to go back to Phoebe," she said, though no one had asked her. Mary smiled, and Camille was silent until she said, as if just remembering that she should say something, *anything*, to Maybe, "Don't be too late. Gigi's planning dinner."

Maybe didn't say, *She always does*, but the words circled in her mind. Instead, she nodded and crossed the hot sand, straining to hear if Mary and Camille would speak, but if they did, it was too low for Maybe to make out. She turned back to see if Camille was watching her, but she was focussed on Mary, smiling brightly at her. She glanced up only briefly in Maybe's direction, raised her arm in goodbye and then turned back to Mary once again.

❖

Robin's bedside table had a pile of books, and at night, while Alan snored contentedly, his pyjama-striped back wide, Robin curled on her side, a book cradled in her hands. She read novels, books of poetry, essays, short stories. She felt her tenuous connection to the outside world—the real world? Was this all not real?—was strengthened when she read. The ones she loved she kept, stacking them in a corner of the living room, despite Alan's suggestion that she get a bookcase to contain the mess. She liked to see the books bumping up against each other in unexpected ways—Alice Munro meeting Langston Hughes or Flannery O'Connor. There was a smaller pile of her favourites, the ones she went back to again and again. There was Sylvia Plath, Agatha Christie, a small collection of Shakespeare's love sonnets, Harper Lee, Pablo Neruda and, most recently, Betty Friedan. Those first lines—*a strange stirring, a sense of dissatisfaction, a yearning that women suffered... Each suburban wife struggled with it alone*—came to Robin, thick and swampy, at odd times, surprising her. When she read them—alone in the house, sure that Alan would be at his office all day, so she could curl up in the corner of the couch uninterrupted—something snapped open within her, a quick widening, a breaking apart. She'd thought simply, Yes. It was clear, uncomplicated: there were others as unhappy as she was. She'd never seen it laid out so simply, articulated just so. She imagined other women on the street, other mothers who stood in the playground waiting for their children, also reading those words. Feeling elated, comforted. Suddenly sure that something was not wrong with them. It was a powerful feeling.

Robin spent the day immersed in the book—she left the dishes, decided they could order pizza for dinner, drank cold cups of tea she'd forgotten about—and finally closed it half an hour before Phoebe was set to come home with Gigi. She felt restless, her hands now empty, her mind thrilling. She could go back to school. She could find a job. Things would be different. She would be different.

She decided to have a shower, wanted the feeling of the hot water, the sharpness of the scent of soap, the way everything seemed new and possible after a shower. She washed her hair, soaped her body; after, wiped the mirror clear. She looked younger, shiny, hopeful.

When Alan came home, Robin and Phoebe were in the kitchen, slicing the pizza onto plates. Robin had opened a bottle of wine—a good one—and had just poured a second glass. She took a sip and smiled at Alan. "How was your day?" She felt generous, magnanimous, and she poured Alan a glass of wine as well. "One slice or two?"

Alan put his briefcase down—quintessentially professorial, aged and faded in just the right way—and took his jacket off, slinging it on the back of a chair. He took the wine, glanced at Phoebe, who happily munched away at her slice of pizza. "Pizza?" he said, and Robin heard the surprise—the question—in his voice. "Great idea. You need a night off." He scooped up a slice, took an exaggerated bite and was left with cheese on his chin. A night off.

Robin swallowed the remainder of her wine, refilled the glass. A night off. A night. This was the exception: tomorrow, Alan would expect laundry on the line, dishes gleaming, a bowl of spaghetti or a pot roast waiting. This was her night off. This would not be her life.

She went to bed angry but quiet, not willing to give Alan any portion of her day, the way she'd felt after finishing the book, the way she'd imagined her life might look in five years. Alan was happy with their life the way it was; he imagined their life together continuing exactly as it was now. She was angry at his contentment, at his inability to see her unhappiness, so angry it seethed and simmered just below her skin. She kept her back to Alan as she pulled her nightgown over her head, told him that she had a headache from the wine. He patted her leg and asked her no questions.

The next day, Robin tucked the book into the middle of her pile, far enough down that Alan would be unlikely to see it, would not casually flip through it, offering approval or disdain, as he often did—assuming, of course, that his opinions on literature were superior to hers, were wanted—and later she'd glance at it when she moved past it, vacuuming or pulling back the curtains on a sunny day. Sometimes she touched the spine, expecting the same flash of insight she'd had, that burrowing thrill, but it did not occur. She didn't read it again, didn't feel like she had the capacity to hope for more, even momentarily. She felt the world spinning, while she was standing completely still. Rooted.

Now, after reading Camille's book, Robin had an urge to open *The Feminine Mystique* again. Acknowledging the desire for more—more than laundry hampers and lemon tarts and endless, endless cleaning products stacked in the cupboard—the want for work or interests, Robin understood. But the idea that children alone were the reason for unhappiness, for duty, for the quagmire of any woman's complicated emotions, did not feel true to Robin. Camille's claim that putting yourself first, finding what made you happy, what made you whole, even if it meant leaving your children—suggesting that it was *helpful* to leave them—made Robin shudder cold. When she'd read Camille's book, she'd turned the pages searching for insight—for a regret at abandoning Maybe, for a way to align being a mother with being an individual—but she found none. She read and reread the passages, thinking, She must mean something else, but then she got to the end, to Camille reclaiming her identity and encouraging other women—no, other *mothers*—to do the same, and Robin snapped the book shut, pushed it away as if it were bright hot. She pushed the book under her bed, tried to forget about it. It screamed against everything else Robin had read,

Friedan and Steinem and Greer, all of them. She had never exactly considered herself a feminist, but after reading their words she thought, Yes. Their words made sense, and she felt less alone. They emphasized choice as the great equalizer, and at its most base, becoming a mother was also a choice. What was Camille saying? Just the opposite. Robin could not reconcile her words.

I made the only choice I could. We all must find our voices and use them, for what greater gift is there to give? Giving voice to those of us who have for so long been silenced.

She hadn't placed *The Other Mother* in her stack of favourites; she'd left it under the bed, hoping it would gather enough dust to be unrecognizable.

Phoebe asked her about the book once or twice—"But what's it *about,* Mum? Can't you just tell me? I'm not a baby anymore"—but Robin had brushed her off, unsure of how to explain it. To say Camille didn't want to be Maybe's mother—didn't want to be a mother at all—was too simplistic. To say it was about anger or patriarchy or the strains of society wasn't correct. To say it was just about Camille herself, about wanting to get attention and fame, was the closest she could manage, but she could not bring herself to say the words. She didn't want Phoebe to understand that not all mothers loved their children—that lesson was too hard, too messy, and Phoebe, despite her protests, was still so young— but more than that, she didn't want Phoebe to understand it and tell Maybe. She saw the way Maybe looked at Camille—sidelong, quick and hungry when she thought no one was watching—and she knew what it meant. Love. Anger. Longing. She couldn't let Maybe drift into hate.

She'd been so careful with her words until the barbecue. She'd tried to be kind, had even lied, saying she'd liked the book. She was fascinated by Camille, wanted to understand how she could have written what she did, how she could have simply left and not looked back. Had wanted to celebrate her ability to make that choice. But then there was Camille with her eyes rolling over Robin—just a housewife, just a mother—and dismissing her. It had been too much. When she closed her eyes, she could still hear Mary Quinn's laugh, her quick clap when Robin said "derivative." For that moment, Robin had felt vindicated, lifted. She'd made Camille feel small and she hated that she enjoyed it. Comeuppance, Robin's mother would have said. The word was old and musty, but the only one that worked.

Robin pulled the curtain back from the bedroom window, looked out onto the treetops that separated her house from Aidan's. The great, wide, green expanse, looking feathery enough that she might be able to step out the window, tiptoe across it silently. She squinted, trying to catch any glimpse of Aidan. A flash of arm. Rake moving across the grass. There was nothing but the tree limbs, branches still in the warm afternoon, the edges of shade below. She considered crossing the grass and knocking at his door. Aidan bare-chested, just having finished mowing the lawn, dusted with sweat. Her hand on his chest—the warmth of his skin, the particular texture of his hair beneath her palm—and the slow spread of his smile. *Come in.* It would be so easy.

A swell of shame came over her and Robin dropped the curtain, stepped away from the window. Camille wanted fame, wanted a career, wanted to be admired, more than she wanted her daughter, and was Robin really any different? She wanted something else, something more, as well; only, she wanted Aidan, felt it thrum through her when she caught sight of him, the gentle curve of his head, the muscled expanse of his shoulders. Wanted him so badly it shocked her. She was just as selfish as Camille.

❖

Camille's swims became more frequent as the summer went on; she dripped the sea across the kitchen floor, and Maybe followed the trail from the door to her room. She'd watched her swim in early morning, the light from the sun just edging up, the sky burning into red and pinks, promising more sun, more heat, but it was the night swims that Maybe was really interested in. Camille slipped from the house when everyone was asleep. The night was deep and dark, an inky blue that edged into black. The beach would be long abandoned, with moonlight the only marker, hovering over the sea.

Maybe wondered what Camille saw in the sea at night, what she felt wrapping around her legs.

It was not difficult for Maybe to wait until Camille slipped out of the house one night. Maybe lay on her bed, staring up at the long white ceiling, watching the hours slide by. The house settled, creaking a little, relaxing into night, doors shut tight. Maybe heard Gigi shuffle down the hall, heard her bed moan under her weight. And then Maybe waited, waited until the sky got even darker, and she heard Camille's footsteps down the hall. The back door sighed open, then clicked softly shut, and Maybe knew Camille would be walking quickly across the lawn, angling toward Lear Street.

Maybe avoided the spot in the hall where the floor creaked, she tugged the door shut with a twist of her wrist, she lifted the latch of the back gate and let it rest again just as gently. She was silent. Camille was already almost all the way down the street, her pale hair and beach towel bright in the dim moonlight. Maybe stayed far enough back that Camille wouldn't notice her. She kept close to the trees, walking softly on lawns. It was dark, and Maybe had long ago learned how to be a shadow.

Once she got to the beach, Maybe paused. She wanted to make sure that Camille was already in the water, where she'd be so focussed on her strokes that she wouldn't see Maybe crouched by the log. She was still as stone, only a speck on the beach. Camille had dropped her towel onto the sand, and was swimming out into the dark sea. One pale arm appeared, then the other, as she swam the crawl, moving dutifully into the inky water. Camille did not look back; she was focussed on moving away.

Maybe skirted the logs to the water's edge, pausing in between Camille's strokes. She pulled her shorts and T-shirt off quickly, tucking them behind a large piece of driftwood. She shivered in the cooler night air, her navy bathing suit slick against her skin. She slipped into the water soundlessly, swimming deep under the lip of the surface. She swam until her breath finally gave way, and she had to come up. She gulped greedily.

Camille was much farther out, far to Maybe's left. She was no longer swimming, but seemed to be treading water, her head tilted back to look up at the moon. Her neck was a smooth column, white in the light, and Maybe instinctively looked up, too, expecting something more than the almost-full moon. But the night sky was as it had always been, long and lean and continuing on forever. Maybe kept herself mostly under water, her chin and mouth still submerged, and watched Camille shift onto her back, float on the calm sea.

What did Camille think about, starfished under the moon? She came out here, swam, floated, as if this was her own private world. She kept so much of herself from Maybe, from everyone. It seemed that they stayed this way forever, Camille looking up to the moon while Maybe treaded water and watched her. Her legs started to ache. Then, Camille shifted, started swimming in Maybe's direction, and Maybe dunked under the water.

Maybe did not know exactly what happened—perhaps she'd moved too suddenly, perhaps she instinctively took a gulp of water rather than air—but she felt herself go down, go under, and push back toward the shore in panic. But her breath caught, her legs tangled in seaweed or reeds or something else cloying and claustrophobic, and she was disoriented. She pushed hard with her arms, but she didn't know if she was going toward shore, or away from it. Her lungs complained, and yet Maybe pushed forward still. She kicked, her chest ached, she could no longer hold her breath. Her air was gone, but she needed to push further. She had to reach shore.

When she finally came up for air, she was parallel to the shore, farther away from Camille than she had intended. She gulped in air. She gasped. She could see Camille on the shore, wrapping a towel around her. She was so far away, Maybe might have missed her if she didn't know where to look.

Once Camille had walked across the beach and back toward Lear Street, Maybe dragged herself from the water. She lay in the shallows on her back, looking up at the sky. It was still dark, still dotted with stars. And the moon still hung low, watching them all.

❖

Maybe and Phoebe lay on Maybe's bed, under the open window that let in the fragrant night air. Maybe could hear Gigi, Walter and Mrs. Eames in the garden, speaking in low, warm tones. It was the sound of so many of Maybe's childhood nights. Walter asked the women if they wanted more wine, and then there was the sound of him coming into the house and searching through the fridge for another bottle. They'd stayed out in the yard after dinner— after they'd all gorged on the strawberry pie that Mrs. Eames had brought—and Maybe and Phoebe had retreated to Maybe's room, tired of listening to the unending conversation about the sinkhole in Quebec, the life sentence for the FLQ terrorist, and, as always, Prime Minister Trudeau. Gigi snorted about him, crossed her arms, and Mrs. Eames said, "I can see the appeal for the young women." Walter laughed.

Phoebe's shoulders had burned in the sun, and now she peeled back papery-thin strips, holding them up to the light. "Did you know they made lampshades from skin during the war?" she asked.

"Gross."

"Yeah." Phoebe put the strips in a pile on Maybe's desk. Maybe handed Phoebe the tube of Noxzema that Robin had sent with her, and Phoebe absently applied the lotion, her skin turning opaquely white. "Help me," she said, motioning to her back, where there was a strong, red strip, shoulder to shoulder. "Can't reach."

Maybe smoothed the lotion on Phoebe's back, the heat from her skin searing up into Maybe's hands. Phoebe leaned forward, toward the fan, its cool air pulsing around them. Outside, Gigi laughed, and Maybe imagined her cheeks pinking from another glass of wine.

"Wanna play Life?"

Phoebe set up the game—insisting on the red car, stacking the cards just so—on Maybe's bed, and they sat opposite each other, cross-legged.

Gigi, Walter and Mrs. Eames's voices trickled in and out, some-times growing louder—Walter told a joke, Mrs. Eames sang the cho-rus to an old love song—and Maybe and Phoebe spun the clacking wheel of Life, snapped their cards down, collected husbands and houses and babies (Phoebe squealing when she got twins). Maybe was hoping she'd get to go to Millionaire Acres when she heard Gigi shout, "And that damned book!"

Mrs. Eames hushed her, but Gigi's voice carried on the last dregs of her wine—all their voices were louder, clearer than they might have otherwise been—and both Maybe and Phoebe paused, their hands stretched out over the board game.

"They're talking about her," Phoebe whispered. They waited for the next words, but for a moment they were quiet outside. Thinking, weighing their next words, or taking another sip of wine, each waiting for the next to speak.

Maybe and Phoebe abandoned the game and kneeled in front of the open window, straining to hear more. The air outside was still warm, feathery, the smell of roses and lilacs coming along the breeze. The girls put their hands on the sill, balancing against one another. Finally, they heard the low, low rumble of them talking again—purposefully quiet, suddenly aware of themselves. Maybe leaned a little out the open window, but could make out only single words—*again, stay, ridiculous*. Glasses clinked, Walter chuckled, and finally their voices grew again, rising high enough that the girls could hear every word clearly.

"She can call it whatever she likes—she abandoned her." Gigi. Voice firm, no soft edges, no forgiveness.

Walter said, "She was young."

"Was. Was. That was nine years ago. She's twenty-eight now, for Christ's sake."

"Maybe she's learned something. Maybe it took her this long to realize what she'd done."

"Doesn't seem to me she's realized anything. Don't know why she's here at all."

"For Maybe," Walter said.

Phoebe looked quickly at Maybe, a soft, hopeful look. A look that made Maybe's stomach roll.

"Nothing Camille does is for anyone but herself," Gigi said. "Never has been."

"But surely this is different," Mrs. Eames said. "She's come back. That's something, to have her return."

Maybe thought of Stanley Eames, who had never returned, and knew by the silence that followed that Gigi and Walter were thinking the same thing. *That's something, to have her return.*

"It's selfish," Gigi said, more quietly than before. "To leave Maybe for that long and then to come back, as if it were nothing. It was nine years. Nine birthdays, and Christmases, new teachers, and doctor's appointments, and nightmares, and Mother's Days."

"She had you, Gigi. You know she never felt like she was missing anything. She was so young."

Was this true? She'd known she was different, certainly, and had been able to see it every time she watched the children in her class rush out of the schoolroom door to their mothers. They were not greeted by grandmothers, but by young mothers, their smiles stretched wide across their faces, drawn into their arms. She'd known her life was different. But had she been able to pinpoint what exactly she was supposed to miss?

"You know it's not the same," Gigi said. "Maybe lost her mother. And I lost my daughter." Maybe heard the sting in Gigi's voice and realized she'd never even considered this, what Gigi had lost when Camille left.

Mrs. Eames said, "I always wished we'd had children. That would have been something, at least." Mrs. Eames's loss had made her thankful for anything that was possibly good. It was unfair that she'd never had children of her own, babies in yellow hand-knit bonnets.

"It's too late," Gigi said. "Camille squandered Maybe's youth, just sent those damned postcards, and she's too blind to see what she's lost. That you can't always get time back. It doesn't work that way."

Walter said quietly, "I think you have to let her try, Frances."

They stopped talking. There was the clatter of dishes, the sound of a chair scraping the limestone patio, and then the radio flipped on, snippets of songs coming at Maybe and Phoebe until someone settled on a station, old jazz songs that Maybe vaguely recognized, and she knew the night had taken a turn away from Camille, that she wouldn't learn anything else from them tonight.

You can't always get time back.

"Sorry," Phoebe said as she flopped back against Maybe's bed.

Maybe shrugged. "It's okay. I mean, I knew all that." It was the first time Maybe lied to Phoebe; it was embarrassing to admit she still didn't know Camille, despite having her here for the last two months. Phoebe knew everything about her own mother—was privy to her good moods and bad, all her beauty and brightness and kindness—and could take her very presence for granted. A hot surge of jealousy flared in Maybe, and she said, "Let's just finish the game."

She suddenly hated the tiny family in her blue car, hated the two kids in the back with their smooth, plastic pegs. She watched Phoebe spin the wheel—the quick clipping of it—and clap her hands, pleased at her luck.

❖

The weekend disappeared, Monday shimmied into itself, and then Tuesday found Maybe back at Mrs. Eames's house, staring up at the leaves in the maple tree. Maybe closed her eyes and listened to everything around her, the birds in the trees, the sea in the distance. Camille was still keeping her distance, leaving early to swim in the sea, coming back late at night. If Maybe had acted that way with Gigi, she would have sat Maybe down at the kitchen table and told her how disappointed she was; after they had talked, they would have made dinner, ate it in the backyard with music playing low. Gigi would have forgiven Maybe quickly. But Maybe and Camille did not have this history, and so they moved around each other with caution and unease.

Maybe rolled over to look at Robin Hollis's copy of *The Other Mother*. The photo of Camille was large on the back cover, and Maybe squinted at her. Hands on her lap. Heavy necklace at her throat. Hair curled and piled, a single lock coming down to touch her cheek. All posed. All purposeful. Maybe closed one eye, then the other, trying to trick herself into seeing different parts of Camille at once. Eyes. Cheek. Mouth. But they remained parts, rather than a whole. She opened the book again, as she had practically every day since Phoebe had left it for her, and flipped to a random page. *Society asks us to give up the most central part of ourselves: our voice. Our value and autonomy as individuals.*

Reading the book unearthed a new, specific anger in Maybe. Camille's voice was practised, polished, and the gloss of it was like nails on a chalkboard. How false, she thought. It didn't sound like other books she'd read; Camille was an anomaly in the pages of the women's movement, even Maybe could see that. She thought there had been a mistake, that this book had been shelved in one section when it was meant for another. She wanted to be able to put it aside, slough it off. Yet she kept flipping through it, her fingers smudging the print, the edges of the pages turning silvery and soft. She kept thinking she'd missed something, that there was more within Camille's story, if only she could find it. The words felt hollow, and she kept looking for a line that might clarify everything. She tried to imagine all the women who'd bought the book—"A bestseller," Camille was fond of repeating, "for ten weeks!"—reading these same words. She wondered if all women felt this way secretly, deep down. Did Robin? She held the book to her face and breathed in deeply. It smelled like ink and grass and, beneath that, a hint of something soft and vanilla, Robin's perfume. She breathed in again. She let her arms go slack, the book covering her face. The words disappeared.

"Hard to read that close."

Camille was standing above Maybe, her arms crossed. The sun streamed down from behind her, casting her in a pale yellow glow. It was as if Maybe's one possible memory had been made new—Camille backlit like this, her hair fanning out—but it was broken just as quickly when Camille shifted from one foot to the other, tilted her head. "You'll ruin your eyes that way." She was trying to be funny, to charm Maybe.

Maybe tossed the book to the side, on top of her bag. "I'm not reading it."

Camille put her hands on her hips, her gold bangles jingling together to make a bright sound. "I don't mind," she said, smiling. "I had a feeling you would want to read it."

Maybe heard it, clean and true, in Camille's voice: pride. She wanted Maybe to admire her. Perhaps to want to be like her. Was this what Camille had wanted from her all along? It seemed too boring, too easy. Maybe held her hand up, to shade her eyes from the sun. Camille was in her white pedal-pushers, her legs tan and smooth against her shimmering gold sandals. Camille didn't crouch down next to Maybe, but stood tall and straight, like she was simply waiting for Maybe to gush her admiration, ask about her life, her book. "I read a little bit," Maybe finally said.

"Did you like it?"

Maybe shrugged. She knew Camille wanted to hear that it was wonderful, that it was the best book she had ever read. But Maybe couldn't say that. "I don't know. I mean, I don't really get it."

Camille said, "Well, it's about freedom. About needing something more than what everyone expected of me. You know?"

Maybe looked at Camille's gold sandals, the criss-cross of leather across her slim foot. Maybe did not know. "But it's about being a mother, right? And I'm your daughter. There's barely anything about me." She waited for Camille to say something, to explain or apologize. She waited for a flicker of anything—anger, disappointment, dismay. But Camille was just looking down at Maybe, smiling.

"What do you want to be when you grow up, Maybe?"

The question startled Maybe. "I don't know. Maybe a teacher? Or a reporter?" The real answer was a writer, but that felt like too much to admit to Camille.

"See, that's the thing—you can be whatever you want. You have options. That's what I wanted: options. Every girl from my class got married to their high school boyfriend and had babies. A couple got jobs as secretaries. And that's what everyone expected of me: to be someone's wife and someone's mother."

The words were hard as a slap. Maybe thought, But you were already someone's mother. You are. Camille lowered herself to the grass and sat cross-legged beside Maybe. Their knees did not touch, and Maybe wished they had. To feel that little electric jolt.

"It terrified me," Camille continued, looking up toward the trees. "Being stuck here, in a kitchen I hated, packing lunch for a husband I hated. I couldn't do it. I saw my whole life, and how it would shrink, would keep shrinking until there was nothing left. I could *see* it." She looked at Maybe, raised her eyebrows as if waiting for Maybe to agree. "You know?"

Maybe didn't know, didn't understand, but she shrugged. Smiled.

"So that's what the book is about. The kitchen and the lunches and why I had to leave." She put her arms out behind her, leaning on her hands. She closed her eyes and let the sun warm her face.

Maybe could see the kitchen, too. It was Robin's kitchen with its cheery curtains, and ceramic frog, mouth open wide for the sponge. But she couldn't see Camille there. When she thought of nineteen-year-old Camille, she was on the ferry, the water choppy below. She was on the deck, holding her jacket closed in the wind.

Maybe said, "So why did you come back then? If you knew—if you *know*—you don't want all that. To be here."

Camille sighed, and opened her eyes. "I'm not really sure. I think I had to see if I had been wrong. I mean, I'm not nineteen anymore." Maybe waited, expectantly, for Camille to say she would stay, she would be able to do it all—writer, mother, woman. But finally, Camille said, "It was hard, writing the book. It was hard to be the person everyone thought I was. I guess I was escaping a little."

Escape. Maybe saw her again, on that deck, her back to the island and Lear Street.

Camille said, "Let's go to town and have lunch. You can tell me all about your life. About all the secrets on Lear Street."

Something in Maybe's core swooned. Camille wanted to spend time with her, and while Maybe knew this was an ordinary thing, nothing that should surprise her so much, it seemed like a gift. It swooned and Maybe wished she could push it down. Was she asking for forgiveness? Did she regret, even for a minute, leaving? Maybe watched her, waited, but Camille did not say anything. Maybe said, "Okay. Sure. Let me just tell Mrs. Eames." Maybe nodded toward the chair where Mrs. Eames dozed in the shade.

Camille picked up the book, thumbing through it while Maybe went across the lawn. She put her hand on Mrs. Eames's shoulder;

she'd be worried if she woke and Maybe was simply gone. "Mrs. Eames?" Maybe shook her a little, but she slept on. "Mrs. Eames?" There was no movement, not even the sound of her steady breathing. There was silence, a heavy, thick, uncomfortable silence.

Maybe felt Camille's hand on her arm before she even realized Camille had crossed the lawn to her side. "Maybe," she said softly. "Go phone the ambulance." Camille turned her away from Mrs. Eames, pushing her gently toward the house. "Go."

Maybe watched Camille hold her fingers to Mrs. Eames's neck, the soft, crepey skin there, and then reposition the light blanket over Mrs. Eames's shoulders. Camille moved calmly, her hands graceful and cautious, while the birds twittered in the trees above, and someone's sprinkler ticked in the distance, as the world continued on its steady, unstoppable pace.

small deaths

The funeral was small and brief, full of pale pink flowers and everyone dressed in black, standing shoulder to shoulder. Gigi took care of most of the arrangements, making phone calls and ordering flowers, cooking casseroles and pies for the reception that would take place in her own backyard. She was worn out, exhausted from all the effort; Maybe could see it in the slope of her shoulders. Walter took photos of Mrs. Eames to the copier and had programs made, also in pale pink, and so while the minister spoke, they all looked at a young Evelyn Eames, her dark hair waved close to her skull, and her hands folded primly on her lap. On the back of the program was a more recent photo of Mrs. Eames, sitting in her back garden. The youthful Evelyn that Maybe had only ever heard stories about, and the Mrs. Eames that she sat with every Tuesday of the summer. The changes seemed impossible, improbable.

They set up long, thin tables in the garden, piled them high with food. Camille made a huge punch bowl of iced tea and started on the coffee and tea as people started to trickle into the back garden. Walter set out bottles of wine. The gate creaked with each guest, announcing their arrival before they awkwardly made their way to empty folding chairs or stood in small clusters, speaking in low tones.

Everyone from Lear Street attended, and then there were the other people that Maybe did not recognize, Mrs. Eames's relatives, travelling to the island for the day. They mostly stood together, holding glasses of wine or cups of coffee, their skirts and trousers pressed and starched. They were the kind of relatives that showed up at weddings or funerals respectfully and dutifully, but had not seen Mrs. Eames in all the years Maybe had known her. Perhaps there had been phone calls or letters, starting with *Dear Auntie Evelyn*, but none of the relatives had visited.

The afternoon had a coolness to it, and the grey edge to the sunny skies they were used to seemed appropriate. They still had bare arms and short dark skirts, but no sunshine streamed through the treetops. Maybe moved between the tables and the guests, her feet aching in uncomfortable, black patent shoes. It had been months since she'd worn anything but sandals or worn-in sneakers, and now the sight of green grass and her black Mary Janes seemed wrong, out of season. It made Maybe think of fall, going back to school, not the bright days of August.

While adults crowded around Maybe, balancing wineglasses and coffee cups as they talked, Mary Quinn appeared at the back gate. She came in quietly, in a sleeveless black dress, and searched for a face she recognized. Robin had her back to Mary, talking to one of Mrs. Eames's relatives, and Gigi had disappeared into the house again. Aidan Felles was talking to Camille, but Maybe watched as Camille noticed Mary. Her face brightened, and she smiled before turning back to listen to Aidan. But her eyes flitted back to Mary again and again. Mary started across the lawn toward Camille, nodding at people she recognized along the way. She did not stop next to Camille, but Maybe saw Mary reach out and brush Camille's hand as she passed. It was just a brief touch of fingertips, but deliberate. Camille smiled, but did not turn to look at Mary; she nodded at something Aidan was saying, her face full of pretend interest. The look shook something in Maybe: she recognized the way Camille could pretend to be one person when really she was another. She'd done it with Maybe.

For all those years, Maybe had been trying to hold on to the memory of her, memorizing the blurry photo of her, reading and rereading her postcards for anything that would give her away. Maybe had finally put the book away, tucked tight back under her bed. She wanted to give the book back to Phoebe, to be rid of it, but found herself unable to do so. Every time she put the book into her bag, intending to hand it over to Phoebe, something stopped her. But now, she recognized that look from Camille. The elsewhere look. She knew this, at least, about her mother.

Maybe stepped quickly into the house, away from Camille and everyone in the yard and into the quiet. She breathed in the familiar scent of Gigi's leftover baking and, below that, the lemon cleaner that continually lingered. She traced her hand against the wall as she went down the dark hallway. She could not stand outside anymore, worrying about Camille or Mary, watching Gigi pile the tables with food, or Walter laugh with the older men, all remembering Mrs. Eames. It seemed fake, all the people who had not seen Mrs. Eames in years but who now gathered in their dark Sunday best. Maybe wanted only to think of Mrs. Eames as she'd known her, pouring milky tea.

Camille had left her bedroom door open, and her yellow notepad rested on the unmade bed. Maybe pushed the door wide and put one toe into the room, just over the threshold, and then pulled it back. Forward. Back. The notepad was covered in Camille's handwriting, several pages rolled back and packed with her scrawl. Maybe took a step into the room, and then paused; she was half in and half out, not really committed to what she knew, deep down, she would do. She could still turn back, turn away and go back out into the yard. Sit in the shade with Phoebe and watch the adults as the adults ignored them. But she would not. She knew she would step into the room, would sit on the edge of the bed and take Camille's notepad. Three quick steps and she was at the bed, sitting precariously on the edge, as if the less room she took up, the less guilty she would be.

The notepad was lighter than she'd imagined it would be. She flipped back to the beginning. It started in the middle of a sentence, so it was not the first notepad for the new book: *and now, I see all these other stories, these other lives, and it makes me ask myself: Who do I want to be?*

Maybe read greedily, hyperaware that she might only have a few minutes before someone would come into the house in search of the washroom or even in search of Maybe herself. Maybe read as fast as she ever had, skimming over words and stopping on others, flipping the pages forward and back, forward again. Her eyes stopped on the word *daughter*. A description of a girl desperate for her mother's attention. It stung. All their stories were on the pages—Robin, Mary, Gigi, even Mrs. Eames and her long, sad story. She read the last two pages quickly, waiting for there to be a revelation there, a reason why Camille had stolen their most secret moments, but when she turned to the last page and the last line, it was incomplete. *I have come back, to write this book and to—*

Maybe put the notepad down. Camille had come back to write another book. Another bestseller. She had come back for her career. Not to tell Maybe how she would have done things differently if only she had known, not to look at Maybe and say, You've grown so much. Not because she'd felt a hollow ache, where Maybe should have been. Remembering the weight of her in her arms, missing it. It was all about a new book.

I have come back, to write this book.

She heard Phoebe's voice from afar, asking where Maybe was. She knew she would have to get up, leave the room, go back outside to where the mourners would be starting to leave, checking their watches and talking about ferry schedules. They would trickle out in twos or threes, their heels loud on the back alley, until only the people from Lear Street were left, unwilling to go home and sit with their grief, thinking about Mrs. Eames and their own dark, slow mortality. The day would end and Robin would make dinner and watch Phoebe and Professor Hollis eat. Walter would pour himself a whisky and stare out at the darkening sky. Gigi would stay in the back garden until every table was wiped clean, each chair folded up and put away, even the grass smoothed.

Maybe knew all this. But she felt a shift in the air when Phoebe called, "Maybe?" and she stood up from the bed, her knees weak, and made her way out of the cottage.

girl with a seashell

August arrived and, with it, the new disappointment that summer was closer to ending than beginning; it was sliding into fall so quickly, no one could stop it. All these things were inevitable, Mary knew, but still the promise of fall felt like a rebuke.

August was still hot, still sunny and humid, but now the nights brought a sharp edge of chill with them, the cool of West Coast summer evenings. The sea breeze reached open windows to shiver curtains and wind chimes, demand an extra quilt on beds at night. The shady areas of Mary's back garden grew cooler, and the longer into early evening she worked, the more layers of clothing she wore: tank top, men's button-down, cardigan with deep pockets, shawl. She wore the shawl that had been Kay's, the white-and-cream one threaded through with gold, the one she had held to the light in the tiny shop, trying to see the sky through the material.

Mary felt a new, acute need to finish her paintings. To finish anything. Rationally, she knew she had plenty of time—there was no need to finish before fall arrived, she had time—but still she found herself working for longer and longer hours, until her hands cramped and her eyes ached and her back protested. Perhaps it was because September heralded routine, a shifting away from the strangeness of the summer, and then Maybe would go back to school. It was simple now to catch a glimpse of her as she rode her bike down Lear Street or walked the beach with Phoebe Hollis. And, of course, she still came on Wednesdays, standing in the yard with Mary to paint. Those days, though, Mary worked on other paintings—one of Saint Clare in her bare feet, another of her memory of the back door of the house in Vancouver, the way it sagged, exhausted just as she had been, with Kay waiting impatiently inside. It would be too awkward for Maybe to see the painting of her at the beach. She worried that Maybe would feel uncomfortable being the subject of the work, worried that she would not see herself in the same way Mary saw her. Would find something false in it, a distortion. But it was the only painting Mary really wanted to be working on, the one that woke her in the middle of the night with an idea about the shading of Maybe's hair against her back, her shadow long on the sand. So, instead, Mary watched the way Maybe stood, memorized the line of her neck, or the angle of her arm, and then worked on the painting when Maybe had gone. She closed her eyes to recall Maybe's brow furrowing in concentration just as Camille's did. She had the beach; she had the sea; she had the trees beyond. She had even, finally, managed the texture of the sand—layers of thick paint, grey and yellow and white and brown, countless layers. What she could not get quite right—what she had painted and painted over again—was Maybe herself. Maybe's stance was not quite right, her angles and shadows and lines off. The face hers, but not quite hers at the same time. The shadow of someone else. And Mary needed to get Maybe herself, Maybe as she actually was, now, this summer.

She worried over Maybe's arm, her elbow, the position of her feet in the sand. She'd already thought of a title—a nod to Renoir, *Girl with a Seashell*—but it seemed the girl portion of the painting was not going to co-operate.

Mary wiped her hands on her shirt and stretched her back, holding her arms high in the air. It was the first painting she'd been really excited about in a very long time, the first one that she could visualize as complete. She'd hoped it would happen with the saints, but she'd found herself bored by their sameness. Was this necessary for goodness? All these beatified women with their tragic, horrible stories. And they merged together, indistinguishable in their very sameness. The thrill of possibility for a painting hadn't happened since Kay, since the days she'd painted in the house in Vancouver.

The room had been too small, too hot, and she'd pushed open the window to the sounds on the street below. Cars on the street, the whir of tires, beyond that shopkeepers yelling to one another about dragon fruit or the price of oranges. The last painting there—Kay's hands, the knuckles thick, her rings heavy and golden and raw looking—still sharp in Mary's memory.

Mary shook her head, rubbed her hands, trying to push the memory away. Vancouver was another planet, another lifetime entirely. She would not get it back. Mary stepped back to look at the canvas. Maybe's head was right—the tilt and the angle, the golden shade of her hair—but everything else was forced. The expression on her face was all wrong. She'd never held her body that way; she'd never posed her leg at that angle. It was pretentious. None of it felt natural. It suddenly seemed like an impossible feat, to get any of it right. To see anyone as they actually were. Had she ever been able to do that? Certainly not with Kay. Maybe not with anyone.

In four weeks, summer would start to really disappear, and fall would make itself known. There'd be no more painting outside; Mary would be confined to the indoor studio, to the white walls and long windows, the paint on the hardwood floors. Fall.

Mary had promised she'd have a collection ready. It had been too long; they were all more than impatient to see something new from her. Mary hadn't been able to paint for days after the funeral; there was something about Evelyn Eames's death—alone, Mary tried to forget, how alone she'd been—and she couldn't help but see herself in Evelyn Eames. She knew Evelyn had had a husband who disappeared, who vanished and left her so startlingly alone, and this, too, made her think of herself and Kay. One day, she would be alone, too. No one to witness that last breath. Alone.

When Mary finally picked up her brush again, her mind went blank. She couldn't shake the thought of Kay. She was supposed to be painting; the island, this house, the distance from that previous life was supposed to shake Kay from her, was supposed to inspire her, to push her work in a new and exciting way. But instead, she was worrying about a simple, traditional painting, something even mundane, a girl on a beach, a painting she never thought she'd attempt. And she was worrying about Maybe Collins, the tilt of her head, the way her arms crossed. Capturing her in any way that was honest.

And, also, she was thinking about Camille Collins.

❖

Gigi said, "School's coming," and Maybe had the sudden vision of desks lined up in neat rows, the smell of newly cleaned classrooms, not yet smelling like sneakers and bologna sandwiches and wet bookbags. It seemed too soon, suddenly, as if the summer break had only just started.

"You'll need new clothes," Gigi said, putting her hand on Maybe's hair, lightly. "You're growing like a weed."

"I have things that fit." She didn't want to spend an afternoon buying sweaters and sneakers and new denim pants at Hudson's Bay, when she could be at the beach with Phoebe, or painting at Mary's.

"Can't wear sandals and shorts all year." Gigi bent back into the rhododendrons, her shears making their tidy, metallic clicks. A withered lilac branch fell. A rose limb came free, petals fluttering to the dirt.

The door to the house slammed shut, and both Gigi and Maybe turned to see Camille standing at the edge of the lawn. She was wearing a short peach-coloured dress, her legs long and tan, her feet bare. She said, "Do you ever leave the garden?"

"Takes work," Gigi said, turning back to the plants, shears snipping at the blooms that were tired, exhausted from the high sun. Gigi let the words hang in the air between them. *Takes work.*

"We're going into town," Gigi finally said, still not turning to face Camille. "Need anything?"

"What's in town? Fertilizer or pâté?"

"Clothes. Back to school for Maybe."

Maybe watched Gigi's hand as she continued to trim, checking buds, touching glossy leaves. She did not turn around, and Maybe imagined herself standing in a hot dressing room, pulling itchy sweaters over her head, staring at eight reflections of herself.

"I'll take her."

Gigi and Maybe both turned to look at Camille, who simply shrugged. "I could use a day out."

Gigi put her shears down. She wiped her hands on her thighs, long smears of dark dirt. She looked at Camille as if she were seeing her for the first time. "You wouldn't know what to buy."

Camille raised her eyebrows, gestured to her own dress. "Fashion, I know about."

"Not *fashion*. What an eleven-year-old needs."

Camille looked steadily at Gigi, who stared right back. Finally, Camille smiled and said, "Maybe can show me." She looked at Maybe for the first time, hopeful. Maybe felt her cheeks burn and immediately hated herself for it; one look from Camille, one kind word, and she burned, thrilled by the attention. "Right, Maybe?"

"Sure." The word was a reflex, the need to please Camille. Gigi was looking at Maybe astonished, as astonished as Maybe herself. Maybe couldn't bear to return her gaze. She was angry with Camille, but still she said yes. She'd said yes, and she'd somehow sided with Camille, she'd made some sort of decision she hadn't meant to make. The word *sure* had never seemed so complicated.

"I mean, I guess," Maybe muttered.

Gigi adjusted her straw hat, looked between the two of them. Then she picked up her shears again, and turned back to the rose bush. "That's fine, then. Enjoy yourselves." She smiled at Maybe over her shoulder, as if to reassure her.

Camille said, "It'll be great."

"Great," Maybe repeated, the word sticky on her tongue. The drive into Victoria. Hours spent trying on uncomfortable clothes. An awkward lunch where Maybe would pick at her food, wishing she'd ordered something else. The trip back. The whole day, stretching ahead. Just waiting to be filled. Camille would ask her questions, and Maybe would have to find ways to answer, to explain the last nine years, to avoid saying, I know why you're really here. I know that you are a fraud. Maybe felt a swell of panic; there was no way she could spend a whole day with Camille.

"I'll just get my things," Camille said, disappearing into the house.

Gigi's shears continued clicking. There was the distant sound of cars on Lear Street. A mower somewhere. The clap of a door, shutting. Maybe shifted from one foot to the other, trying to decide what she should say to Gigi—that she was happy to go? Nervous? Nothing seemed quite right to describe what she was feeling. And so she stayed silent, knowing that Gigi was waiting, too, letting Maybe take her time, assuming she'd say something eventually.

"What will you do while we're gone?"

Gigi's shears paused, only for a brief moment, and then the clicking returned. Click, click. Click, click. "Finish up out here. Make some lunch. Don't worry about me." Maybe wished Gigi would turn around—if she could look her in the eyes, she'd be able to see everything Maybe was feeling, all these tumbling, confusing, irrational feelings—but then there was the sound of Camille coming back outside, the jiggling of car keys, Camille's gold sandals on the stone.

"Gigi—" Maybe started.

"Have a good day. Don't forget a backpack, Miss Maybe." Gigi turned to look at them, and Camille stood next to Maybe, her tasselled purse slung over her shoulder. She smelled warm and spicy, maybe patchouli. If Maybe shifted a little, her arm would graze Camille's. They were as close as they'd ever been.

"Ready?" Camille swung the keys in her hand, the silver flashing.

"Yeah, sure."

They didn't speak on the way into Victoria. Maybe looked out the window, at the clear blue of the ocean, the pale sails of the boats, the green mounds of islands beyond. Camille fiddled with the radio, before settling on Helen Reddy's "I Am Woman." She hummed, tapped her thumbs on the steering wheel. The sun coming through the windshield warmed them, while the ocean air swirled in through the open windows. Maybe closed her eyes, let the sunshine burrow into her.

Once they reached Victoria, Camille parked the car and they walked from store to store, Camille holding up lacy, gauzy things,

Maybe shaking her head no. Camille pointed out miniskirts, peasant blouses, glittery sandals. *Those are things for you, not me. You don't know anything about me.*

Maybe selected a T-shirt, two pairs of pants (one denim bell-bottom, one corduroy), and agreed to a white blouse with embroidery across the front. Maybe wanted a sweatshirt and Camille frowned, said, "They're so boyish. You're too pretty for that."

This was something Camille was not supposed to say, was not even supposed to think. All the women at the marches, even the beautiful Gloria Steinem with her big glasses and perfect hair, and Maybe knew this was something Camille was not supposed to value. She wasn't supposed to say this to Maybe. *You're too pretty for that.*

Camille paid for the clothes and then Maybe carried the bags, the plastic handles quickly turning her palms sweaty.

"Oh, look," Camille said, pointing toward the harbour, "there are vendors down there. Let's take a look."

There were stands that had second-hand books, oil paintings, tie-dyed shirts, handmade beaded necklaces. The tiny stands were close together, tightly packed, and Maybe felt disoriented as they weaved between them. Camille touched just about everything, considering each item before letting it slip from her hands. She flipped the pages of a paperback, read the back cover, moved on to the next stand. There was no pattern, no reason to the items she chose, but Camille seemed unable to devote her attention to any single item.

"I think I'm hungry," Maybe said as Camille picked up another book. "Maybe we should stop to eat."

"We'll get lunch after," Camille said. Behind her, people were spread out on the slim line of grass that bordered the harbour. A man sat on a multicoloured, patchwork blanket, playing a guitar. Maybe didn't recognize the song, but a few people around him swayed to the music.

"Maybe, you'd like this one. How much?" Camille asked the bookseller as she dug into her purse. She paid him and moved to the next stand, a display of woven necklaces. "Look how pretty," she said, and proceeded to hold different coloured strands up to her neck, red, blue, yellow. She considered her reflection solemnly in the mirror. She picked up the purple necklace.

Maybe followed slowly, some distance from Camille, until she realized that Camille hadn't turned around to make sure she was there. She wasn't paying attention to Maybe at all; she assumed Maybe would simply follow. As Camille looked at more items—a wind chime, a hat with a bright blue feather—Maybe stayed farther and farther back, trying to guess how long it would take Camille to realize she wasn't beside her.

Now. After she puts the vest down.

But Camille kept moving, talking animatedly to the vendors, flashing her beautiful smile. She touched scarves, handcrafted silver bangles.

I have come back, to write this book.

A wash of anger came over Maybe, and she stepped back, away from the stands with their musty items, all the things that belonged to someone else and still smelled like those other houses, and stood near the man with the guitar. He was still playing, singing with his eyes closed, plucking at the strings. He wore frayed denim shorts and a bright yellow shirt, his hair long and in need of a wash, a bandana around his head. His guitar strap was purple, his feet bare, deeply tanned.

"Want a turn?"

Maybe hadn't noticed that he'd opened his eyes, and had seen her watching him. She took a step backward, bumped into one of the women who lazily swayed to the music. "No, thanks."

"Have a seat," he said, nodding at the blanket. "I don't bite." He smiled a wide smile, his teeth yellowing and small, and Maybe shook her head. He was too old to ask her to join him. He was old enough to know that. A queasiness edged up in Maybe as she watched him. She tugged at her shirt, newly self-conscious of her own body.

Maybe turned and caught sight of Camille trying on a large, floppy hat. She posed, smiled at her reflection in a small mirror. Maybe wanted to move away from the man with the guitar, to go back to Camille and the endless stands of things they didn't need, but something about Camille's smile at her own reflection kept Maybe rooted even though she was uncomfortable. He was still singing, tapping his foot in time on his blanket, and he smiled again at Maybe.

"Take a load off. Plenty of room."

Maybe didn't know how to say no. Didn't know how to say, This feels strange—I don't know you. And so she sat, as far from him as she could, one leg completely off the blanket, her bags puddling beside her.

He said, "A shy one, hey?" and reached over to put his hand on her knee. His fingers were rough and grimy all at once, his touch alone leaving an invisible mark on her skin. She wanted to push his hand away, fiercely, but was afraid that would insult him. There was a strange sense of obligation that she must allow this touch, and Maybe knew it was wrong even as she felt it. What was it that made her feel she owed this man anything? His hand was still on her leg, another moment too long.

"Maybe?"

Maybe looked up at Camille, her cheeks pink, standing in front of the blanket. "What are you doing?" She looked from Maybe to the man with the guitar, then back again. She looked at his hand on her leg. "What are you doing?" she repeated.

Maybe thought, I don't know, but she didn't say anything, just stood up, rubbed her hands on her shorts and picked up her bags. She shrugged, trying to look unfazed. "Nothing. Waiting."

The man looked up at them, smiling. "One just as pretty as the other," he said.

Camille put her hand on Maybe's shoulder and turned her away from the man and his guitar, the packed stands, the harbour all blue and innocent. Maybe looked down at her leg—at the spot where he'd touched her—and saw a smudge of dirt, something dark. Greyish. Worn looking. She rubbed at it while Camille spoke—something about Maybe being inconsiderate, scaring her like that—but it only made the dirty mark spread.

❖

Maybe did not tell Gigi about the man in the harbour, about Camille becoming distracted by the stalls. Nor had she told Gigi what she'd read on Camille's notepad. The secrets piled up around Maybe, and something about this felt shameful. She was sure that if Gigi knew what Camille was writing, she would make Camille leave, and the idea of that thrilled Maybe: Camille *should* be cast out, after what had happened at the harbour. It was the least that should happen. And then that made her feel guilty as well. Camille had given her so little, but Maybe had been prepared to exist on scraps. Her need was embarrassing.

Maybe's cheeks burned, remembering the man's hand on her leg, Camille's obliviousness as she tried on yet another necklace and gazed at her own reflection. This grown man's hand on her thigh, the danger of it obvious in the way he looked at Maybe. She felt the burning in her chest turn deeper, darker, red-hot, when she thought about it.

Maybe knew now that Camille would never be the kind of mother she had envisioned. She would never be like Robin Hollis, baking macaroons or slathering suntan lotion on bare arms, always aware of Phoebe in the easy way Maybe had seen other mothers with their daughters. Ease in the quiet, the everyday. Ease came from spending your life around that other person, every day of your life. Maybe could never have that with Camille.

The last time she'd been at the Hollises', she'd made the mistake of saying this to Robin as they sat at the kitchen table. Robin had made them soggy tuna sandwiches, and even that seemed endearing to Maybe, that Robin could be bad at something so simple and still smile so brightly at Phoebe. When Phoebe went to the washroom, Maybe picked at the edge of her sandwich and said, "I wish Camille was more like you."

Robin kept stacking dishes in the dishwasher, only glanced sideways at Maybe before sighing, "Oh, Maybe. No, you don't. Everyone wishes for something different sometimes."

She watched Robin's dark ponytail move across her back as she worked, the quick twist and flick of it. She was about to say something else, something about wishing Robin were actually her mother, but then Phoebe returned and the room took back its normal shape and pace, with Phoebe picking up dropped bits of tuna and Maybe pretending she hadn't said anything to Robin. Phoebe chattered and Robin responded and the minutes ticked by until Maybe could almost believe she'd never said anything at all.

After lunch, the girls draped themselves over the family room floor and watched *Let's Make a Deal*, Phoebe muttering, "Zonk, zonk," over and over again. Maybe was restless, and even though she loved *Let's Make a Deal*, and loved Monty Hall even more, she didn't want to be watching TV. She wanted to run, or hold her breath under water, or scratch her leg so fiercely it bled. It was a restless, terrible feeling. Instead, she closed her eyes and listened to the contestants talk, their voices mingling and separating in waves.

Maybe opened her eyes when she heard the doorbell. Phoebe didn't look away from the screen, but Maybe caught the dark shadow in the amber glass beside the front door. Robin didn't look through the peephole, instead simply pulled the door open as if she'd been expecting the interruption. Maybe couldn't see who was outside, but watched Robin lean against the door frame. The soles of her feet were a pale, snowy white compared to her coppery tan.

She was far enough away that Maybe couldn't make out what Robin was saying, but she could hear her laugh, light and high and clear, and then tilt her head back so that her ponytail grazed the centre of her back. Robin remained at the door, talking in low tones and occasionally laughing. Maybe watched the shadow behind the amber glass, the stretch of an arm, the bulk of a torso. It was a man, Maybe could tell. A low laugh came up now and then, much deeper and richer than Robin's. The familiar rumbling of a man's voice, and Robin's floaty laugh, and a knot that formed in Maybe's stomach, refusing to let go. *Everyone wishes for something different sometimes.*

Phoebe said, "Zonk, zonk," and pulled at a piece of bubble gum, stretching it out long before snapping it back, but her eyes never left the screen. Only Maybe was paying attention to this moment, watching Robin at the door and listening with dread for the voice of the man she couldn't see. She couldn't say why she felt certain this was something she had to pay attention to, but she did. She squinted. She waited.

routines

Robin looked up at the ceiling, as she did almost every morning, waiting for the day to really start, for Phoebe to ask for French toast or crepes or some other equally time-consuming dish, and for Alan to drive away from the house with a wave, a smile, leaving her staring after him. He was happy to go to campus every day, happy, she assumed, to have those hours in his small office with the windows that looked out and over the green lawns of the campus. She imagined him sitting at his desk, pen raised, nodding as he read another term paper, so far and so distant from her long days of washing clothes that were not her own, endlessly wiping counters, watching the hours tick by more slowly than she thought possible. She didn't imagine that he thought about her days at all; he was too busy with grading and students and colleagues and a life that had shape and structure to it. He did not lie awake and stare at the ceiling waiting for something, anything, to happen. Things already happened to Alan.

Robin listened to the sound of the shower running, Alan getting ready for an early meeting or a consultation, some student crisis or administrative decision to be made. She could smell the soap just barely, coming in light and fresh. She closed her eyes.

Robin liked to think this was why everything with Aidan had happened (she could not bring herself to call it an affair, could barely think the word without a queasiness coming over her in waves). She liked to think it was this inattentiveness, Alan's inability to notice her or anything really about her, that had pushed her into this uncomfortable territory. It had seemed inevitable in the way that

Christmas was inevitable—whether or not you actually believed, the day still came. And so she knew somewhere within her that this would happen, that she'd be pulled away from Alan until she felt like she was looking at her life from a distance. It had happened too easily, too simply, for it to be planned; it just happened. No. That was not exactly true. She had made it happen, had made the decision that it would happen the moment she looked up at Aidan and saw him looking right back.

Alan was working late tonight, and Phoebe having dinner at Gigi's, and so Aidan would appear just past five, cutting into the backyard through the side fence. His face would startle her, as it always seemed to do, because somewhere deep within her she expected it to be Alan's face, smile broad and wide and genuine, crossing the yard to her. She was married; it was supposed to be Alan. It took her a moment to get her equilibrium back, to remember that this was her life now, her crossing the warm concrete to take Aidan's hand. There was some degree of privacy in the yard, but they did not touch each other—not really—until they were in the house, curtains drawn, lights off. It made her feel more safe, the darkness and the cool interior of the house as dusk approached.

Where there was familiarity and routine when she and Alan made love, there was only surprise with Aidan. His touch was more confident, more demanding, than she had once assumed it would be; he did not hesitate or fumble, but moved across her in a way that made her feel wanted, and she was greedy: she wanted more and more of him. She was not cautious or demure. She was eager to kiss him, to slide her hands across his back, to tug at the shorts he wore, and they would lie together after and talk quietly in the dark. Those were the moments that frightened her, because suddenly it seemed like so much more than just sex. He told her about the woman he'd been engaged to, that Robin was the only other woman he'd been with in nearly a decade, and Robin scoffed, disbelieving. She'd assumed that he had plenty of other lovers, that that would explain the way he touched her, the way her body responded, and he'd been hurt by this. Robin had laughed it off, but was aware that the moment had shifted everything between them from something casual, without expectation or rules, into something else entirely. He wanted her. Really wanted her. She had been a choice.

Later, he would kiss her beside the gate, where the trees dipped low and they were obscured from the street. He'd hold her against him longer than he needed to, and she would like it, would want to stay just like that pressing her breasts against him, her body still humming, her thighs aching, her mouth feeling bruised and swollen. And this want turned her stomach to liquid, and she'd imagine— only briefly—if there could be a life where she stepped away from Alan and made a new life with Aidan. If she could feel this every day. But then she'd hear Phoebe at the front door, calling, "Mum?" and Aidan would slip away, and the night would turn a little deeper, a little darker, and Robin would go back into the house, holding her hand to her mouth to see if she could still taste him there.

Alan was working late more and more—a hiring committee, honours students, a new course planned for fall—and Robin must have seemed to him like the picture of the understanding wife. She felt guilt rise up in her when she thought about it, Alan ensconced at his desk, believing she was at home alone, waiting for his return. But then the guilt turned a corner and became ambivalence: he didn't ask her what she did the nights he worked late, didn't call, didn't suggest he'd been spending too much time away. Robin wondered if he was having an affair as well, if they were both confusing comfort with trust.

Phoebe came down the stairs and asked Robin to tie her hair in French braids, and so the two of them sat on the couch, as they had when Phoebe was very small, and Robin brushed her hair out. "It's getting so long," she said.

"I want to grow it until I can sit on it," Phoebe said as Robin parted her hair, exposing the palest pink of her skull. "Maybe even longer."

Robin took her time, revelling in this window of normalcy, her hands on her daughter's silky dark hair, the sureness of pulling one section over the other, seeing the tidiness of her work. She secured the end of each braid with a tiny yellow elastic, and then hugged Phoebe against her, breathing in her still-young, soapy, good smell.

"Mum," Phoebe half whined, half laughed. "You're going to choke me."

Robin loosened her grip and smoothed Phoebe's braids once again. "Sorry, couldn't resist."

"Can I stay over at Maybe's? Gigi says it's fine."

Robin thought, Aidan could stay later, and then hated that it had been her first thought. *I've become that woman.* Her happiness seemed suddenly like something to be ashamed of, something beyond Aidan and the affair; that any desire outside of being a mother and a wife was greedy in a hot and pulsing way. She knew this wasn't true, couldn't be true, but still the old pulse carried through her. "Sure," she said. "Take a pillow."

She watched Phoebe cross the street in the evening light, the tall trees shading the street from the high moon, and tried to memorize the moment, as she had since Phoebe was a baby. It wasn't ever the big moments that crystallized for her—she couldn't remember anything about Phoebe's first birthday party other than all the people demanding something of her, and how flustered and sweaty and incompetent she'd felt trying to concentrate on Phoebe and make dinner and serve cake and clean up spills—but she could remember the way Phoebe's head felt on her chest in sleep, how Phoebe's face slackened into babyhood long after she'd moved out of baby years, how Phoebe looked spinning in a red-and-orange dress that had an especially wide skirt. This moment—with the light fading, and Phoebe stepping lightly across the street, and the heat of the day still lingering so that everything felt close and moist—seemed to sharpen before her eyes, until she was certain she would be able to recall the exact outline of Phoebe's body.

Once Phoebe disappeared into the Collinses' yard (after turning and waving a quick, precise goodbye) Robin turned and went back into her own house, quiet and still with only her body inhabiting it. The clocks ticked, the refrigerator hummed a little in harmony with the bump of the dryer, spinning. The house wouldn't know if she was there or not; she could curl into a corner and disappear. Soon, the stillness would be broken by Aidan's light rap at the sliding door, by his first step into the house, Robin standing to greet him, pulling him down onto the couch. But for now Robin was completely alone, listening to the crickets beyond and the skipping of her own heart.

❖

When Maybe woke each morning, she wondered if this would be the day Camille would be gone, her book finished and her need for Maybe and Gigi finished. *Goodbye, see you later, thanks so much.* Maybe had snuck back into Camille's room whenever she could to see new words appearing on the pages of her notepad, the words crowded and pinched together. Maybe saw more of herself on the page—the description of the death of a close friend, her own attachment to this wise woman—and stiffened. Camille was using each day she spent with Maybe as material for her book. There was a passage about the way men valued young girls, the way they looked at them with a dark longing in their eyes. It felt like everything was filtered through a heavy-bottomed glass, distorted and swimming upside down. This was Camille's reinterpretation of what had happened, what she must think readers would want to see in a mother who returned to her child after years away. Pretend remorse. Another distraction, and just like the first book, another lie. The dark pit in Maybe grew. She wanted to wound Camille, like she had wounded her.

Maybe tried to distract herself, but some days even the beach and Phoebe weren't enough. Phoebe wanted to go for a walk or talk about which class they'd be in in the fall, but Maybe could not concentrate. She felt like she had nowhere to go to be away from the reminder of her mother and the book; it circled in her mind, a new endless loop. They were all simply characters. She made judgments about them, about their lives and their choices, and cast herself in the most flattering light possible. Maybe had even stopped following Camille when she went for her late-night swims. All she wanted was to just be away from her. But everywhere Maybe went, Camille followed in some strange way; everything was touched by her.

And then the idea came to her—whole and perfectly formed, as if dropped into her lap from above. She didn't know why she hadn't thought of it before now: Mrs. Eames's house.

Since Mrs. Eames's death, the house had stood empty, as if they had forgotten that she was not coming back, as if she had disappeared just as Stanley Eames had. Gigi had a key, and once a week she walked down to the house, collected useless mail, opened the windows and doors and aired it out. Then, Gigi came home and tucked the key back in the deep ceramic bowl by the sink. And that was where Maybe found it, tucked it in her pocket, and used it to open Mrs. Eames's house for herself.

She waited until Gigi had left for work on a Tuesday (no longer Mrs. Eames's day, now a day when Maybe was expected to stay with Camille) and Camille was sitting cross-legged on the iron garden chair, her notepad bulging in front of her. She waited until Camille hunched forward in concentration, and then Maybe stepped out of the kitchen and let the door bang noisily behind her. She paced, squatted by the roses, came back to lean against the maple in the shade. She sighed. She sighed again. She knew her efforts at appearing bored were clumsy and false, but also that Camille would not know this. Finally, Camille looked up, squinted at Maybe in the shade and said, "What's up, Maybe?"

Maybe shrugged, picked at her nails. "Nothing. Just bored."

Camille glanced at her notepad, then up at Maybe. "See what Phoebe's doing?"

"Not home."

"A book?"

"Nothing new to read."

"I don't know what to tell you, Maybe. What do you want to do?" Her irritation was clear.

Maybe shrugged again, feigned indifference. "Maybe I'll go for a bike ride."

Camille smiled, obviously relieved that she would get a reprieve from Maybe's sulking and would be able to concentrate again on her new book. "Sure," Camille said. "Just be back for lunch." Camille never made lunch, and Maybe recognized the empty gesture. It was what she thought she was supposed to say.

Maybe pedalled away from the yard, circled the block once, making sure no one was on Lear Street, watering their lawns or clipping their rose bushes, talking over hedges, before she veered into Mrs. Eames's yard. She parked her bike in the shade of the side yard, out of view from the street, and took the key out of her shorts pocket. She'd never had to use a key to come into Mrs. Eames's house before; she had simply just knocked and then pushed the door open, welcomed by Mrs. Eames calling out, "Maybe, dear, is that you?"

This was different. There would be no Mrs. Eames in her favourite chair, only the yawning gap of a house unused. There would be ghostly imprints where furniture had once been, and the lonely, sad leftover pieces that no one had wanted. She felt a sudden caution at opening the door and stepping into the house. This ghostly space. Maybe put the key in the lock and turned the knob.

Gone were Mrs. Eames's sideboards cluttered with vases and ceramics, gone were her velvet couches and patterned slipper chairs, gone were her plush rugs and huge paintings of sailboats and lakes. The only things that did remain—the things that her relatives had decided they did not want or could not use, the things that they had not yet decided just what to do with—seemed smaller, faded by daylight. They had asked Gigi if she wanted anything, and she had only smiled and asked for the picture Mrs. Eames kept in the sitting room, of her and Stanley when they were young, standing in front of the house. No one had wanted the photo, and that had made Gigi angry and Maybe sad: they wanted the oak hutch and the four-poster bed and the rolled writing desk, the *things* that had occupied her home, the things they deemed of worth, but they did not want the things that mattered the most to Mrs. Eames. They did not want the things that told her story.

Maybe had found old black-and-white photos in one of the lonely dresser drawers and pasted them carefully in her journal, smoothing and resmoothing them so that there would be no creases, no bubbles, no folded corners. Mrs. Eames in front of an old-fashioned car. Mrs. Eames smiling at the camera, her hand up against the sun. Stanley Eames in shirt sleeves, in the back garden, leaning on a shovel. All these moments that no one else would remember. Mrs. Eames so young, younger than Maybe could ever have imagined.

Today, though, there was no possibility of going again to Mrs. Eames's with Gigi determined to add mulch to the beds, planning ahead for fall, stubbornly staying around the house. Maybe paced her room, not wanting to go out into the yard with Gigi and Camille, where she'd have to pretend to be interested in Camille's incessant stories about the years she'd been gone. "The Woman Problem," Camille said with a flourish. "Equal rights. Health care. Abortion. Contraception. It is everything. *Autonomy*. What else is there? When I met Germaine Greer, she said—" and Gigi would scoff, her face hidden by the yucca leaves. Maybe had grown weary of Camille's stories, unconvinced that any of them were actually true. People could lie as easily as tell the truth.

But still, Maybe's journals bulged with Camille's postcards, raw edges, gummy backs. Sunsets, pretty boats, a bunch of wildflowers, harbours. New York. The Golden Gate Bridge. Washington. She randomly picked one journal up and leafed through it. The postcards that she had been saving all this time, thinking they gave her some clue to Camille, but they were calculated fabrications, just like everything else in Camille's life.

Maybe started slowly, peeling one postcard away from the thin page of the journal. It was satisfying to see the page made bare again, as if everything could be erased. She pulled away another, and then another, until she was no longer pulling just the postcards free but ripping whole pages from her journals. The floor was littered with postcards. Stories were ripped apart, the past accumulated beneath her feet. Maybe gathered the pages and postcards in her hands and shoved them hastily onto a shelf, pushing them behind the books.

The idea came to Maybe quietly, not with the rage or force she might have expected. There was no epiphany, but a slow bubbling up. The image grew in her mind from black and white to Technicolor, until she could see it perfectly, completely; she knew what she would do, and she felt mildly horrible for knowing it.

late-night phone calls

She knew it was Kay when she answered the phone and heard only breath; no words, no silence, but the thick intimacy of breath on the line. "Kay?" she said softly. "I know it's you."

The first few times it happened, she held the receiver away from her ear—the breathing was too much, a reminder of all those times before when Kay had lain next to her, her lips at her throat— and waited to see how long it would take for Kay to say something. It felt like the least she could do, just listen to Kay breathing. Mary understood why Kay needed to make the calls. There was so much that had been unsaid between them, so much of their relationship unfinished, and the silent phone calls felt necessary. And Mary could give her this, could offer herself in a way she had been unable to when they were still together. It was a gift, an apology, all the hours Mary spent with her ear pressed to the phone, listening to Kay breathe. And so Mary answered the phone when it rang, tucked it against her shoulder, listened. Kay never hung up; each time she'd called, it had been Mary who had finally, her neck aching, gently put the receiver back in its cradle and waited for the next call.

Today, when the phone rang, Mary thought it would be Camille, calling to ask her to go into Victoria, maybe have lunch or go shopping or *just get away from this damned street.* Camille had been calling more often, stopping by the house, finding Mary in the garden or, other times, at the beach at dawn. A tentative friendship had blossomed; tentative on Mary's part at least. She saw the way Maybe watched Camille, the hurt in her eyes, and she understood it: Maybe wanted her mother to be interested in her, to be following her to the beach or asking her to go shopping for culottes. But Mary understood something else, too, something that Maybe was still too young to understand, and Camille was too afraid to ever vocalize: it had been painful for Camille to return, tail between her legs, as it were. Her presence at Gigi's cottage alone seemed to say, *See, you were right. I didn't know what I was doing.* Camille told Mary how much she hated being in her mother's house, having to ask her mother permission for everything from using a bowl to driving into town with Maybe. "She's my daughter," Camille said one day as they sipped white wine under the leafy trees, and Mary hadn't contradicted her, hadn't reminded her that all her years away trumped any kind of biological tie she had to Maybe. Instead, she listened to Camille complain like a contrary teenager, and she poured wine or offered cheese, and sometimes held her hand. Mary convinced herself that she was doing this to help Camille and, in turn, to help Maybe. What she couldn't admit—even in the darkest hours, when she was happy for the memory of Camille in the chair next to her, for the sound of her voice in the quiet house, for the way she laughed, so easily, as if she had never been wounded—was that she wanted Camille around. She needed some sort of normalcy, some sort of companionship, after everything that had happened. She didn't think, After Kay.

Mary picked up the receiver and said, "Hello?" in a casual, bright way. She waited for the rush of Camille's words, the way she never seemed to ease into a conversation but jumped into the midst of an anecdote or request. But only silence greeted her. For a moment Mary thought it was a problem with the line, and she said, "Hello? Hello, is anyone there?" but then it happened, the exhalation of breath she knew too well, the moist, unhappy sound clear even across all that distance, ocean and land and thick, stone walls.

"Kay," she said. "I know it's you; I always know it's you. Please, say something." Mary said the same words every time, and always received the same answer: breathing that never changed in pace or depth or sadness. Just breath.

She didn't know how Kay had gotten her number, or if anyone even knew who she was calling. She just stood there, like some lame animal, holding the phone in her hand and listening, Kay's breath reminding her of what had happened and her own complicity in it.

After a while, like every time Kay called, Mary could hear the dull sound of a tinny announcement in the background, the shutting of doors, sometimes a buzzer going off in the distance. She tried to piece together what was happening, imagine where Kay was sitting with the phone pressed up to her ear, but found she couldn't; she no longer knew the shape to Kay's days, to her life, and if she was honest with herself, she wasn't sure if she wanted to know.

She never said goodbye before she hung up; she just placed the receiver in its cradle and watched it for a few seconds, wondering if it would ring again. *One, two, three...* She had gradually started counting longer, watching the phone for a moment or two more than the last time. A part of her believed that Kay would call again and again; a part of her believed that this was something much bigger than a simple, silent phone call.

"Mary?"

She hadn't heard the knock, hadn't heard the knob twist open, but now here was Camille, all bright and smooth in a peach-coloured dress, amber beads at her neck and wrists, golden sandals on her feet. She had a paper bag in her hand, and she held it up, jostling its contents. "Hungry?" She smiled.

She wasn't, but she smiled at Camille and nodded, looking at the phone once more before following Camille out to the garden. It was warm out, but silvery in the shade of the garden; it was cooler here, all the leafy trees offering privacy and moisture and lushness. Mary wiped off the table with the corner of her shirt and Camille flopped into the chair opposite. She unrolled the top of the paper bag and revealed two cherry glazed pastries, still steaming, giving off the too-sweet smell of sugar and fruit and hot kitchens.

"Where did you get those?"

"My mother is baking," Camille said, kicking off her sandals and crossing her legs under her. Her skirt pulled up high enough that Mary could see the tops of her thighs, soft and pale. "She's keeping herself busy by baking. She's trying to bake me away." Camille bit into the pastry, leaving flakes on her lips. "But, bless her, she can bake." She licked at the cherry centre as Mary took the other one for herself, tore shreds of pastry and popped them into her mouth.

"God, this reminds me of being young. My mother bought— *bought*—pastries like this from the corner bakery. Warm. With milk."

"I always wanted Gigi to buy my birthday cake. I hated that they were homemade. I wanted the boxes like everyone else had."

"Kay used to bake," Mary said, immediately wishing she hadn't. It had come out before she'd meant it to, her mind still on the phone call, Kay's breath in her ear.

"Kay?"

"A friend of mine. She used to bake all the time, cakes and tarts and cookies, we were practically smothered by sugar."

Camille looked at her steadily, raising one eyebrow. "We?"

It was that simple: a pronoun, and her world laid bare. We, when she should have said she. We, when she had practised so many times not saying Kay's name, not offering anything about her. We, when that word was heavy, laden with implication. We, when Mary wore Kay's shawl, even now, when Camille had seen it around her shoulders and had touched it lightly, her fingers at the tender skin there. She wondered how she had made such an easy mistake—we instead of she. And then, wondered if it had been deliberate.

"We." She looked at the pastry in her hands, the red jelly on her thumb. She licked it off and glanced up at Camille. "Yes, we."

Camille kept steadily eating her cherry pastry, licking her fingers for the crumbs. The moment stretched, elastic, until finally Camille wiped her hands on her skirt and said, "I wondered."

Mary tilted her head. "No, you didn't."

"Of course I did. You mentioned her a few times, and you never mention anything about your life. And you had that shawl. I knew it wasn't something you would buy."

"That doesn't mean anything."

"Apparently it did." Camille smiled.

Mary leaned back in her chair and felt a wave of relief flood through her. Her whole life, she had been cautious, careful; she'd never offered too much about herself, who she lived with, who she slept beside. It had never seemed to matter to her, but she'd learned early on that it mattered to other people. Her mother had believed she could be cured, and then there had been the activism, the violence of the late '60s. It all exhausted her. She hadn't wanted any part of that, hadn't wanted to make a political statement about feminism or experimentation or freedom or choice. She had just loved Kay, and had quietly made her life with her in their tiny house in the east end of Vancouver. Until she hadn't.

So she had been purposefully ambiguous about her life now that she had moved to Lear Street, where there was such history and routine with the residents, where there was the Old Side and the New Side; she had been quiet, solitary, but it seemed that a solitary life did not suit her. Here was Camille, arriving with pastries and making her remember the days with Kay when the kitchen would get so hot she would wind up baking angel food cakes in just her pale blue slip, her bare feet covered in flour, leaving ghostly impressions throughout the house. If she closed her eyes, she could see Kay in that blue slip now, the crescent moons of sweat beneath her breasts, could feel her hands diving into her hair, the flour that was left behind.

"What happened?" Camille asked.

Mary opened her eyes to the garden and Camille, watching her intently. "With Kay?"

"Yes."

Mary shrugged. It seemed impossible to put into words, to explain in a way that really made sense, though in the end it was as predictable, as commonplace as any love affair: it ended. The details could change—she left, I left, there was another woman, she hated my career—but none of them would alter the landscape of the present. "It ended."

"Badly?"

Camille leaned forward, and the edge of her dress dipped forward, revealing the top of her breast. She held Mary's eye, aware of what she was doing, and lightly touched her chest with a finger, drawing it across her breastbone. Mary said, "Badly."

"You can tell me. I want to know."

It was possible Mary could tell her, could lay the past on the table like an ancient offering: This is my life. It was also possible she could lie, give Camille any number of explanations for why she had left Kay, why she had moved here, why she answered endless phone calls. But she found herself wanting to tell Camille the truth—all of it, the messiness, the violence, the guilt—just to see what Camille would do with it, whether she would pack it up and carry it with her like some kind of shared burden, or if she would hold Mary at arm's length, wary of her now. Mary thought, I want to see if she's playing at this. Camille was being obvious, flirting in the way she would with any man—in the way she likely *had* with any man—and Mary saw it suddenly as an act, a facade that Camille had built for herself. The charming ingenue. The beautiful bestseller. Mary swallowed and tried to arrange the words in her mind. "I ended things, she tried to kill herself, and then she was committed. Electroshock."

Her words had had the desired effect: the coyness disappeared and Mary could finally see Camille herself. Her eyes widened, one hand dropped to her lap and the other unconsciously touched her left temple. "Oh."

"I left, and she's still there."

"I see." Camille's tone was flat, and she did not look at Mary. She brushed crumbs from her skirt, scratched her knee.

It disappointed Mary in a familiar way, the ease with which Camille had been deflated by the admission. Disappointed. It made her believe—as she had in the corners of her mind for some time, in that far-off place where she tried not to go—that she should be ashamed by this story, that she had made mistakes too grave to correct. That she had been a coward. She was about to open her mouth again, to explain the phone calls to Camille, that she was compelled to answer them and have the memory of Kay's mouth, but Camille stood up suddenly, pushing her chair away from the table. She crumpled the paper bag that she had brought the pastries in and tucked it into her pocket. She touched her hair, then straightened the placket of her dress, her hands swiftly brushing over her breasts. She stood tall, and looked at Mary.

Mary felt more exposed than she had in months, since she had watched them put Kay on the stretcher, since she had told them, *I found her like that*, since she had opened the door to the remnants of steam, the shower full on and Kay on the floor, her eyes accusing. She withered a little under Camille's direct gaze, and watched as Camille moved around the table.

She's leaving. Of course.

But she did not leave. She skirted the table to stand beside Mary. She looked down at her for a minute, then another, as if she was trying to see something, as if there was a decision to be made, and then Camille bent down toward Mary and took her face in her hands. She kissed her, softly at first, but then with a startling urgency that made Mary put her hands on Camille's hips and draw her down further. Camille kissed her and Mary tasted the butter from the pastry, the tang of the cherry on her tongue.

possible prayers

The pool shimmered and shivered in the sun, a blue reminder of cooler temperatures, cooler months. The specific shade of it made Robin remember one crisp May when she had been pregnant with Phoebe and Alan had gone to a conference in Toronto for three weeks. She had been nervous, anxious that the baby would come early, that she would be alone in the hospital, terrified and in pain, while he was talking about obscure authors or the use of landscape in Canadian fiction. The blue sky out the window of their tiny apartment, though—was it turquoise? Cerulean? Aquamarine? It seemed like it was all of them at once, and still something more—had made Robin sink into something like calm, believe that things would unravel as they were supposed to, the baby arriving pink and fat and cooing with Alan next to her. And it did; Alan was home for over a week before Phoebe arrived, all downy dark hair and furious cries.

Now, the exact blue of the pool seemed to accuse Robin, reminding her of days when she had believed that her life would follow a certain path, the order of it reassuring. She had assumed that by now she would have settled into a comfortable routine, that she and Alan would be more quietly and steadfastly in love; she had never envisioned Aidan, or anyone like Aidan. If anything she had blandly worried that Alan would have an affair, might take up with a graduate student in a predictable way. That would have been more bearable.

Robin squinted at the pool now, noting the blue and, listlessly, the two towels that had been left out on the stones after the girls had gone swimming. There was something dark—another towel? Pool toys?—at the bottom of the pool, and Robin cradled her coffee in one hand as she stepped out of the house and into the yard. The closer she got to the pool, the more shape the dark mass took on: a bathing suit? A deflated inner tube? When Robin got to the pool's edge, she knew what it was and felt her stomach roll, recoil, lurch. A possum, bloated and dark and drowned, eyes wide and staring straight ahead, there at the bottom of the deep end.

"Alan!"

It was the hole under the fence, the gaping hole they had been lackadaisical about, noting the hole beside the gate each time they passed, one of them mentioning that they should do something about it, but nothing ever happening. Alan scooped the possum out of the pool and into a garbage bag ("But where will you put it?" Robin asked. "It can't just go in the trash with paper towels and soup cans. It's a *possum*.") and then it disappeared from the backyard. Robin didn't know how it happened, but the men were assembled quickly: first Aidan coming in through the gate with a smile and a tool belt, and then Walter. And so, quickly and with crossed arms, the three men began to make a plan to fix the fence.

It started with a lot of standing, further crossing of arms, looking at the fence from various angles. Walter suggested a new panel. Aidan wanted to pull it out, pour cement, secure the fence back in place. Alan wanted to use wooden ties, patch the hole up that way. His choice was purely aesthetic; there was no real concern for solidity, maintenance. Robin knew that Alan's suggestion would be the one that ultimately won out. There would be no real compromise, she knew, without even having to listen to them talk. She could see the negotiations by the tilt of their heads, the way Aidan crouched low to look at the footings, how Alan looked up—into the trees? the sky?—instead of really listening to either of the two men.

The men disbanded for a while, Aidan and Walter getting into Aidan's truck while Alan collected shovels and hammers, nails, and started cautiously wiggling the panel, measuring the width.

Robin watched, on and off, the progress of their work all morning. The sound of saws, the heave of hammer, occasional laughter. Alan came into the house twice for beer, cradling them under his arm as he went back out into the heat. She watched Aidan wipe his forehead with the edge of his T-shirt, saw the smoothness of his abdomen, suddenly, tanned against the whiteness of his shirt. She watched him take the beer from Alan, twist the cap off and then take a long, deep drink. He smiled at Alan in thanks, and then glanced toward the house, looking for Robin. She stood exactly where she was, rooted in her spot at the sliding door, where she imagined he might be able to see her. She briefly held her hand up to the glass, then realized her mistake—a wave meant for Aidan? For Alan? Both?—and let it drop, quickly, to her side.

At half past two, Robin carried a platter of halved sandwiches out into the yard. "Come on," she called to the men leaning against the fence. "Lunch!"

Alan patted Aidan on the back, the gesture too familiar, too comfortable, and Robin felt a queasiness rise up in her. They moved across the grass, Alan slightly ahead, Aidan's strides slower, even with Walter. Alan smiled, proud of a morning of work, and from behind him, Aidan smiled as well. His eyes locked with hers and she couldn't look away. It seemed too plain, too obvious, so after a moment she looked at the ground, busied herself with arranging the plates. Surely, Alan would think she had been looking at him; only Aidan would know otherwise.

"Looks great," Walter said as they crowded around the table, collecting sandwiches and plates, munching on chips. Robin handed out napkins as the men sat down, Aidan taking his time so that he was the last to sit. He took a spot beside Robin, his leg bumping hers as he sat, soon followed by his hand, settling on her knee beneath the table. Robin breathed in sharply. Slowly, excruciatingly slowly, Aidan's hand moved up her thigh, higher and higher, until his fingers came to the edge of her panties.

Robin pulled away as if she'd been stung. Alan looked up at her quickly, questioningly, and she went so far as to rub her leg, grimace a little as if she'd banged her knee on the table. She turned toward the house and said over her shoulder, "I'll grab a couple more beer."

Inside, she turned the corner into the dim kitchen and leaned against the wall, her heart quick in her chest, her breath shallow. Aidan was sitting out there next to Alan, talking about the fence or summer plans or something else men talked about together. They would not be talking about Robin, but Aidan would have the clamminess of her leg on his fingertips, and the intimacy of that gesture would be there just below the surface. Robin breathed deeply, trying to calm herself enough to collect the cold bottles of beer and take them out to the men. She might even take an extra one for herself; that might dilute her worry and guilt enough so that it would go unnoticed.

Outside, the three men were complimenting one another on their work on the fence and taking big, hungry bites of their sandwiches. Robin placed a beer in front of each of their plates and then sat at the far side of the table, popped open her beer and took a long sip. She put her feet up on the empty chair next to her, and asked Walter how Camille had been lately, if things were any easier for Maybe. "She won't really talk about it," Robin said.

"Not much to tell," Walter replied. "Same old, same old."

"Is Camille going to stay?"

Walter shrugged. "Hard to say. Don't know that Camille even knows what she plans to do."

They settled into an easy camaraderie, Robin and Walter continuing to speculate about Camille while Alan talked to Aidan, asking about his renovations and, finally, his love life. Walter was talking about Camille's new book or, rather, talking about the mystery of her new book, when Alan said, "Seeing anyone?"

Robin knew Walter was still talking; she could hear the comforting bass of his voice, the lilt of laughter when he mentioned Maybe, but the words swam in her ears. She strained to hear what Aidan would say, if he'd be cautious or cavalier, and so she felt like she was in two places at once, failing miserably at both.

"Gigi's worried, of course," Walter said.

Robin nodded and made some kind of acquiescing sound, training her ears to listen for Aidan's response. Dully, from somewhere that seemed far away, he said, "Yeah, I guess I am. But it's fairly new."

She relaxed a little at his purposeful vagueness, allowed herself a glance over. He was leaning forward, elbows on his knees, dangling his beer bottle from one hand. He didn't look at her, did not even motion in her direction, but she knew that he was aware of her eyes on him. She could see the slim white line on his back where his tan faded away into the recesses of his T-shirt. She could see the dirt streaked on his shorts, where he had wiped his hands. And his hands, the hand that had been on her thigh, touching her so gently but purposefully that she had jumped, loosely holding the bottle.

Robin turned back to Walter, saying, "Of course, this has all shook Maybe up." She thought she had been casual, had only acted innocently, interested for a moment in a new neighbour's life, but as soon as she saw Walter's face, she knew she had revealed herself. Walter had seen her watching Aidan. She had been plain. There was nothing specific, no accusation or sly rising of eyebrow in understanding, but something in the way he held his head, looking at her from an angle. His eyes narrowed slightly, momentarily, and then were the laughing, comforting eyes of Walter Keane again.

He said, "Of course, this summer's been full of surprises." He chuckled, as if this were a joke both he and Robin were in on, but Robin could not concentrate on feigning normalcy. She had been obvious, and now Walter knew something, at least suspected something.

Phoebe trundled out the sliding glass door, all tanned and glistening and yellow in her romper, and begged Robin to go into town, to get an ice cream, a cold drink, a breeze. "I'm melting," she said as she pretended to collapse beside her father, leaning against his arm.

"Yes, of course, that's a great idea. Get us out of here for a bit." Robin gave Alan a quick, light kiss as she followed Phoebe back inside, thankful for the distraction of her daughter and the insistence of a young girl's boredom. It seemed the only thing that had saved her.

❖

In August, other kids from Maybe's class at school went on vacations with their parents: the Oregon coast, the interior to visit aging grandparents, long, uncomfortable plane trips to exotic locales like

London or Newfoundland or Disneyland. When they went back to school in September, Maybe would be forced to listen to stories about these journeys, about the cramped cars and the funny accents and, worst of all, the rides at amusement parks. She would listen, pretending to be interested when, really, she wondered when it would be her turn, when she would get to bring in photos of Big Ben or Mickey Mouse and tell the class about air travel. Once, Phoebe had gone to Mexico with her parents and had come back with strange marionettes, but that had been so long ago that it almost didn't count anymore. Each September, Maybe and Phoebe would try to think of new ways to say the same things: I went to the beach, we rode our bikes, we ate a lot of pancakes. This year, though, Phoebe said things would be different for Maybe: people would know about her mother and that would be something special for her to share. "You can tell them about how she came back. And how she's famous!" But Maybe wasn't interested in revealing anything about Camille to her class.

She was wary of what Camille actually wanted from her. Just another story. Her story bumping up against all the others from Lear Street. Once, when Camille had asked if she wanted to walk down to the concession for ice cream, Maybe had replied, "Why? What do you want to know?"

Camille tilted her head to the side, looked at Maybe as if she'd never seen her before. "What do I want to know? What a question."

Maybe wanted to scream at her, I know about your book! She thought that if she told Camille that she knew the book was full of lies and half-truths and stories she had stolen from everyone around them, then Camille would leave as quickly and quietly as she had come. Morning, bags gone, bed smoothed as if she had never been there at all. It would be easier that way. It would be better. It had to be better.

But Maybe didn't say anything. She bit her nails and watched Camille from the corner of her eyes and snuck into her room to read the new snippets of her book. She went to the library and read the books in the back garden. She rode her bike and spent time at Phoebe's and watched Robin touch her daughter's long braid and felt a dark pit open up inside her that couldn't be calmed by Gigi's lemon cakes or poached eggs on brioche.

Maybe watched Camille leave the house late at night, swimsuit on under her sundress. She watched her leave, turning into Mary Quinn's driveway. She watched the women sharing a bottle of wine in the early afternoon, passing it between them on the beach, their laughter high like schoolgirls'.

And Maybe knew what she had to do. What she perhaps had always known she would do. What she perhaps had always been preparing to do. But this did not mean she felt good about it.

Maybe went out into the back garden, across the small stepping stones, past the hydrangeas and the always wilting peonies and the day lilies. She crouched low beside the statue of the Virgin, as she had done as a small child, and looked up at the smooth eyes, these eyes that looked but could not see. She touched the side of the Virgin's face. She whispered, "What I want to do is horrible and unforgivable, and I know I shouldn't. But I want to. I think I need to."

She could not tell anyone else, so here she was crouching in the dirt talking to a statue. Maybe waited for a response that she knew would not come. She stared at the statue, and imagined what a response would sound like. She stared at the statue, only turning away when she saw Camille, coming out the front door. Maybe could tell by the way she twisted the doorknob and pulled the door shut slowly that she was sneaking out. Maybe had done the same thing herself. Camille held her sandals in one hand as she picked her way down the path that led to Lear Street. Maybe watched Camille's barefoot escape and knew something had happened, and she had just missed it.

❖

The drive from Lear Street into downtown Victoria was not long—only about fifteen minutes, depending on the day and time—but Mary took the longest way she could, skirting the sea, slowing at Oak Bay Marina to watch the boats bob on the glassy surface. Some days she stopped at the local galleries to see what pieces hung on the walls. She never spoke to the owners or introduced herself as a fellow artist, but walked the edges of the rooms, looking at the pieces from different angles. Some names she recognized, some names she did not, but she liked the cool interiors of the galleries, the way seeing other artists' work made her remember what she was trying to accomplish, why she spent so much time standing in her garden working on the looming painting of Maybe. She knew she could capture something in Maybe, the essence of something that Mary had long ago lost, not quite innocence but something closer to hope: Maybe still hoped that things could change with Camille, still hoped that her whole life could change, could flip like a slick trout in water. And it was that, precisely, that Mary thought she might be able to reveal in her painting. It was more than she realized she could accomplish with the saints. They felt predictable, forced.

The last time Mary had stopped at one of the galleries, it had become clear to her—in a way that both surprised and saddened her—that she would have to paint Kay. Not Kay herself, exactly, but something about what had happened with Kay. Nothing as literal as her sliced-open wrists, the bloody floor, but perhaps the bathroom door to carry on from the painting of the door of the East Vancouver house they had shared. And, perhaps the locked door of the hospital later. The doors might tell her story, and Kay's too, and then she might be able to put it aside, move forward to other pieces that she dreamed about, but was unable to paint. Her hands were cautious. Her mind was dulled, stuck on Kay and those last, awful days. They'd fought over everything, slamming doors and yelling words Mary never thought would cross their lips. Kay had cried almost continuously, accusing Mary of having an affair, of not loving her enough, of being cruel when she poured cream in Kay's tea instead of milk. *It's the small things!* Kay yelled, balling her fists into tight, tight knots of anger. *You don't know me at all, and you don't even pretend!* Mary remembered the sheer exhaustion of sleepless nights, the depth of Kay's need consuming her. She tried sleeping on the couch, even on the tiny back porch when it was warm out, and still Kay sought her out, humming with new grievances. Somewhere within those hazy days, Mary had felt the switch go off within her, and as surely as she knew her own name, she knew she could no longer do this. She did not love Kay, might not even like her, and at one point her rage at Kay's endless, inexhaustible tirade scared Mary. She thought, *Just stop fucking talking. Close your mouth.* And then, *I could kill her.* And she believed it, could almost imagine it and the silence, the blessed, dreamy silence that would come after. That night, Mary packed a small bag and went to stay with a friend. She told Kay she'd come get her things the next afternoon, when Kay would be at work. She had left Kay wailing on the front step, her red hair tangled and matted, smelling musty and dark from lack of washing, collapsed on her knees. *You can't leave,* she cried. *I don't know what I'll do, you can't leave.*

They were the words of a young woman's fury. Mary thought that Kay was only being dramatic, worried what the neighbours would think of her shrieks, loud in the night. She never thought Kay was serious. She never thought suicide.

Mary wasn't sure why Kay was so determinedly on her mind today, why she couldn't seem to shake the image of her. Since the kiss with Camille, she had been thinking of little else; perhaps it was as simple as the presence of another woman, the intimacy and plain sympathy in the kiss, but Mary had been running over the last months of her relationship with Kay. Picking apart every detail, each slight and hurt, each moment that lacked kindness or patience. She knew it was pointless, ridiculous even, but she seemed unable to stop finding her own faults: a day when she had been sharp with Kay, an evening when she had stayed longer at the studio than she needed to, just to avoid Kay at home. Rationally, she knew that these things mattered little, that she could have done any number of things and the outcome would have been the same, but it didn't feel that way to her. She felt that she had broken Kay, was as culpable as if she had cut her thin wrists herself.

Mary rolled down the window in the car; the morning heat was already almost unbearable, and she could feel the back of her blouse sticking to her skin. She wanted to look presentable for this lunch with her agent; he'd come over on the earliest ferry and insisted he just wanted to "check in," but Mary knew it was more than that. The deadline she'd given the gallery in Vancouver had come and gone, and was incredibly close to passing again. She'd told Henry that she was working on the last couple of pieces, that she'd be done any day now, but she knew by the moment of silence before he responded that he did not believe her. He'd known her long enough to know better. That had been three weeks ago, so when Henry had called to say he'd be in Victoria on Monday morning, Mary couldn't honestly say she was surprised. Flattered, frustrated, guilty, yes, but not surprised.

Seagulls cawed and swooped down low to the sea, pausing to perch on masts and survey the water beyond. She watched one lift off, spread its wings wide and glide out over the ocean until she could no longer see it. She was jealous of its ease, the graceful way it departed. It would know that mast, that beach, the curve of the bay there. It would return. She hadn't felt certain of anything in such a long time.

Henry had insisted on lunch at the Empress, and Mary hadn't refused, even though the idea of such a formal venue made her feel tired even before she arrived. She would have suggested a nondescript pub, somewhere she might slink into a corner and avoid the glaring truth between them: she wasn't painting.

Mary saw him the moment she stepped onto the veranda—*Such a lovely warm summer, it would be sacrilege to sit inside,* he'd said on the phone—but still Henry stood up and waved, as if he was uncertain that she would stay. He smiled brightly, waving her over. She picked through the tables that littered the veranda and took the seat Henry gallantly held out for her. Henry Babineau was in his late fifties, an impeccable dresser and finder of new talent. He always seemed a little too formal, a little too stiff, as if he belonged in another era; bell-bottoms and clogs were not the way of Henry Babineau.

"So lovely to see you," he said, taking his seat across from Mary. He had a tumbler of something dark—Scotch? Bourbon?—in front of him, and he immediately waved a waiter over to take Mary's order. "A glass of red, nothing too heavy, a Chianti, perhaps?" He glanced at Mary, knowing her preferences but waiting for her approval. She nodded and the waiter disappeared into the background of the bustling veranda. Mary always felt like she was out with her father when she was with Henry; her father had been protective in the same way, holding doors, offering his jacket, insisting she walk on the inner sidewalk. It comforted her some, her father being gone for so long, to have Henry fill this void when she saw him.

"Nice day for a ferry ride," Mary said, toying with her silverware.

"Oh yes, yes. I was on the deck most of the time, hoping for some sort of mammalian adventure."

Mary smiled and thanked the waiter when her Chianti arrived. "Well, cheers," Henry said, touching his glass lightly to hers. She took a long, deep drink—more than she should have—and tried to quell her nerves. She felt like she was nine again, in the principal's office, just waiting for the punishment to be doled out. *Two weeks late again, that will be a week of detention, young lady.*

"I was hoping—"

"Before you say anything, Henry, I know I'm behind on my promise to the Mind's Eye. But I'm almost there; I just need to finish this one painting, maybe two, and then the exhibit will be ready."

Henry smiled. "Ah, I see I don't need to offer the lecture. You're already hard at it."

Mary smirked. "Yes. I've been busy berating myself all the way over here."

"Then no need for me to remind you how important this show is. After…everything. We haven't seen anything from you since you came over here. This would be a nice reminder that you are still active."

After…everything. She'd called Henry two days after she found Kay, and cried into his shoulder when he came to see her. She remembered the rough texture of his sports jacket beneath her cheek, the comforting scent of tobacco that he carried with him. He'd helped her pack up her art supplies, had made some calls about finding her a quick rental apartment. He'd never once asked her anything about Kay, but had let her spill the sad story out to him at her will. He'd simply listened and poured strong gin and tonics—*You need a serious drink at a time like this*—and patted her hand. Of course, her situation wasn't a new one; love affairs ended all the time. But Henry knew, as well as Mary did, that she would not simply brush this off and carry on. These things had weight, had heft and depth, and Mary would carry it with her, clumsily, sadly.

"Of course," Mary replied. "And I do appreciate their patience. It's just…I seem to be stuck. I've met this girl, and I'd like my painting of her to be the final piece in this show. I just can't seem to get it right."

Plates of steak and roasted potato and overcooked beans arrived, and Henry dug into his meal happily. Mary picked at the steak, wishing for something lighter in the heat, and waited for him to say something. He finally nodded, looked up at her and said, "Well, it's got to be right. But, Mary, it's also got to be soon."

She understood what he meant—the people at the Mind's Eye were getting impatient, other galleries were understandably cautious. Mary needed to do this, and do it well. As they ate, Henry made small talk, inquiring about her new house, updating her on the other painters she'd known in Vancouver, and Mary listened, mostly, but also looked out, beyond him, to the tourists who flocked to the Empress and the facing harbour, taking photos in their shorts and sneakers, little children running with balloons and dogs. She watched the boats moor in the harbour, watched a few pull out into the steady blue. She watched a man in a bright green T-shirt and a beaded headband take a seat on the Empress's lawn and begin to pluck at a guitar. She couldn't hear the words, but could almost imagine the lazy, low sound of his voice. And then, she caught sight of the long, wavy red hair, hair that she would recognize anywhere, beside the man. The woman—Kay, it had to be Kay—was dancing, barefoot on the grass, in a long, layered skirt that seemed to move in three ways at once. She had her back to Mary, but she moved her hips in a slow, low way that Mary remembered. She held her pale arms above her head, and Mary almost lost her breath when she saw the woman's wrists were covered by stacks of bracelets.

Surely, if Kay had been released, someone would have told her? Someone would have called, would have written. *But who?* Mary had cut herself off from almost everyone she knew; they all knew her as part of Mary and Kay, Kay and Mary, and Mary knew, even before she called the ambulance and held Kay, her blood staining Mary's jeans and T-shirt, that she was no longer Mary and Kay. Would never be again. So, no, no one would call, no one would write, no one would know about the breathy calls Kay made from the hospital, no one would know about any of it at all.

"Don't you think?" Henry asked, taking a sip of his drink. He was smiling at Mary, expectant.

She turned away from the man and the dancing Kay and said, "Sorry, Henry, I blanked out there for a moment." Henry laughed and said, "Yes, yes. I was saying that I think Esme Moore's photographs are…"

Mary looked back to the lawn, trying to listen to Henry, just as the woman turned in her dance. She straddled the man with the guitar and kissed him, deeply, wrapping her arms around him. When she broke away she threw her head back, laughing, and her face was full, soft in the sunlight.

It was not Kay. Of course it was not Kay.

The woman raised her arms above her head again and jingled her bracelets, and the man laughed as well. They fell back onto the lawn together, and Mary finally turned away. "I adore her photos," she said, as if she had not just seen a ghost right there on the Empress Hotel's verdant lawn. "Perhaps I'll buy one."

Henry wiped his mouth and smiled. "Do it now, while you can! She's on the brink, on the brink."

Mary had another glass of wine, and watched the dancing woman on and off until she and the man stood up and walked, shoeless, away from the hotel and Mary's sightline. She felt her shoulders burning in the sun, felt achy and cranky and overtired from the afternoon. When she and Henry parted ways, Mary promised him she would be ready in another two weeks, just in time for the end of summer. "Still a fall show, then," Henry said, nodding. "Very well. I'll let them know."

Mary declined Henry's offer to walk her to her car and, instead, she embraced him there on the sidewalk in front of the Empress and said she would be in touch soon. Henry winked at her, and then said, "Fourteen days. "

When Mary got back to her car, she slumped into the driver's seat with her hands on the wheel. It was too hot, claustrophobic, but she did not roll down the windows. She let the heat sink in, making her feel heavy with it. She tried to breathe normally, but found she could not. She couldn't stop thinking about the dancing woman, the woman she'd been sure was Kay, and her own dull disappointment when it hadn't been her. She didn't know what it meant, didn't understand why she still answered the phone every time Kay called, and didn't know how to stop it.

Finally, Mary sat up straight, brushed her hair out of her eyes and started the car. When she rolled down the windows, cool ocean breezes greeted her, and for a moment her arms turned to goose-flesh, as if she really had seen a ghost.

behind closed doors

Aidan's mouth on her neck, her shoulder. Ribs. Knee. Thigh. Light coming through the open window, pale yellow. Smell of the sea. Cry of birds, low caw. The creak of the bed. His hands in her hair, salt of his skin under her tongue. Car tires on the road. Car doors slamming. Voices. Sheets rumpling, strained. Her own cry, her voice strange, her hands tight on his back.

Afterward, Aidan leaned back against the headboard the same way Alan did—one arm behind his head, smiling, pleased—and Robin had to look away. It was too much, being in her bed with Aidan, feeling the same crush of sheets beneath her as she did every other night, and now seeing him posed as Alan would be. Satisfied. Happy. She wondered if it could be that, really, all men were the same deep down, so easily placated. It seemed cruel, suddenly, to think that Aidan and Alan were more the same than different, that she had made a mistake in ever thinking otherwise.

Robin shrugged her tank top on, and wriggled back into her panties and shorts. The room was hot—too hot, for this time in the afternoon—and Robin knew she'd have to open the windows wide, air the room out before Alan came home. He'd said, "Late, late," meaning that after his meetings he would likely go to a pub with a couple of colleagues, eat greasy pub food and drink a few cold beer before coming home after Robin was already asleep. She still had hours ahead of her—eight? Maybe even nine?—before Alan would stumble into the bedroom, fall heavily onto the bed and almost immediately fall asleep. More than enough time to change the sheets, air the room, pour herself a large glass of wine to ease her nerves, pour herself a second over dinner. She wouldn't be asleep when Alan came home, but she would pretend to be. She knew how to do that.

Is this who I've become?

It startled her, this realization: she was the woman who planned how to feign sleep and erase all signs of her infidelity. And she did it well, easily, and this frightened her all the more.

Aidan touched the small of her back where her tank top did not quite meet her shorts. She turned a little, smiled when she saw the softness in his expression. She knew—had known for some time, if she was going to be truthful with herself—that this was more than an affair for Aidan. He meant it, each touch, each kiss, and she knew that he expected her to make a choice, to walk away from her marriage and start a new life with him, or to not. And then it would be over. This grey area, this in-between land they inhabited, would not be enough for Aidan for long. Already she felt the shift, even though Aidan had never vocalized it. He loved her. He had imagined his future with Robin, had never dreamed that she would stay with Alan. And she had never told him otherwise.

He brought his hand up to cup her jaw. His palm was warm and comforting, and she leaned into it, closing her eyes. His kiss was deep, long. She wanted to curl up next to him, listen again to the sounds of the world outside coming through the window, and pretend that everything was perfect, everything was as it was meant to be. She wanted to be with Aidan, needed him on some primitive level, but she also knew that leaving Alan, really making that decision and committing to it, was likely more than she could bear. There would be legal battles, custody of Phoebe, the house, all of their money, and the hate that Alan would feel for her, for ruining the life he had thought was perfect. She could imagine how he would turn cold and mean, asking for petty things that meant nothing to him, hurt and shamed by what Robin had done. It was too much, knowing how separating would devastate Phoebe. Her life would be unequivocally broken. She could not even imagine what that hurt would look like. But she also could not imagine seeing Aidan with another woman, living on the same street as him and being unable to touch him, to feel his body against hers in these hot, stifling rooms.

"I'm going to have a quick shower," she said, moving away from Aidan. "This heat."

He smiled and stared at her, the look that reminded her that he had just seen her naked, had been given permission to touch her as he wished, and she had to look away. "Sure," he said. "I'll be here when you get out."

She wanted to cry in the shower, where he wouldn't hear her, wouldn't be able to take her in his arms and tell her it would all be okay. She knew if he did that, once she felt his muscled arms at her waist, once she smelled the solid, earthy smell of him, she would believe—even if only for a brief, flashing moment—that it was true, that things could be all right. She would be tempted, consoled. And she knew, deep down, that that was not the truth. Things would never be all right; from the moment she first kissed him, in the dark yard behind his house, feeling dangerous and exciting and fated, nothing would ever be all right again. It would be messy and painful and chaotic. Robin had known this when she leaned in to kiss him, when they leaned against a darkened tree and his hands moved from her breasts to her ass, pulling her against him, and had done it anyway.

She shut the bathroom door tight—wanting to lock it but resisting, knowing that small click would tell Aidan something, everything, about how she was feeling—and turned on the water, cool. The sound lulled her a little and she took her clothes off again slowly, holding her top to her face to smell Aidan's smell. What did she want? It seemed like such a simple question, but the answer was as tangled and maddening as a neglected ball of yarn. She wanted Aidan, needed something that he provided. The something between them was almost impossible to name, to explain. Chemical. She had been drawn to him in some sort of primal way, had wanted him, and had kissed him beneath those trees. He touched her and light expanded inside her. He looked at her and she felt like a better version of herself. She dreamed about him, about his lean body and low voice, about the way he moved against her, and awoke astonished. It felt so real. Every time she resolved not to see him again, to end things (It's the right thing to do, I'm married, you understand), she would see him in a simple, everyday act—raking leaves from the lawn, carrying a bag of groceries into the house—and she would need him with a force she had never known before. She wanted to feel the stubble of his almost-smooth head underneath her fingers. Wanted to hear him say *Robin*, low and greedy. Just wanted him.

But she had Phoebe to think about. And her marriage. What she wanted was to turn back time, to have found and chosen Aidan earlier, to have Phoebe with him. She wanted the impossible.

The cool water felt good against her too-hot, too-sensitive skin. She thought she could feel every place Aidan had touched her, amplified under the stream. She closed her eyes and leaned into it, her hair turning silky as it snaked down her back. She heard Aidan moving around the bedroom—gathering clothes, straightening the bed sheets—and then she heard something else, something that she wasn't supposed to hear until almost seven o'clock, when Phoebe was scheduled to return from a day in Victoria with Maybe and Gigi and Camille. The front door banged shut, and Robin's heart stopped for the briefest of moments.

"There's someone here." Aidan pulled the shower curtain back, his face cut with panic. There was nowhere to go, nowhere to hide. Robin heard feet on the stairs.

Her mind went blank. Phoebe would walk in and see them in this tableau—Aidan Felles with only his underwear on, chest bare and summer brown, holding the shower curtain back to reveal her mother naked in the shower. She would cry, she would blame and hate Robin for destroying her family, and everything would crumble over itself.

"Shut the door," Robin finally said, coming back to herself. "Lock it."

Aidan did this in one, swift move and then leaned back against the linen closet doors.

"Where are your clothes?" Robin whispered.

"In the bed? On the floor? I don't know."

Robin could not focus on anything; she looked at the yellow towels hanging lazily, limply, on the towel rack, the fluffy white bath mat, still holding the impression of her foot, the toothbrushes in the glass cup—hers purple, Alan's green, the bristles used, in need of a new one—her perfumes corralled on a mirrored tray, the cap off one, and her hairbrush, left on the counter, strands of her hair caught in it. It was all too normal for the few moments before Phoebe would appear and it all would become painfully real. Robin heard the soft shuffle of Phoebe's feet, then the sound of her trying the knob on the bathroom door. She twisted it once, twice, then stopped. "Mum?"

Robin put on her bright, happy mother voice. "In the shower, honey! You're home early." Aidan was so still beside her, Robin thought he had forgotten to breathe.

"Camille got bored. Me and Maybe are going to go down to the beach, okay?"

Robin relaxed slightly, relieved. Phoebe would exit the house as quickly as she had entered, and then Aidan would go out the side door, walk between the trees to his own house as if nothing had happened. The day would go back to its normal shape. "Sure," she said.

There was a long pause, and then Phoebe said, "Mum? Why is the door locked?"

A household that never locked doors. Phoebe often came in when Robin was showering, sat on the edge of the toilet and told her about her day, confessed what was worrying her or giving her happiness. Robin said, "Must have bumped it, you know how finicky that lock is."

It was a lie. The lock wasn't finicky, but Robin thought that if she said it this way, it would make it so. She waited, could hear the blood pumping in her chest, the loudness of it in her ears. Everything else in the room was quiet as she waited for Phoebe's reply.

"Okay," Phoebe said. "I'll be back in a while." She thumped away from the bathroom door and Robin and Aidan stayed in their awkward poses until they heard the front door slam shut again.

Robin turned off the water, covered herself with a towel.

Aidan smiled sheepishly. "That was close."

She said, "Yes," and then stepped past him, checking to make sure that Phoebe was actually gone. Aidan waited in the bathroom, until she nodded and beckoned him out. She found his T-shirt and his shorts, tossed them to him, and he dressed quickly, wordlessly, bending to kiss her again—a kiss filled with remorse or understanding or apology—and then slipped quietly out of the room.

Robin sat on the edge of the bed, and pulled at the stray threads on the towel. There were three, four, and she tugged at them until they ran the edge of the towel, unravelling before her eyes. When had she become so comfortable, so lazy? How had she let this almost—*almost*—happen? *She would hate me*. She started to cry, heavy, hot tears, and she wasn't sure if they were from relief, or grief at what she knew would happen next, how it would all go, what she would have to do. *Want* was not a word that she could use; it was not a word she could even think anymore. She had almost let Phoebe find her with Aidan, had almost let her see her that way, cut off her unconditional love and childhood as surely as if she had sliced it clean through with a butcher's knife. The moment Phoebe would see her as a woman, as someone flawed and complicated, no longer just as her mother. And she could not bear the thought of that.

She dressed quickly, and then set about stripping the bed. She pulled the pale blue sheets free and then balled them up, tossing them out into the hallway. She replaced them with a white set, dotted by purple flowers. Smoothed the sheets, bounced the pillows into their cases, returned the light summer blanket to the end of the bed.

For the next two hours, Robin cleaned. She did the laundry, replaced used towels with new, banged the rugs out on the porch, washed the breakfast dishes in the sink, wiped down the counters and swept the floors. The house smelled like lemons and sunshine and clean, clear air coming in from the open windows. It smelled like all this and yet nothing, all at once. It was wiped clean. She cleaned until her hands were red and starting toward raw, until all she could feel was the stinging in her fingertips.

❖

Maybe got up early, before anyone else had so much as stretched into the new day. It was dark still, the sky hanging low and deeply blue. Maybe walked down Lear Street with her bag slung over her shoulder.

The nicked kitchen table remained in Mrs. Eames's house—the table Mrs. Eames had sat at each day, where she read her mail or wrote letters, where she ate dinner and, sometimes, a flaky pastry delivered by Gigi in the middle of the afternoon—and the sight of the table all alone made Maybe feel new sorrow.

A sole mahogany cabinet remained in the back sitting room. Mrs. Eames had kept soft, old books on the low shelves, and a vase of flowers from her garden on the top. The lower shelves were now bare—one of the relatives had boxed up all the books, tucking them into the trunk of her car—and the top empty, dust powdering it. Maybe wiped a finger through the dust, then tugged open the drawer where she'd found the old photos.

A few old telephone bills, a subscription letter from *Reader's Digest* and a property tax bill. A grocery list in Mrs. Eames's own handwriting: *milk, potato, butter, bread.* She looked at it a moment longer than the others, the fancy loops of her handwriting, the way the *b* and the *r* came together and the smudge at the edge of *milk*, where her fingers must have glided over the letters.

Maybe put the list in her back pocket, and from her patchwork bag, she pulled out Camille's book and the stack of her own journals, bursting with Camille's postcards and Maybe's stories. Camille in a rowboat, crossing a vast lake, her strokes strong and sure. Camille at an outdoor café in Italy (Maybe had had to look up Florence in the encyclopedia, and then she imagined Camille sitting near the Duomo, with its pink and green marble panels) sketching people as they walked by her. She didn't want the journals. Could barely look at them, but still could not make herself throw them away. The idea of them in the garbage bin made her feel queasy. She looked at the book and journals only briefly before shoving them into the drawer and pushing the door shut with a definitive click.

Maybe went out into the yard, lay down on the grass and looked up at the sky. She'd always loved this view, the way it made her believe that there was something waiting beyond Lear Street, that she might find it. Mostly, though, it made her believe that this tangled-up way she felt would not always be with her. There was the outside world, beyond Oak Bay. There was more than this summer. There was more than Camille coming back, all the confusion she brought. There would be more.

She didn't want to go back to the cottage. Every time Camille looked at her, she saw the question behind Camille's eyes: "What were you *doing* with him?" The afternoon in Victoria had changed something between them. Camille had looked at her, and then at the man's hand, as if Maybe had done something wrong, as if she'd wanted his touch. The many rules, the expectations of adulthood, of being a woman, were too complicated. Maybe didn't understand any of it. She watched each of the women she knew with wonder; they had all made choices, had certainly made mistakes. Their lives were marked and defined by them. What kind of girl was she supposed to be? Had she already made mistakes? Everything felt like quicksand.

She put her sneakers back on and went out the way she had come in, touching the same walls and furniture, locked the door and tucked the key back in her pocket. She biked quickly down the back lane and dumped her bike on Gigi's lawn, just as Camille came out of the house in her thin nightgown. "Early bird," Camille said quietly, smiling at her.

Maybe didn't reply, but slipped into the house, where it was cool and dark and held the new morning scent of coffee and butter. The summer was almost over. Sixteen days until school would start again, life returning to its normal, predictable shape.

Maybe had sixteen days to do what she needed to do; sixteen days left to plan how.

open doors

Camille didn't knock any more. Mary would know it was her by the shushing sound of her pushing the heavy wooden front door open, the swish of her slipping off her shoes. Camille dropped pieces of herself as she walked through the house—scarf, earrings, bracelets, hairpins, earrings—searching for Mary. It was as if Camille took over the house, leaving her scent in each room as she went. Mary found her perfume on her bed sheets, on her damp towels, on Mary's own blouses where Camille had pressed up against her. Later, Mary would turn in sleep and be overwhelmed by the sudden sensory reminder that Camille had just been there, curled against her. Camille never spent the night; she did not want to explain her absence to Gigi or Maybe. "What would I say?" she asked. "They wouldn't understand."

Mary felt herself turn cold when Camille said this; she already assumed this relationship was a momentary, convenient distraction for Camille, and her inability to articulate their relationship to anyone in her life only furthered this belief. She said as much to Camille, and Camille was quick to deny it, but Mary understood Camille, understood what this relationship meant.

And yet, still she snuck out every time she could and appeared at Mary's door, abandoning her amber necklaces on the coffee table. Mary let her in, tugged her silky dresses off. She understood Camille.

Mary Quinn did not share the painting of Maybe with her. She kept it tucked away in the studio where Camille rarely went; she thought Camille would have too many opinions about it, would question the shading and the composition, which, Mary knew, would really mean that Camille was questioning why Mary was painting Maybe at all. *Why not me?* She never said it, but Mary knew the words would be the first thing out of her mouth if she saw the huge canvas, Maybe in a white dress, her hair loose and her feet bare.

And still, Mary could not finish the painting. In the days since she'd had lunch with Henry Babineau and believed she saw Kay—there was still some part of her that held on to the notion that she *had* seen Kay, that it had only been a trick of light, the appearance of the man with the guitar, that made her doubt herself—there had been a flurry of painting, furious and fast and seeming to come to her as if in a dream. The paintings came fully realized: she could see the work as it should be, and her hand obeyed. There were now three new works detailing Kay or, rather, the unravelling of her relationship with Kay. It hadn't been the doors as she'd imagined, but abstract images of Kay. There was one of a bandaged arm, the edges of it peeling back from wear, another of a telephone's handset, the cord trailing off the painting, and a third of her shawl, the same shawl that Mary sometimes wore, twisting around her shoulders as Kay once had. They were complex enough that she did not feel she was betraying Kay, telling a story that should be theirs alone, but she had felt something release within her when she put the last curl of white highlighting on the telephone cord. They were her love letter to Kay, her acknowledgement of everything that had happened, and everything that would never happen again.

The phone rang late one night while Mary was in the tub and Camille was sitting on the edge, talking about her new book, how close she was to finishing it, and Camille got up to answer it.

"Leave it," Mary said, reaching for her towel as Camille stepped out of the bathroom, heading toward the bedroom. "It's probably just a wrong number."

"It's no bother," Camille said with a flick of her wrist. Her silk robe billowed out behind her like some great set of wings, all pale yellows and roses.

"Camille, really, leave it—"

But Camille picked up the handset and said breezily, "Hello, Quinn residence." She stood with her hand on her hip, one breast exposed where the robe fell away from her. She smiled at Mary, waiting, and then her brow furrowed. "Hello? Is anyone there?"

Mary wanted to sink below the water where she would be unable to hear what would be said next. She wanted to hear nothing, to avoid this long, stilted moment where her past and her present met, Camille standing in her bedroom listening to Kay breathing. But she slowly stood up from the tub and wrapped a towel around herself. She crossed the room to Camille's side and held her hand out for the phone. Camille mouthed, "What?" but passed the handset to her. She curled up on the bed and looked at Mary, her gaze direct, as if waiting to see what Mary would do, how this moment would alter the path their new, tenuous relationship was on.

Mary held the phone to her ear, unsure of what she would say. She wanted to plead with Kay to finally stop, to just stop calling and start a new life, but she still felt the pull of obligation. Camille had never asked about Mary's past, only wanted her to listen to her worries about the new book, to feel her bare thigh against her, to press her mouth to her hip bone. Mary listened to Kay breathing, and in this silence knew that she was responsible for where Kay now was, how her life had unfolded. She would call, and call again, her breath enough of a reminder; Mary could never forget what had happened, and every time she answered the phone she would see it all over again: Kay's face contorted in pain as Mary left their home and, later, her wrists red and impossibly bare, her dull eyes saying, Because of you. Because of you.

Camille looked up at Mary, her breast bare to the cool air, her nipples turning hard and vibrantly pink. She smiled, and let her head rest gently, so gently, on the pillow. She pulled the robe open, letting it drop to her sides. Her breasts, the flat plain of her stomach, golden hair between her legs. Here was the warm reality of Camille. Not a silent phone call, haunting Mary. Mary took a deep breath, long and low, and hung up the phone.

partings

"Mercy Mercy Me" played on the radio and the afternoon seemed to hum: the air was electrified, made into a sizzling mass by the heat of the sun. Lear Street had turned quiet. Birds did not chirp. Cars did not roll over the hot, bouncing asphalt. Doors did not open or close, did not even bang loosely behind children or lazy hands, bicycles did not whir toward the beach. Even the sky seemed still, the blue more consistent than Robin had ever seen before. When she looked up, she hoped for soft white clouds that would lend themselves to the game she had played as a child, turning clouds into animals or fairytale scenes or the worn pages of her favourite books. But the sky was cloudless, hostile to her hope for distraction, and so she closed her eyes, still seeing the bright spot of the sun behind her eyelids.

Phoebe was inside somewhere, complaining it was too hot, too hot, and waiting for Maybe. They wanted to do something—*anything,* they pleaded—but they were unable to decide what that might be. They were bored of swimming, there was nothing to do at the beach, it was too hot to ride their bicycles anywhere. Robin had offered to drive them into Victoria, to sit in the shade and read a novel while the girls ate ice cream or pulled a kite through the wind of the harbour. But Phoebe had looked at her and wrinkled her nose as if to say, Mum, no, in that low, whiny voice that she sometimes had, that she seemed to have more often now that she was leaning into her teen years.

Teen years.

Robin could not believe she was the mother of an almost-teen-ager. She had been the mother of an infant, then a toddler, a preschooler and then a child in that awkward age when they were indistinct, when they could be seven or nine or ten. She remembered all those ages, and could feel the weight of Phoebe in her arms, her fingers sticky, her kisses spontaneous and serious. She wasn't sure when the transition had happened, when Phoebe had turned into this other creature, this person with all her own wants and desires and opinions; when Robin had become so essentially unnecessary to her. She wanted to go back and relive all those early days, when Phoebe cooed and mewed into her neck, when they could spend whole days curled up in bed together, dozing and simply looking in each other's eyes. It seemed only a moment ago—a flash, a thunder clap—and now Phoebe was leaning into the years she feared most, the years when Phoebe would want independence and privacy and a sure, safe distance from her mother.

And what will I have then?

Robin's years were marked by Phoebe's; Phoebe's accomplishments were her own, a direct connection to her ability as a mother. Where Camille Collins had run, Robin had sunk deeper into motherhood, being pulled down lower and lower until she could no longer see the surface. In some ways, she admired Camille in her ability to claim what she wanted, the way she would determine how her life would unfold. She could almost see herself step away from it all, move somewhere far north with Aidan and pretend that she had left nothing behind. The cold would help. The slate could be wiped clean, and she could do all the things she had failed to do, all the things she had been too afraid to do, and change the path of her life forever. It wouldn't take much to finish her nursing degree (did she even want to be a nurse anymore?), and they could go anywhere, all the places she had never been (where did she want to go?). But there was one distinct difference between Robin and Camille: Robin could never leave Phoebe. She loved her to distraction. She would miss too much in Phoebe's life, would never be able to reclaim those days or months or years, and that would be simply unbearable. Not to see her face in the morning, still sleepy, when the face of her as a baby was still visible. She could not miss those moments.

Robin felt a hand on her knee and slowly opened her eyes, expecting Phoebe's lopsided grin, her hair still waved from yesterday's braids, but instead there was Aidan, tanned and smiling and leaning down over her, closer than he should have been, the scent of his warm skin distinct.

"Aidan," she breathed as she sat up, awkwardly readjusting her bikini top. He'd seen her naked countless times before—the acknowledgement made her blush—but it was too bright, too average, here in her backyard, for him to see any part of her exposed. "What are you doing here?"

"I saw Alan leave." He sat on the edge of her lounger, close enough that their thighs touched, warm and sweaty and sticky. She looked at the tan line from his shorts, where his skin was a vulnerable creamy colour. She made her hands into fists, resisting the urge to touch him.

"Phoebe's here. She hasn't gone yet."

Aidan touched her stomach lightly. "She's not out here."

"Aidan." She whispered it, but even she knew her voice was not convincing. It held the remnants of desire, and when she looked up at Aidan she knew that he had heard it too, and her plain desire for him embarrassed her. "Aidan," she said again, swatting at his hand, but also nudging it closer to her thigh, everything mixed up and complicated and uncertain.

He traced his finger down her inner thigh, and smiled. She smiled back instinctively, and then felt his hand rest just there, in the space where her bathing suit bottom met her thigh. Not the gesture of a neighbour, a friend; a gesture that told a whole story in its familiarity. He put one finger under the elastic of her bikini bottom and tugged.

She heard the gate swing open, but she felt tethered to her place on the lounger. She did not so much as push Aidan's hand away, did not turn to look who she knew would be standing there, witnessing this moment, who would understand what a man's hand on a married woman's thigh meant. She knew Maybe stood there, saw it all, and held her breath, waiting until Robin would exhale, or turn, or make some lame excuse to explain what was plain to see.

All Robin could think was, Thank God it wasn't Phoebe.

"I…uh…Phoebe said she'd be around?" Maybe's voice was soft and embarrassed, and Robin wished she could have saved her this moment of gracelessness. Robin turned to her, smiling, Aidan's hand falling away.

"Sure, honey," she said. "She's inside hiding out somewhere. I need a cold drink, anyhow, I'll come with you."

Aidan sat awkwardly on the lounger as Robin rose; he looked down at his hands, and then glanced back at Maybe. He mumbled, "Hey, Maybe," and Maybe smiled at him.

Robin put her arm around Maybe's shoulders as they walked across the warm flagstone pad toward the sliding glass door. Robin opened it with a shush, and they stepped together into the cool kitchen. Robin had kept the drapes mostly closed, and fans whirred from the corner. She liked the white noise of them, the way they soothed the otherwise too-quiet house. She could not hear Phoebe moving around upstairs, so Robin knew she had a few minutes before Phoebe came trudging down, complaining that Maybe was late. Robin pulled the sliding door shut and turned to face Maybe.

"Maybe, sweetheart, look, I know what you saw, or what you think you saw, but I want you to know, I mean, I want to explain that…well, sometimes, you know, adults are friendly, and Mr. Hollis has been working so much, so Aidan—Mr. Felles—he's been helping out a bit, you know, with the yard and the fence when we found that possum in the pool and—thank God you girls weren't here for that, it was horrible—and then…" Robin knew she was rambling, was talking too quickly and saying too much, but even as she thought it she knew she could not stop; the words came tumbling out before she even thought them, leaving her lips half-formed. She paused, smiled apologetically and brushed a strand of hair from Maybe's forehead. Maybe looked up at her, clear and direct and without even the slightest suggestion of anger or disappointment or shame in her new knowledge. "What I am trying to say is—"

"It's okay," Maybe said quietly. "I won't say anything."

Robin felt the room hush around her, as if the fan did not

stir the warm air around them, as if the house did not creak and groan, as if Phoebe's footsteps were not just there, above their heads, finally impatient. Maybe smiled at Robin, a quiet smile, and Robin felt her own face lose its forced cheer and fall into sadness. She had not wanted this for Maybe, to saddle her with a secret she was too young to really understand. She had not wanted to be the source of any pain for Maybe, who had certainly already had more than her share of it. She cupped Maybe's cheek in her palm—that same cheek she had held when Maybe was younger, rounder, her tears hot over a skinned knee—and Maybe tilted her head a bit, welcoming the touch. "Oh, Maybe," Robin sighed as Phoebe came trundling down the stairs. Before she could round the corner into the kitchen, Robin gave Maybe's cheek one last light stroke, and then she took her hand away and readied herself to face Phoebe.

"Like a herd of elephants," she said as Phoebe appeared, her hair in a ponytail and her legs seeming long—too long, surely—in their denim shorts. "Maybe's here. Now you don't have an excuse to be *so bored.*" She smiled, but she was aware of what had passed between her and Maybe, that they were now on the same side of a rapidly rushing river, that Phoebe was held separate, still safe on the shore.

"Finally," Phoebe said as she opened the refrigerator. "Grilled cheese?"

"Too hot," Maybe said.

"Hot dogs? Watermelon?"

"I'll make you sandwiches," Robin said, crossing the kitchen to open the refrigerator.

"It's okay, Mum." Phoebe said. "We can do it."

Phoebe and Maybe moved silently in the kitchen, gathering bread and cold cuts and mayonnaise, until they were side by side, giggling about something Robin had missed, and creating an assembly line of ingredients. Maybe bumped Phoebe's hip with her own and Phoebe tripped a little, righted herself and continued on, the room consumed by their laughter and youth, and Robin felt the breath go out of her. The girls were no longer just girls, but leaning into something much more treacherous, something they would have to negotiate on their own. She wanted to yell, *Not yet, not yet! You're too young, stay young just a while longer,* but she knew it would do no good, had done no good when she was their age; they would continue to become foreign, less and less the children she had held and comforted and encouraged. They were little changelings. And Maybe already had secrets to keep, perhaps the first adult secret she had ever held close. Robin felt the tears coming and blinked them away as quickly as she could, stunned by these two young women, their bony knees and just-beginning buds of breasts, and Maybe, already stepping with her into the swirling waters of adulthood.

Robin left the girls giggling and talking and making a mess, and went back out into the yard. She'd half wondered if Aidan would have been frightened off by Maybe's appearance, but he sat where she so recently had, angled on the lounger. And this stopped her. It was too familiar, too comfortable, and she whispered, "Aidan, you have to go. The girls are just inside."

He looked up at her, a smile fading from his lips. "Maybe already saw us, it makes everything—" Robin knew he was going to say easier, and she held up her hand, stopping him before he could. It wasn't easier, not for her, but she saw with sudden clarity that it was for him, that he thought this was the inevitable: a breaking apart of her family, a new restructuring of Robin and Aidan and Phoebe, with Alan renting an apartment by the university or moving in with a new girlfriend, that their lives would alter, yes, but that they had been working toward this all the time. That somewhere within her, perhaps, even she'd thought it possible. But then she'd seen Maybe's face—the change, the shift, her new, clear understanding of Robin as unfulfilled, disappointing—at the sight of Aidan's hand on her leg. *No.*

"Aidan," she said quietly, gently. "No."

He put one hand up over his eyes to block out the unrelenting sun, and looked up at her, his brow slightly furrowed. "No?" It wasn't quite a question, not a statement, but the edge of it told Robin that he had been hopeful, and that his understanding about what this *No* meant would be slow, excruciating.

"No," she repeated, shaking her head. She squatted down next to him, so that their faces were even with one another. His eyes were the warmest golden brown she had ever seen, and the thought of never seeing them again, never seeing his eyes close in sleep or pleasure, cut through her swiftly. He leaned forward on his elbows, watching her closely. She almost changed her mind, her whole body turning liquid, but then she remembered Maybe's eyes. "No," she said, barely audible. She took his hand in hers in what she hoped would be comfort, but what turned out to feel insubstantial.

Aidan pulled his hand away. "Did you ever intend to leave him?"

"I did. Or thought I did. I don't know, Aidan, I didn't plan any of this. It was just *you*, you know?"

Their first kiss, the canopy of trees, the way she'd seen him look at her for all those months before, the way he did not look away when she caught him staring at her, how she knew just from his gaze that he wanted her. That he would, eventually, have her. That she would do this, that she *meant* to do this. That first kiss had felt inevitable, necessary in some primitive way. She had kissed him, held him closer, believed for a moment that she could have everything she had ever wanted.

Aidan stood up. She looked at the scar on his knee, remembered him telling her about the forest fire, the white-hot branch that fell and caught him just there, cutting through the layers of clothing and protective gear. His knee, then, the white sheets draped around him, and her fingers on the scar, believing she could almost feel the residual heat.

"Leave him," he said. "You don't love him."

Robin straightened, stood to face Aidan. She could smell the warmth of his skin, and held her hand up to touch his chest. "No," she said carefully. "But I don't hate him. And I do love Phoebe." She took her hand away. She had made her choice.

Aidan looked toward the house, as if just now considering Phoebe, and Robin thought for a moment that he might go into the kitchen, sit at the table laden with turkey and mustard sandwiches and glasses of lemonade and say, "Your mother loves me," but he did not. He looked toward the house for a moment, then another, and then said, "Robin."

He had said her name many times before, but not in this way. His voice was full of sorrow. She knew he would not beg for her to leave, he would not beg her for anything, but the sadness when he said her name made her understand that this was not only her sacrifice, that she was insisting he make the sacrifice as well.

Aidan looked at her in the same way that he had for all those months before they became lovers, and then he bent forward and kissed her, a kiss so deep she felt herself falter, wondered how she would grow old knowing that she had done this, had had this surprising love, this man who only wanted her, only wanted to please her, and she had said no. She had to let it go.

He didn't say anything as he walked away, did not look back, but Robin stood in the yard long after, watching the spot in the trees where he could return, where he might fight for her, insist that she leave Alan, do this one thing for herself, and she thought that if he came back, if he took her hand, she might.

Then the girls came out into the yard, filling it with their giggling and whispering, and the branches of the trees did not move, did not part.

the return

The temperature dipped at night, requiring shawls or blankets when they sat outside, and Gigi said, "That's it. Summer's turned its back. So long."

The days remained bright and warm, but there was an edge that reminded you that soon daily life would return, school and sports and band practice, and soon after rain would come, and then fireplaces would be lit and blankets heaped and summer would be entirely forgotten. Fall meant real life. Fall meant Maybe's life returning to normal, the house with just Gigi and Maybe in it, turning back into the life they had shared together.

Camille said that she was looking for an apartment in Victoria, but Maybe had not seen any papers with advertisements circled. Gigi took the claims more seriously, eyeing Camille suspiciously, asking questions about neighbourhoods and rent. She was softening, Maybe could see, getting used to having Camille here. Camille was her daughter, after all, and whatever Maybe had lost when Camille disappeared, Gigi had lost as well. Maybe knew that Gigi would feel differently if she knew what the new book was really about, that she would feel foolish, betrayed by seeing her own life unfurl on the pages, but Maybe couldn't bring herself to tell her. It would be like Camille leaving all over again, only this time with the added insult of their lives in the new book.

Gigi and Walter played rummy on the iron patio table, using walnuts as currency. The dinner dishes had been piled inside, waiting for Maybe to go inside and wash them, and Camille had remained in her room, saying she wasn't hungry.

"But it's mussels," Gigi had said through the closed door. "Your favourite." Gigi had been doing this more often, making things Camille would like, and Maybe knew Gigi would think she'd been conned by Camille. More disappointment, more sadness that would do her in. Camille had not come out for dinner, had instead said she'd eat later. The sight of a blue plate, full of soft bread and olives, covered carefully by a tea towel, on the kitchen counter made Maybe heartsick.

"Raise you three," Walter said as he popped a handful of walnuts in his mouth.

"Stop eating the money."

"Won't need it. Won't need it."

Gigi said, "You're a terrible bluffer," but smiled behind her cards.

Maybe had barely seen Phoebe in the last week; she was too afraid she'd blurt out what she'd seen between Robin and Aidan Felles. She knew Phoebe didn't know what was going on, still saw her mother as perfect, or close to it. Sometimes, Maybe felt so much older. So, instead, she ate, she slept, sometimes she cooked with Gigi, on a good day she found an excuse to go to Mrs. Eames's house, but mostly she just waited for the day to be over. She watched the Xs take over the calendar's month of August, and felt the pit expand in the bottom of her stomach. Robin had waved to her a couple of times from across the street, and Maybe had waved back. Once, Robin had even jogged across to the front yard and asked if Maybe wanted to go with them for fish and chips. But Maybe had lied and said she'd just eaten. "Well, next time then," Robin said before she went back to the car, but Maybe knew she was secretly relieved. Maybe knew something that Robin must be ashamed of, her one mistake. Now, Robin was just a little less perfect, a little more like every other adult, and this made Maybe heavy-hearted. Was every mother, every woman, burdened with these kinds of choices? Was every choice a new action or reaction to be judged? The idea of it exhausted Maybe.

"You're all here, great. Here, here." Camille came out of the house, balancing glasses and a bottle of wine in her arms. She was smiling, a smile so bright and big that Maybe saw nothing but how beautiful she really was, all glowing and golden.

Camille put the glasses on the table, pushing aside some of the walnuts, and quickly poured the wine—three full glasses, one only a mouthful—and then handed the glasses to Gigi and Walter and, finally, walked across the lawn to Maybe and gave her the last, small glass.

"Oh, Camille," Gigi said. "She doesn't need any wine."

But Camille ignored her and said, "Come over here, Maybe," as she crossed back to the table and picked up her own glass. "You'll want to be a part of this. It's important."

Gigi and Walter exchanged a look. Maybe crossed the grass and stood next to them at the table.

"Raise your glasses," Camille said. "You'll want to make a toast!"

"To what?" Gigi asked. "What's happening?"

"It's done," Camille said. "I've finished the book!"

She put her glass out, waiting to be congratulated and cheered, but they all sat still and silent before Walter said, "Great news." He clinked her glass with his own, and then Gigi followed suit, smiling at Camille. Maybe did not move, but Camille touched her glass to hers as she laughed, pleased with herself, happy with their attention.

With the first sip of wine, Maybe's eyes began to water. It was tart and thin and it made her throat burn. She closed her eyes and drank it all, one long gulp, just to be rid of it. When she opened her eyes, Camille was looking at her, laughing. "That's good," she said. "I liked it too much the first time I tried it."

Maybe's stomach rolled. Gigi took the glass from her, and set it down on the far side of the table. "I'm watching you," she said.

"So, tell us, what happens now?" Walter asked Camille. She sat cross-legged on a chair, her skirts bunching up in her lap.

"Well, my agent reads it, and then there might be some editing. Then we find a publisher. I've called it *The Return*. Here's to another bestseller!" She was giddy, practically humming with pleasure.

"That's just great," Walter said, refilling his glass and Camille's. "Cheers again."

Gigi was quiet, looking into her wineglass, and finally Camille said, "Cat got your tongue?"

When Gigi looked up, her eyes were bright with tears. Walter reached across the table to pat Gigi's hand, but Gigi waved him away, wiping quickly at her eyes. She said quietly, "I'm proud of you, Camille."

Camille spun her silver ring on her finger and looked down at her lap. Maybe thought she might cry, and this surprised her. Soon enough, they would read the book, and then everyone would all know what she had been doing for these last months. Stealing their lives, their stories. The hurt would be fresh, astonishing. Gigi would be crushed, and the very memory of this moment would be especially painful. Camille looked up, her eyes twinkling but dry, and said, "Thank you, Mum."

They refilled the glasses and toasted Camille again, and she talked more about the book and Maybe only half listened. Their lives were going to be laid bare, through Camille's eyes. But Camille smiled, tilted her head, told them the book was about her finding out who she really was—emphasizing *really*, and smiling at Maybe—and drank her wine. Maybe watched her, watched Walter chuckle and ask more questions, and watched Gigi look at Camille in a way she hadn't seen before, a softer, hopeful way, and Maybe felt the anger rise up in her, souring everything.

"I need to celebrate," Camille said, getting up from her chair. "I'm going to go out with Mary Quinn." She dashed into the house, returning with her gold sandals and a tasselled bag. She put her sandals on, and attached a turquoise earring. "Don't wait up!"

She blew a kiss to Walter and then smiled at Gigi. Maybe kept her arms crossed over her chest. Finally, Camille reached out and touched Maybe's forehead, brushing her fingertips across the hairline. "Be good," she said before she disappeared around the side of the house and into the night. Good. There was no more goodness in Camille.

After Camille had disappeared out to the dark street, Gigi and Walter finished off the bottle of wine. Gigi brought a blanket out for Maybe, tucked it around her in the iron chair. The night was cool with a breeze, and the smell of salt on the air, the night soft. Maybe's eyes grew heavy, and she dozed in her chair. Gigi said, "For heaven's sake, go to bed." But Maybe didn't want to, opening her eyes for a while before they became heavy again, watching Gigi raise her glass to her lips, smile across the table at Walter.

Walter drained his glass. Gigi tapped the rim of her own, pursed her lips. "I have to admit, I'm curious," she said.

"Ask her," Walter said. "Could be good for you. For the two of you."

Gigi stared up at the dark night sky, the stars bright. "I should read it."

"Ask her," Walter repeated.

"No, I should just read it."

Maybe turned to look at Gigi. Read it. She couldn't tell if Gigi was serious or not, if it was simply the after-effects of the celebration and the sweet wine. Gigi stared into her nearly empty wineglass.

"You can't do that, Frances. Ask her."

"I can," Gigi said. She took a sip of wine. "After the last one, I need to know what she's saying now."

Maybe knew Gigi shouldn't read the book—she'd looked so hopeful tonight when Camille said she'd finished her project; she'd be broken when she read Camille's words. A whole summer reimagined, the people of Lear Street appearing in the pages. And always Camille as the shining star. But still, that dark, hard part of Maybe wanted Gigi to read it. To share in her rage, the sharp slap of seeing themselves on the page.

"It's a bad idea," Walter said.

"Probably."

Maybe rubbed her eyes, and said she was going in to bed. She poured herself a glass of water from the tap and drank it straight down, refilling the glass. Gigi couldn't read the book. But.

Camille's door was open a crack, the bedside light on. The room glowed warm and amber in the dark house. Maybe pushed the door wide. Open dresser drawer. Chair tilted away from the desk. And the notepads, sprawled out, a coffee mug ring on the top of one. She stacked them. She put them neatly on the bed, where they could not be missed. She stepped back to stand in the doorway.

"Out." Gigi put her hands on Maybe's shoulders and turned her toward her own room. She pulled Camille's door closed. "It's late."

She should have stopped her, should have said, Wait, please don't read it. She could have told Gigi everything, but she let herself be propelled down the hallway, each step further away from the truth, as if she had no role in what would inevitably come. She could have said anything, but instead she crawled into bed with her clothes still on, the knot in the deepest pit of her stomach twisting and untwisting.

❖

The house was silent. There was no kettle whistling, no frying pan sputtering with butter, no vacuum spinning across the living room carpet. There was only the creaking of Maybe's bed when she rolled over in the morning.

Camille's notepads were on the kitchen counter next to a hastily scrawled note from Gigi: *Gone to see Camille.*

Of course this would happen. She should have warned Gigi, she should have begged her not to read it. She should have hidden the notepads, torn each page out.

Maybe could hear their voices from the street. The flowers shivered in their copper pots, and Mary Quinn's house looked the same as it always did, but with each step Maybe took up the driveway, the shouting grew louder. Everyone would be able to hear Gigi and Camille and their hot, angry words.

Maybe pushed the side gate open and stepped into Mary Quinn's backyard. Mary was standing at the edge of the patio, her back to Gigi and Camille. Camille sat in one of the Adirondack chairs in her nightgown, and Gigi stood over her. Her face was pinched with anger, turning pink and a deeper pink still. Her voice shook when she said, "Go home, Maybe. You don't need to be here."

Camille did not look at Maybe, but Mary Quinn turned. Her smile was strained and unconvincing.

"I already read it."

Gigi's eyes snapped to Maybe. She recognized the look: it was the same one she'd given Gigi when she'd admitted she'd read *The Other Mother*. Surprise, doubt, disappointment. Disbelief. Maybe repeated, "The new one. I read it."

"You shouldn't have," Gigi said.

"But I did."

"Well then, we're all caught up," Camille said. Gigi looked back to her.

"Are you proud of yourself? Proud of that garbage?"

"It's the truth, Mother. It's how I see things."

"It's a lie. Every blessed word of it. You put us all on the page, but none of it is true."

Camille shrugged. "It's how I see things. It's exactly what I've experienced being back here."

"And to think I congratulated you last night—I was proud of you. If I'd known what you'd written, if I'd known that you'd written about all of us…"

"It wouldn't matter. You'd find a way to hate it, no matter what I wrote. Just like the first book. Like everything always."

Then the shouting started again, Gigi and Camille's words coming faster and louder, shouting over each other, indecipherable. Gigi yelled about the truth, and Camille yelled about everything. Every word was a sharp shard.

"You should be ashamed of what you've done!"

"You have never understood anything about me."

Mary Quinn skirted the edge of the patio to Maybe's side. She put her arm around Maybe, and said, "You don't need to hear this. Come on, let's go inside." She smelled spicy, warm, as if she'd just rolled out of bed, perhaps been woken by Gigi's fists on the door.

"No," Maybe said, "it's all my fault."

"Your fault?"

Gigi and Camille continued to yell behind them, but Maybe concentrated on Mary's face so close to hers, her brow furrowed, not understanding what Maybe was trying to tell her.

"I should have told her. I knew what Camille was writing."

"That's not your fault. It's—"

They yelled about the past, ancient hurts, all the ways they'd hurt each other. Nine years of all the things Gigi had wanted to say, calling Camille selfish, immature, unfit. And Camille listed all her complaints, going back to her own childhood. Gigi threatened. Camille threatened. Then, silence. Too much silence.

"Mum? Mum?"

Maybe turned to see Gigi half slumped against Camille, her face gone ashy. Camille stumbled under the weight of her, crying out again, "Mum?"

Gigi did not look up, her face contorted in pain against Camille's shoulder. Camille cried, "Call an ambulance."

refusals

Maybe had been born in this very hospital eleven years ago, on a spring morning. Her first breath had happened here, Camille's hands on her small body, counting her fingers and toes. That had been the beginning. Or maybe the beginning was long before that, before Camille became pregnant, before she was a teenage girl bored by suburbia, before she was a little girl who stood in the surf. Perhaps everything began even before that—before George Collins died, before Gigi first held Camille in her arms, all tiny and furious with the world. Perhaps it all happened long before Maybe's arrival. Their history was long, all the branches entwined, knotty.

And now Maybe stood in the hospital hallway, looking through the tiny window in the door. Gigi was pale and prone on the hospital bed, an oxygen mask on, various wires and tubes attached to her. Maybe tried to follow each of them, tracing them back to the beeping monitors, but lost the thread of them once they snaked under the pale green blanket. A doctor stood beside the bed, gesturing to Gigi. Camille was at the bedside, nodding her head, listening to every word the doctor said. Maybe squinted, trying to read their lips. She had wanted to be in the room as well, but Camille had said no, ushered her out and pushed the door shut with a definitive click. Walter paced the hallway, asked Maybe to get a coffee with him, but she couldn't leave. She needed to stay just there, at the door. She knew it was ridiculous, but she thought if she could keep Gigi in her sight, nothing bad could happen. And so she stood there, watching Gigi take a laboured breath, turning her head to the side.

Her eyes fluttering, closed, exhausted. Mary Quinn had brought Maybe to the hospital, her car trailing behind the ambulance that carried Gigi and Camille, but now she sat farther down the hall. Walter crouched next to her speaking quietly, and patted her knee before coming back down the hall to Maybe's side.

"She's going to be fine," he said, his voice low and reassuring. "They're just running some tests to make sure."

"She had a heart attack."

"Well, yes. And she'll have to take better care of herself. Take some new medications."

"You said it was because of stress."

"Partially, yes."

Walter didn't need to say anything more; Maybe knew what he meant. The summer had been nothing but stress—all the uncertainty that came with Camille, her sudden return, the mystery. Then, the surprise of the book itself. Seeing herself on the pages. Gigi had been in the middle of all of it, holding the tentative balance.

Behind them, nurses busied themselves with other patients, carts full and wheels squealing on the linoleum floor. Machines buzzed, lights flashed, carts stuttered, laden with supplies. But Maybe would not take her eyes off Gigi in the slim hospital bed, so much smaller than she'd ever been in real life. The blue hospital gown overwhelmed her slight form, swallowing her into the largeness of illness. Only when the doctor had come out of the room were Maybe and Walter allowed in. Walter stood at Gigi's bedside, patted her hand in affection.

"Always dramatic," he said with a wink. Gigi smiled up at him before turning to look at Maybe, who was frozen at the end of the bed.

This was not the Gigi she had ever known. An IV ran into her arm, and the oxygen mask had been replaced by slim tubes running to her nostrils. Camille had combed back her hair, a swift attempt at normalcy, but still Gigi had a grey cast to her. She did not look like herself. She wasn't herself. Maybe blinked back tears. Blinked again, hard.

"I'm okay," Gigi said in a new, coarse voice. "Really." She smiled at Maybe with effort, and this made Maybe want to cry again.

"She'll have to take it easy for a while. Take some time off work. But once they've sorted out her medication, she'll be fine," Camille said.

"Right as rain," Walter agreed.

"It'll be no problem, Mum," Camille said. "I can take care of the bills for a while."

Gigi turned to look at Camille and Maybe saw a hardness come into her gaze, the first glimpse of the Gigi she had known all her life resurfacing. The tensions from their argument remained; nothing had been settled, nothing decided between them. "It's not the money I'm worried about."

"We'll sort everything out," Walter said quickly.

"No. If something happens to me, I need to know that Maybe will be looked after."

Camille said, "I told you. I can take care of the bills."

"I'm not talking about bills."

Camille looked away, out the window. Quietly, she said, "I can help out for a bit."

A bit. There was the scent of industrial-strength disinfectants, the slightly stale smell of any number of medications. And below that, skin in need of a wash, or freshly washed, and blankets and cotton gowns and sharply nubbed sheets. Maybe breathed in these scents as she waited for someone to speak. For Gigi to ask for more, or Camille to say, finally, I'll stay. For Maybe, I'll stay. But there was only silence, the beeping of the machines next to Gigi's bed.

"A bit?" Gigi said. "What does that mean?"

"Please, Mum. Not now. Not here."

"I need to know your plans."

Camille sighed and closed her eyes. "I have research to do for my next book. New York. Planned Parenthood. I have the idea to explore—" Camille's voice faltered a little. "It doesn't matter. You know I can't stay."

"You can't stay because of an idea?"

"Frances," Walter cut in, "don't work yourself up. You need to rest and—"

"It's not me I'm worried about. But one day, Camille, one day something *will* happen. And Maybe…" Gigi turned away. There was a window at the far side of the room, and you could see the trees beyond. All the emerald tops of those trees stretching out as if they could go on forever.

Gigi's head was angled toward the window, and so Maybe turned her head that way too, imagined they were both looking at the treeline, wishing they were anywhere but here. The harbour. Lear Street. Home. Not here. Gigi wiped at her eyes, and Walter bent to whisper something to her.

Camille was not looking at Gigi. She was looking at Maybe in a new way, as if it were the first time she'd really, truly seen her. Was she noticing her legs—thinner now from her last growth spurt, her knees knobby in a way Maybe hated, her hair the same colour as Camille's? She was looking at Maybe like she was finally considering the reality, wondering if she could do what Gigi was asking. She looked at Maybe for another long moment, before she turned away. It was the turn that gave her away. Maybe knew what she would say before she said it.

"I can't stay," she repeated.

Camille would not stay because she did not want to stay; she could not be convinced to be domestic, or practical, or predictable. She might have wondered about it for a moment, maybe had even come back thinking she would stay. But Maybe could read Camille's face: she could never do this. She *would* never do this. She wanted to leave, to be someone else.

Could you even understand dedication when you had been gone for almost a decade? Camille would never do anything that other people expected of her. She would be only herself. Untethered. Be anywhere but here. Heat pulsed through Maybe's chest.

Gigi finally turned away from the window and the treeline, but did not turn to Camille. Instead, she looked at Walter and said, "They're keeping me overnight. Can Maybe go home with you?"

"Of course."

"Don't be ridiculous, Mum," Camille said. She was exasperated, as if Gigi were irrational, a nuisance. "Maybe will come home with me."

Gigi turned to Camille. "I never know your plans, Camille." She looked to Maybe at the end of the bed, smiled. It was a sad smile, exhausted. "Well, what would you like to do, Miss Maybe?"

There was no choice to be made. Maybe had to go home with Camille, let Gigi believe that they would be able to continue on without her. It would be a lie, but it was the one thing Maybe could give Gigi now. She'd go home with Camille, eat dinner in front of the TV, crawl into bed and count the hours until she could return to Victoria General and Gigi. She would hate every moment of it. But she would eat overcooked chicken and let Camille scroll through the channels, bored. She would do this for Gigi. When she returned to the hospital, she'd stand at the door, and hold her hand to the glass, watching Gigi sleep. She'd watch to convince herself that Gigi was fine, would continue to be fine, and would come home.

"I'll go home," she said.

❖

Gigi came home with a new prescription, orders to take time off work, limit her stress levels, to rest. Rest. Gigi repeated this to them in Walter's car on the way back to Lear Street, and snorted. "Limit my stress," she said, glancing at Camille in the rear-view mirror. "Rest!" Camille had her hand out the open window, twisting her wrist in the wind. Maybe pushed the hair off her face and watched as Victoria rushed past them. They moved away from the city, skirting the water and the sailboats dotting the lean lines of blue, until the view outside the car turned to bunches of leafy trees. Maybe's anxiety welled up, the closer they came to Lear Street. Gigi was tired, said she wanted to take a nap once they were home, and this highlighted the change in her since that morning in Mary Quinn's backyard. The heart attack had winded her, made her more fragile than Maybe had ever imagined she could be. Leaving Victoria General, Gigi had grasped Walter's arm, let him open the door for her, sat tentatively in the passenger seat. She breathed heavily as she leaned back against the headrest.

One day, something will happen. And then what? Maybe could not imagine what that future would look like. Camille would be gone—there was a long list of cities she might visit, crossing the continent and recrossing again, each location a new reason to stay away. She might return sporadically to see Maybe—mostly out of guilt, trying to lighten that guilt, the way worrying a loose tooth gave equal measures of pleasure and pain.

And where did that leave Maybe? Nowhere.

Robin had dropped off a casserole, and once they returned to the cottage, Walter suggested they heat it up for an early dinner. But Gigi again said that she wanted to lie down, so Camille busied herself with turning on the oven, wiping down the already-clean countertops instead.

For a moment, Gigi stood still, Walter holding her arm, and Maybe thought Camille would not do it, would not cross the room, help Gigi down the hall and ease her into bed. Play the role of the dutiful daughter. But Camille finally put down the blue bowl she was holding and crossed the room to take Gigi's arm. "Come on, then."

Maybe watched the two of them walk slowly down the hall, Camille straight and stiff. They disappeared into Gigi's bedroom, and after a moment the light clicked on, and Maybe heard them talking quietly.

Walter opened the fridge and took out a bottle of wine, searched the kitchen cupboard for the corkscrew.

"She's asking for you," Camille said. She was standing beside Maybe. "Take her some water and her pills."

Maybe filled a glass of water and picked up the yellow bottle of pills from the counter. Gigi was propped up by pillows in bed. She patted the worn quilt beside her. "Sit," she said. Maybe put the water and pills on the bedside table, and then sat cautiously, careful not to put any pressure on Gigi. Gigi said, "I won't break. I just need rest." She took Maybe's hand.

They sat quietly for a while, and Maybe listened to the sounds of Camille making work for herself in the kitchen, and Walter flicking through channels on the TV. He stopped on a news channel and the steady drone of the newscaster's voice filled the room.

"I'll be fine," Gigi said quietly. "*We'll* be fine."

Maybe nodded, but felt her eyes start to fill. She blinked the tears back quickly. In the low light of the bedroom, Gigi fell asleep, her eyes flitting until finally her breathing turned even and her mouth slackened. Her grip on Maybe's hand loosened. Maybe wanted to curl up next to Gigi as she had as a child, let herself drift into a dreamless sleep; she didn't want to go back to the kitchen, set the table and pretend like everything was fine. Nothing was fine. Gigi had her heart attack and the world spun wildly on its axis. Soon enough, Camille would be gone, and their lives would return to their normal routines. Would Maybe feel relief when Camille finally left? Would she wish she had said something else, done something else? She didn't know.

Maybe tugged the blanket up to cover Gigi's shoulders. Gigi would sleep, and then when she woke they would eat, each watching her for signs of fatigue or rising blood pressure, insisting that she rest more. From now on, they'd forever be watching, waiting.

Walter called Maybe's name softly, and she knew she had to go down the hall and face a long afternoon, the three of them watching the clock, half listening to one another's stories. Gigi continued to sleep, and Maybe put her hand to her cheek lightly. Her skin was cool, feathery.

Walter called her again, and she rose from the bed slowly. He had switched off the TV in favour of the record player, and Louis Armstrong cried out about missing New Orleans. She was already missing Gigi, and she was only asleep in her bedroom. What would happen when it was more than that?

They went outside into the late summer sun. Walter read the paper at the table. Mary Quinn arrived, and she and Camille opened two long-necked beers. There were crackers and cheese on a plate, and Maybe picked at a cracker. They all spoke quietly.

Camille laughed at something Mary had said, and Mary looked up to Maybe as she leaned back against her chair. She smiled, and Maybe smiled back. Everything felt wrong without Gigi out there with them.

Maybe looked at Camille—her long legs stretched out in front of her, neatly crossed at the ankles—and she felt her anger bubble up. Everything had started with Camille's book, and this new book would surely break them all. Had already broken them. Gigi in the hospital bed, Gigi so pale. Maybe sat next to Walter and listened to Camille and Mary laugh on the grass. She closed her eyes, gripped her chair. Nina Simone was now singing about being misunderstood in the background, and Maybe imagined Gigi sleeping soundly down the hall. Dreaming of those years before, when everything had been possible still, when the future was not already written.

4:21 a.m.

Nights were longer, even, than the days. Gigi brushed away help, and instead tottered down the hall on her own. And Maybe stared at the ceiling, counting the hours until everyone would be sleeping. When it would be safe. She heard Gigi come down the hall to her own bedroom slowly, her feet shuffling on the floor. Maybe waited, then waited some more, wanting to make sure that Gigi would be deeply asleep.

Of course, Camille was gone again. She might be swimming. She might be with Mary Quinn. She could be anywhere. Maybe felt her way across the room to where she had left her T-shirt and shorts and slipped them on silently. She eased the door open, and when she heard nothing, not the slightest suggestion that anyone else was in the house, she crept into the hallway. Camille's door was open a crack, her bedside lamp glowing.

Since Gigi's heart attack, Camille had been even more sporadic. She exited the house silently, at odd hours, never murmuring a word. And so, now Maybe slid into Camille's empty room—bed unmade, nightgown pooled on the floor, tangled necklaces and bracelets spread across the desk. She touched all these things as if they could change her mind about what she was going to do. But the jewellery held nothing, not even the leftover warmth of Camille's skin. They were just objects, not talismans. She looked at Camille's clock: 4:21 a.m. Four a.m. and still Camille's bed was untouched. Four a.m. and Camille was gone. Camille would always be gone.

Maybe crossed the room to the nightstand, where Camille kept her work. It was strewn with pens and loose paper, a couple of paperbacks stacked up. And beside that were three of Camille's yellow notepads, secured together with a bright red ribbon. Maybe recognized the words from the page on top; it was the first line: *Nine years later, I've come back.* Above that, the title scrawled in block letters. *The Return.* Camille said that she came back for Maybe, to show her what the options were for her as a young woman in these times. Camille said that she was needed, necessary, a "touchstone" of the larger world for Maybe. Maybe had bristled. Camille had reinvented herself on the page and would make everyone believe it, but Maybe knew the truth: Camille was not a woman seeking liberation. She was seeking fame, admiration, and this was her way to do it. She had revealed all their most private stories, twisting them to suit her own story. Women bought her book and thought Camille had revealed some great, universal truth. They read her words greedily, waiting for the moment when they might have an epiphany and see their own lives with clarity. They saw her as a representative of this new movement, but she was not. Maybe's chest burned just thinking about it. She held the stack of notepads to her chest, paused for a moment before she left Camille's room.

The key was where it always was, there in the ceramic bowl. The coldness of it reassured her. It made her believe what she planned to do was right. Necessary. She slipped it into her pocket and slid silently out of the house into the earliest beginnings of dawn.

dawn

Robin was woken by banging on her door and she immediately thought, Aidan. She sat bolt upright in bed, preparing herself for how she would explain to Alan, what she would tell Phoebe, but when she looked down on the front step from her bedroom window, instead she saw Gigi Collins and Walter Keane.

Alan slept on, snoring lightly, and she slipped on her robe as she went downstairs. A third knocking came as she opened the front door. "Gigi, what is it?" she asked when she saw their faces, worried and grey. "What's happened?"

Gigi was drawn, and it was Walter, instead, who spoke. "Is Phoebe here? We can't find Maybe, she's not in her bed, and—"

Robin did not hear the end of his sentence. She was halfway up the stairs, blind panic sweeping over her, by the time she was able to think at all. What if Maybe had told Phoebe about Aidan? What if they had run away together, both of them angry at their flawed mothers? She pushed Phoebe's door open wide, banging it against the wall, and the purest swell of relief flooded her as she saw her daughter, rubbing her eyes from being so rudely awakened, still in her bed, still safe.

"Muuuum," Phoebe whined. "What are you doing?"

Robin sat on the edge of the bed. "Phoebe. Listen to me. Maybe has gone missing. Do you know anything about this? Do you know where she might be?"

Phoebe sat up slowly, numbly taking in what Robin was saying, and finally shook her head. "No," she said. "I don't know anything."

The search party was formed quickly. Alan, Robin and Phoebe were first out onto the front lawn, and Robin touched Gigi's arm, saying, "She probably just got up early. Forgot to leave a note."

Gigi nodded, but Robin could tell from the strict, straight lines of her face that she did not believe this. Gigi was still weak from the heart attack, and this new development made her appear even weaker. Robin took her arm. Alan and Walter said they would get Aidan and Mary Quinn, and they would all find Maybe. Phoebe sat on the grass, plucking at blade after blade, and Gigi leaned in close to Robin and whispered, "Camille's gone too. I—I don't know what to think."

Robin's mind raced, wondering why Camille would take Maybe away in the middle of the night, but knowing that even this scenario would be better than the others that flooded her brain. If she was with Camille, she would be safe, she could be found; Camille was her mother, after all. If something more sinister had happened— had Camille ever spoken about old lovers? Anyone angry with her? They had all heard the news reports about child abductions, seen the faces staring back from milk cartons, and worse—what would they do? How would they go to sleep tonight and wake up tomorrow, not knowing where Maybe was? Robin tried to push the thoughts from her head, and held Phoebe's hand tighter.

They stood in silence until Walter and Alan returned, saying that they should start searching, that Aidan was getting Mary Quinn. Robin felt relief at another moment without having to see Aidan—they had not yet crossed paths, and Robin did not know if she should expect sorrow or anger or, the worst, a shining indifference. They had left things so unfinished. She thought about how much time Camille had been spending with Mary, wondered if she would know more than any of them about what had happened. Camille might have confided in her. They decided to split up, Robin and Gigi and Phoebe taking the "old side" and the men taking the "new side." They would keep searching until there was nowhere left to search. And then they would search again. Farther and farther, as far as they needed to go.

"Camille!" Gigi had stopped in the middle of the road, looking at Camille and Mary Quinn, who were walking quickly toward them.

Aidan was jogging up behind them, and Robin's heart skittered in her chest. Camille was holding her gold sandals in her hand. Walter put his hand out to Gigi, cautioned her to move slowly, to remember her heart. "Where in the hell have you been? Maybe's missing!"

Camille smoothed her hair, looked quickly at Mary, and Robin caught it: it was the same way Aidan had once looked at her, the same pleading in her eyes. "I was at Mary's," Camille said softly. "I was—"

Mary Quinn opened her mouth to say something, but Camille touched her shoulder, gently, and then they all saw it, what should have been plain for the last months but no one had recognized, no one had expected. Robin thought, They're in love, and then watched as Gigi came to the same conclusion, or some version of it, and looked at Camille in a way Robin had never seen before. Camille flushed under her mother's gaze.

Gigi did not look away, and Walter held his hand out, touched her arm lightly.

"Smoke."

Robin twisted her head in Aidan's direction. He was looking up, above all their heads, and he said it again, urgently: "Smoke!"

There was black smoke coming up from the hemlocks and pines at the end of the street. Once they saw it, it seemed impossible that they had not noticed it right away. Black smoke. The crackle of wood burning. It was colouring the sky around it in a haze.

"That's the Eames house," Walter said, already starting to jog toward it. "The house is on fire."

drafts

The fire was like nothing Robin had ever seen before. How do you describe the particular light of someone's past burning? In the hazy morning, the fire burned orange—hard against the grey sky—and it was less romantic than Robin had imagined it might be. It was only destructive, demanding, pulling the Eames house apart, plank by plank.

Aidan was the first to rush into the Eames yard, sprinting across the grass. Alan pushed Robin and Phoebe into the back lane, and then followed Aidan. The fire was busy snaking through the back section of the house facing the garden. Mrs. Eames's sitting room and kitchen, the last reminders of Stanley Eames and his once-strong hands, were now turning to char. Robin huddled at the garden gate with her arm around Phoebe as Aidan dragged a garden hose from the detached garage and sprayed the back addition. There was no hesitation in his movements, no hysterics, only the quick uncoiling of the hose across the lawn, and the water's arc reaching some of the flames. But the fire was persistent, burrowing into the house. Aidan held his other hand up to shield his eyes from the smoke that choked out of the house, and continued to douse the flames.

Alan and Walter hoisted heavy pails, heaving more water on the fire. Robin realized the fire was larger than she'd imagined at first, already eating through the house. It was disorienting, the whole house alight. The flames were raging against the onslaught of water, the air turning ashy. But the damage was already done: the house had been chewed through, leaving a gaping black maw. She held a hand up, instinctively, over Phoebe's eyes, as if it were that easy to protect her.

"Bloody vandals," Gigi said from behind Robin. Robin had nearly forgotten about Gigi and Camille in the lane as well, watching the flames. Mary Quinn had sprinted back down the street to call the fire department, and so Camille tried to help Gigi, taking her elbow to steady her, but Gigi pulled away. Instead, she took Robin's hand, and they stood together, watching Evelyn Eames's things burn away, as if they'd never been there at all. Her table. The place where she'd made her tea, read her mail. Hoping still for a word from Stanley. Was it this easy to erase a life? Robin knew not everything could burn; some things only smouldered, leaving scars.

They watched the fire surge, flailing against the inevitable. The men coughed as they continued to angle the hoses, dump bucket after bucket of water. Sirens punctured the early-morning calm; Walter, Alan and Aidan continued with their efforts at the blackened back of the house, trying to prevent the inevitable end.

"Is Maybe in there?" Phoebe asked tearily, and Robin and Gigi looked quickly at one another. Maybe. She was still missing.

Gigi's eyes looked from the house to Robin, quick with panic. "She couldn't—she wouldn't—"

They turned their backs to the fire, and resumed their search.

Robin and Phoebe ran toward the beach, instinctually believing this is where she would go. Mary Quinn and Camille helped Gigi as they made their way into yards, Gigi calling, "Maybe!" in such a way that Robin knew her desperation to find her, to be certain that she was not in the fiery house.

The beach was strangely abandoned, as if they were really the last people in the world. Gulls cried their lonesome cries, and they both shouted, *Maybe!* over the noise of the ocean. Robin squinted out into the sea, praying she wouldn't see a small, floating body. She squinted, saw the swells of waves, but nothing more. No small, pale head. Breathed out, relieved. No starfished body.

"She's not here?"

Robin hadn't realized that Camille had followed behind them. But now, here she was staring out at the sea. Robin wanted to shake her, slap her, but instead she calmly said, "She's disappeared. And it's because of you."

Camille opened her mouth to say something, but then Phoebe cried out, "Maybe!"

Phoebe was pointing to the far end of the beach where Maybe was on one of the driftwood logs, as if she were asleep. Robin's heart knocked in her chest. Had the ocean washed Maybe ashore?

Phoebe started to run across the beach, and Robin raced ahead of her, sand coming up sharply against her calves. She pushed past Phoebe, her only thought that her daughter could not be the one to find Maybe dead.

Robin kneeled next to the log. Maybe was so still, she put her hand on her chest to see if she was breathing, as she had done when Phoebe was first born. With the touch of Robin's hand, Maybe opened her eyes. Robin collapsed against her, bundling her into her arms.

"Maybe, thank God. We've been so worried—"

"Is it gone? Is it burned down?"

Robin held Maybe at arm's length, trying to read her too-calm expression. "Did you—?"

"Is she okay?" Camille appeared at Robin's side, looking down at them.

"Maybe! Jesus, what are you doing here?" Gigi was flushed, breathing heavily, with Mary Quinn next to her. Walking through the yards on Lear Street had exhausted Gigi; she should have been at home, letting her body catch up. But here she was in the early-morning light, looking at her granddaughter pooled on a log, as a house burned down behind them. Robin moved aside, letting Gigi move next to Maybe.

"Maybe?" Gigi asked again, bending slowly, painfully, to sit beside her on the log.

Maybe stared up at the sky. Silent. Phoebe took a step forward, but Robin held her back. They were only bystanders; this was not their moment.

Gigi said, more gently now, "Maybe dear, what are you doing here? We've been so worried."

Maybe looked at Gigi, finally, but her eyes were flat. She lifted her arm slowly, as if resigned to the fact that she had to make this gesture, that they had not yet put the pieces together yet. She pointed up Lear Street.

"The fire? It's okay, it hasn't spread. The fire department is there."

Maybe still didn't move. Her legs were streaked with sand. She continued to stare down Lear Street, and Robin followed her gaze. Was she imagining the cracked window, where Evelyn Eames had once sat? The firefighters slowly putting the fire out? Or the blackness itself, the way the fire had chewed its way out, left nothing but ruin?

Is it gone? Is it burned down?

The fire had eaten through the house, from the kitchen, or the sitting room that Stanley Eames had built, timber by timber. The fire had not been set by bored teenagers. No. The fire had been set by someone who knew the house.

Camille was silent, standing slightly apart, watching Maybe and Gigi. Gigi took Maybe's hand, rubbing it. "You're so cold."

"Maybe?" Robin said quietly, and Maybe looked to her. Her eyes were damp and her face had softened into an approximation of what she'd looked like when she was small. Robin repeated, "Maybe?" It was the same tone she would have used to ask Phoebe about something she wasn't sure she wanted to hear the answer to. A tone Maybe had often heard in the last handful of years.

Maybe sighed, her voice catching. "I didn't mean to."

Camille stepped forward slightly, and they all crowded around Maybe, forming a half-circle. Robin knew what Maybe was going to say, and wished there was some way she could say anything else.

"I didn't mean to," Maybe said again.

"Mean to do what?" Gigi pressed. She leaned closer to Maybe, more slowly now, since the heart attack.

"The fire."

"The fire?" Camille's voice was incredulous when she finally spoke. "What are you talking about?"

Maybe turned sharply to face Camille. "I started the fire."

"This must have been a mistake. What were you trying to do?" Gigi said.

"I was burning it."

"The house?" Phoebe asked, and Robin thought, Be quiet. Be quiet. Be quiet. She squeezed Phoebe's arm. Phoebe's cheeks reddened. Mary Quinn stood motionless beside them.

The sound of the firefighters grew stronger, the whoosh of water, their calls to one another, punctuating their strange conversation. Camille glanced toward the road, and Gigi put her hands on Maybe's face, holding her still. "Maybe," Gigi said. "Tell me."

They waited. The morning creaked and groaned, the house splintering behind them. The fire department would demand answers that they did not have yet. All they had was Maybe with her sandy feet, her hair smelling like smoke.

"I was burning it in the sink. I had to do it there, or you would have stopped me. I was almost done, and I don't know what happened—I dropped it, or I hesitated, I don't know—and one of the pages got away from me. It happened so fast—"

"Pages?" Camille stepped closer to Maybe. "What pages?"

"Your book. I was burning it." Maybe's voice was so even, so calm and practised, that Robin had a flash of her in her teen years, or even further in the future as a woman somewhere else, responding tiredly to a question she did not want to answer. The summer had changed her, aged her in ways Robin did not yet understand. Maybe said *I was burning it* as if this were the most logical, practical reason for Evelyn Eames's house to be smouldering. Robin ached for the Maybe that she knew, the little girl she'd watched grow.

"You were burning—"

"Yes. I was burning it. It was a lie. You lied about all of us, about everything. You lied about yourself. All you do is lie."

Everything else faded away. Everyone but Camille and Maybe was merely background, the slightly out-of-focus elements in a photograph. The sirens muted. The men with the hoses quieted. Even Gigi, caught between her daughter and granddaughter, became a blur to Robin. It was just Camille and Maybe on the beach, in sharp focus.

"You burned it?" Camille's words were slow and precise, as if speaking them aloud were what made this true and not the action itself.

"Yes."

"It's gone?"

"Yes."

There was silence. Silence as Camille understood what this ultimately meant, what burning meant, the loss. Camille did not yell or cry, but raised her hand slowly and then slapped Maybe hard across the face.

"Camille!" Gigi's fury spooled away from her. "Goddammit, she is a child."

Camille said, "She burned it! The book is gone. Gone. Just like that."

Maybe held her hand to her cheek, and tears pooled in her eyes. "I burned it because it wasn't true. Because you only came back to write it. You want to be famous. You don't care about us. You don't want to be here. It was all lies." Maybe started crying.

"I'm a writer, Maybe. Yes, I want people to read my book."

"You're going to leave. You wouldn't even stay after—" Maybe looked to Gigi, and then Robin looked as well. Robin longed to reach out and take Maybe in her arms, but she knew she could not do that. Still, her arms ached for her. Gigi had turned paler, as Maybe's words hung in the air. Even after Gigi's heart attack. Camille was going to leave, had always planned to leave, and even Gigi's heart would not change this. Even Maybe burning her book would not change this.

Camille looked to Mary Quinn, and Mary looked evenly back at her. Mary didn't move, did not offer solace or apology; she simply looked back at Camille. Robin could see that something had broken between them.

"It was about coming here. Coming back. It was about trying," Camille said.

Beyond them, the fire still burned. Water arced in the air, turning what was left waterlogged. Ashed. Camille touched her hair, looked down the street toward the men who continued to spray the house. Alan, Aidan and Walter were angling toward the beach and their strange group.

Camille turned away and said, "But it's gone now. It doesn't matter what I said. Nothing matters—the truth, a lie, what we once believed." Camille looked at Gigi, whose disdain was plain for them all to see. She had returned, but would leave again. She'd become a memory. She would not stay for either of them. Camille stood barefoot on the beach, watching her daughter's descent, and she did not know how to cross that gulf, how to be Maybe's mother.

Gigi said, "So. You're going then?"

"I tried. I can't stay here. I don't *feel* like a mother, can't you see that?" She looked quickly at Maybe, then back to Gigi. More quietly, "Don't I deserve to be happy? Happy now, not sometime in the future, when it's too late?"

It was simple: Camille thought she deserved happiness, and happiness was not staying on Lear Street, taking care of her mother and her daughter. It was not packing lunches or sweeping floors. It was not bathing Gigi when she could no longer do it herself. It was not taking Maybe to school, listening to her complaints as she grew. Camille did not feel like Maybe's mother, and never would. She was someone else. Her future was elsewhere. It was everything else.

Camille repeated softly, "Don't I?"

The men walked across the sand in a slow procession. Robin looked at Aidan, his shirt dotted with sweat or water. Could she make that kind of choice? Could she make her happiness a priority, the only priority? She'd wake to his warmth beside her, his lips on her spine. He caught her eye, and she thought for a moment that she could do it. She could make this choice. His hands on her, twisting into her hair. The scent of his skin under his T-shirt, still warm from sleep. She could. All the years ahead with Aidan. She could decide on happiness.

Phoebe reached up to take Robin's hand, a leftover, shy gesture from childhood, and Robin pulled her close against her. Phoebe's hair was still mussed from her bed sheets. She had that specific scent of childhood, sun-warmed skin and freshly laundered sheets, the hint of chlorine behind it. Robin held Phoebe to her side and breathed in her pureness, the goodness. It had been only a matter of moments since they'd found the fire, yet it seemed like so much more. Time had slowed as Robin had watched Maybe's heart break over and over. Aidan, Alan and Walter stood stiffly off to the side, unaware of what they were walking in on, and Mary Quinn said, "Camille. There's nothing you can do here now. We should go."

Camille was staring down Lear Street, toward the house and the fire. Robin knew she was thinking about her book in there, nothing but ashes now, and her face was tight with sorrow. Sorrow for the book, or sorrow for Maybe, Robin did not know.

Maybe said, "You should have never come back. It would have been easier if you'd died."

Robin gasped. The air snapped with Maybe's words. *Easier if you'd died.*

Camille looked at Maybe, and Robin thought she saw the sorrow there, but then Camille lowered her eyes, and slowly walked across the sand to Mary. She looked ahead at the smoking house. Robin could see in the tilt of Camille's head that she had made a choice.

Maybe collapsed against Gigi, the tears finally coming hard, running hot and insistent down her cheeks. Her face was transformed, turned back into Maybe as a small child. The hurt was raw. Camille turned around, took a step back toward them, as if she meant to go to Maybe, but then stopped. Robin thought, Just go to her, just go to her. She held her breath waiting for Camille to move. It was so simple, just that one step, one touch. It would be something. But Camille looked out toward the sea for a long moment, and then slowly turned around, walking back toward Lear Street. The decision had been made. Camille moved away from them, and Mary Quinn followed her, the two of them becoming smaller and smaller.

Gigi tugged Maybe up, and they leaned against one another, Walter taking Gigi's arm, and they made a slow progression back up Lear Street, where the firemen still worked to ensure the fire was truly out. Walter would be the one to talk to them later, ready to explain the age of the house, the wiring, the way the house had been abandoned since Evelyn Eames's death.

They walked down Lear Street the way they'd come, the air sooty, eyes clouded by smoke. Maybe and Gigi and Walter turned into Gigi's yard. Camille and Mary Quinn had already disappeared, now only shadows.

❖

None of them moved, not right away. They were stunned, stuck together there on the beach.

Died. Aidan moved a little closer, looking at Robin, and she wanted to reach out, touch him one last time. She could not explain to him what Maybe's words meant. The slap of them. She could not bear it if Phoebe spoke those words to her: the pain was too pure, too acute. She had the distinct memory of pressing her body against Aidan's, the pressure that was familiar, comforting. She could recall the way he breathed against her, the way his lips felt at her neck. Had this been the only moment she'd been happy? Had this act, this refusal of her safe life, been enough? Robin closed her eyes to keep the memory clear. She would keep those memories for herself. She had to.

Easier if you'd died. When Robin opened her eyes, Aidan had stepped back, away from her, and Robin knew she'd never leave Alan. She would never be able to give Phoebe up.

Phoebe threaded her fingers with Robin's, and said, "Mum?"

She faltered, but then smiled down at Phoebe, who curved against her, as she had as a small child, her arms around her hips. That warmth. That pure, even love. "Let's go home," Robin said.

Alan said, "What a morning," and put his hand on Robin's back. They started back down Lear Street, Aidan just a little behind them, careful to keep his distance. She wanted to turn around and look at him, let him see her sorrow too, but she knew she could not. She smiled (could Alan see how false it was?) and walked with him and Phoebe toward their yard. The grass needed to be cut. The trim of the house could use a touch-up. Robin slowed, looking at the house. She could see every crack, everything that needed to be fixed. Alan stopped with Phoebe in the middle of the driveway, waiting.

Alan said, "Robin?"

Robin turned away from him, looking back down Lear Street. She had to do something. There had to be a gesture that would explain it all. As Aidan stepped into his own yard, he looked at her. She wanted her face to reveal everything, but she knew all he would see was Alan waiting for her, leading her back home.

Robin again allowing herself to be led. And so she did not go up the driveway but instead stood there on the lawn, and looked back at Aidan, under the boughs of the trees. He would see her there, fixed in place on the lawn, and he would know what this meant. He would see her. Really see her.

Aidan smiled a slow, sad smile, and Robin felt her eyes well. After a moment, grudgingly, Aidan turned away from her and went up the drive to his own house, alone. When Robin finally turned around again, Alan was there, watching her. The look on his face, just a flash that Robin caught, told her he understood what he had just seen. Would it be enough for Robin that it had happened, that she'd let herself have this one, pure pleasure in life? Would it be enough to hold on to that memory? She wasn't sure.

What she did know was that she would have to allow Alan his anger at her betrayal; she would have to hold all of that in her hands, cupping it like too much water. It would not be easy. It would not be fair. But then Robin glanced at Phoebe's small, tired face beside her father, and she knew she would do it. She smiled at her daughter.

Maybe had lit the fire, had watched it all burn. It was brave. Braver than any of them. Fire was a brand. And what it marked, was marked forever.

ghosts and their stories

The house felt bigger, somehow, with Camille's things in it. More alive. Mary hadn't realized how sparsely she had been living—the knives didn't rattle against one another in the cutlery drawer, she never lost a sock or a hairpin, the coat closet had been impossibly sad with its three limp jackets—until Camille arrived and filled it up. Drawers of amber earrings and turquoise beads, another of silver bangles and pink lip glosses, layer upon layer of silky, sheer underwear, strands of her hair cluttering the bed sheets, the drain. All the things seemed to multiply, Mary finding new items every day. Camille's new yellow notepads were in every room, balanced on tables with cold cups of tea or wineglasses smeared with lip prints.

"Are you going to write it again?" Mary asked one day, feigning a casual tone, as she stood before her painting, her brush muddy with whites and blacks and greys. Once Camille had moved her things in—unceremoniously, dragging her suitcase down Lear Street after the fire, arriving wordlessly at Mary's door—Mary had worried about what she'd say about the painting of Maybe. But Camille had only looked at the painting when she walked past it in the studio. She had regarded it carefully, but had not asked about it. In the yard behind her now, Camille lazed in one of the Adirondack chairs, a floppy hat over her eyes. Mary watched her for any response. They hadn't talked about the book much; there were so few words left.

"No," Camille said from under the hat.

"You're not?"

"No." The hat moved a little as Camille readjusted it, moved it back a bit to look at Mary beside the painting. "No point."

"Why not?"

She shrugged. "I've realized it wasn't the story I really wanted to tell. I'll write something else."

Mary nodded, though she did not understand at all. All those months, all those words crammed onto each page, and then they were nothing at all; they were gone, vanished, erased so completely they might never have been. She wondered if Maybe's words at the beach—*It would have been easier if you'd died*—had had an effect on Camille. When Mary heard Maybe utter them, she'd felt them like cold air in her lungs. Perhaps they'd cut Camille to the quick, even though she'd never uttered a word about them.

"What will you write, then?" Mary asked. She leaned closer to the painting. She'd wanted to bring it outside to finish it. If she could get this right, it might be done. This was what had been missing. So simple, but necessary. It might finally, finally be finished.

Camille sat up in her chair and said without hesitation, "Fiction."

Mary turned away to smile. Fiction. Perhaps what she had been writing all along. Camille would go to New York, or somewhere else, anywhere else, and she'd continue reinventing herself. She'd disappear from Mary's house, from her bed, as quickly as she'd arrived. Mary's realization of this was surprisingly unhurtful.

Mary put her brush on the edge of the painting, the very bottom right hand corner, and drew upwards, a faint, snaking line of grey. In the foreground, there was Maybe, her back to the viewer now, her hair in the breeze, her hands loose at her side. And there was the sea, and there was the beach where she had stood crying, where she'd swum late at night. There were footprints behind her, leading away. Were they Maybe's footsteps? Or were they Camille's? Mary realized it didn't matter. She added more black to her palette, swirled. The smallest touch of white. There. The perfect shade of grey. She retraced the snaking line up higher, let it dissipate into the sea air, just as smoke was apt to do.

❖

Camille did not say goodbye. Really, what else was there to say? Maybe had burned the book, and Camille had walked away from her on the beach. They did not need words. When Maybe pushed open the door to Camille's room, all her things were gone. Gone were the yellow notepads. Gone were the amber beads, the turquoise rings, the heavy silver bangles. The floor was tidy without her suitcase and filmy nightgowns, her embroidered blouses spilling onto the floor. No golden sandals. No damp footprints smelling of the sea. The bed was neatly made, the desk bare. When Maybe crouched down to look under the bed, there was one solitary amber bead. She took it in her hand, watching it roll on her palm. Maybe put it in her pocket; she'd left so little. Camille had left a window open, so that even her scent was gone.

After the fire, Camille had stayed at Mary Quinn's for a while before she actually left Lear Street. She did not talk to Gigi. Had not spoken to Maybe. Maybe assumed it was because of what she'd said, but she could not be sure it would have made any difference if she'd said something else. *Stay. I love you. Please.* Or even if she'd said nothing at all. There were gradations in the spectrum of love. Camille was at one end, just a spot in the distance, but that could be tolerable. Maybe could learn to tolerate Camille's absence the way people tolerated something that had once been painful. It was like an aching bone that had once been broken, never healed quite properly. Pain lessened; in time, the summer with Camille would be nothing but a memory. Hazy. It could have happened. It might have. And that would have to be enough.

Gigi didn't ask Maybe about what she'd said at the beach. They didn't talk about the book, or the now-charred Eames's house. And so they let the fire fade; neither of them speaking of it, they let it burn itself out. The fire department had deemed it accidental, and there had been an unspoken agreement among the neighbours to pretend that it had never happened.

Gigi might not ask about the fire, but Maybe thought about it every night when she closed her eyes. How it had felt to hold Camille's pages in her hand, to touch the match to the corner and let it burn. The whoosh of flame to paper. They shrivelled before turning to nothing but black char. They disappeared so easily.

It was only when she got down to the last handful of pages that Maybe had felt remorse coil up within her. The words had burned away as if they had never existed, and with those last pages in her hand—the corners already lit, the flames starting to snake up—Maybe felt cold remorse. She panicked, intending to reach the faucet and douse the pages with water. She could salvage these; she could leave the soggy pages for Camille.

Maybe slipped, twisted her arm the wrong way, and the pages fell to the floor, the flames quick to spread, to claw their way through Stanley Eames's addition. They were quick, dedicated, in spite of Maybe's attempts to stomp out the flames.

Or perhaps she let the pages drop. Perhaps she knew that Evelyn Eames would forgive her for this, just to be rid of those words. Perhaps she needed to do this, to let her hopes for Camille go.

Maybe saw the fire every time she shut her eyes. She saw the burning pages, the words turning to ash. What she did not see was Camille's face. Not her face at the beach in darkness. Not her face on the beach, backlit, that golden glow from childhood that Maybe had held onto. Those memories had all been burned away.

Gigi grew stronger, recovering slowly, steadily. She still could not go back to work, but Camille sent cheques that Maybe took to the bank. She no longer looked at Camille's signature, the looping C at the bottom. Maybe and Gigi took walks up and down Lear Street as the doctor had ordered, slowly at first, until Gigi could walk without help, the colour coming back to her face. She said, "I'll live to be a hundred, you'll see," and Maybe chose to believe her.

Camille wrote letters, and Maybe watched Gigi tuck them away to read later, in private, as if the letters themselves would further hurt Maybe. The last one postmarked from New York, Maybe saw, understanding that Camille had finally made good on her promise and had actually gone. She imagined that Gigi tore them into small pieces after she read them, pressing them into the garbage bin between coffee grinds and orange peels.

August disappeared as if it had never been there at all, and instead there was the burrowing down for autumn. Cars tucked away, quietly humming, doors shut tight against the unfurling of fall. The air was cooler. The sun was thin. Maybe closed her eyes when she walked Lear Street with Gigi, and imagined how someone else might describe it. How they might miss the statues in the garden, the cut-out flower on the back gate. Or the path to the Hollises' backyard, lined with stones. Mrs. Eames's leafy trees, under which Stanley Eames had once stood. The rose bushes in Walter's yard. The way Lear Street ran straight to the ocean, as if everything was destined to go that way as well, its waters and all the places beyond, so many options. No one else would ever know Lear Street the way Maybe did.

When school started again, Maybe chose her outfits the night before and packed her bag carefully. She prepared for the questions about her summer, and created answers in her mind. There were so many versions, depending on what she wanted them to believe. She could say nothing had happened—she'd swum in the sea, gone to Victoria for the day, listened to a man play a guitar. Or she could say she'd had art lessons with a famous painter. She could say she'd watched a house burn down, taking all the memories with it. Or, she could say she had seen a ghost, briefly. A ghost dressed in white, all golden hair and a face shadowed by the sun behind. A ghost that was more of a memory, as ghosts tended to be. A ghost that had now vanished. A ghost she had let go. That would almost be true. She could tell any story she wanted. Stories, after all, were the easy part.

Acknowledgements

Writing a novel is a long and solitary journey. There are many people who provided laughter, encouragement, insight, feedback, sanity and general goodness along the way.

Thank you to my amazing friends (and book club, wine and gossip members) Allyson Gonzalez, Amy Read, Kristine Waddell, Jennifer Prodanuk, Sara Forte, Tara Mulldoon, Andrea Gross, Erin Byrne, Serina Townsley, Nicole Schroeder and Stacy Ewing—the finest friends (and mothers) I have ever known. Loyalty and fierceness, you have it in spades.

Thank you to my extended family for literally *everything*. You have been my greatest supporters, lifelines when I needed them the most. You know who you are, and you know how deeply thankful I am. I am winking at you in solidarity right now.

Thank you to the incredible Jen Sookfong Lee, trusted first reader and friend, who has gotten me through some very dark moments (Leos, always); Jane Silcott, for writing traditions and talks. Thank you to the University of the Fraser Valley, for providing me with time and space to work. Thank you to my colleagues at UFV, especially Karen Selesky, Rajneesh Dhawan and Jackie Taylor. And thank you to my amazing students, who inspire me, and buoy me with their enthusiasm.

Thank you to my research assistant, Jess Wind, who provided research for another project that somehow also snuck in here. You are incredible.

Some other books that were important to this novel include: *On Lies, Secrets, and Silence* by Adrienne Rich; *The Feminine Mystique* by

Betty Friedan; *The Female Eunuch* by Germaine Greer; *Sexual Politics* by Kate Millett; *As If Women Matter* by Gloria Steinem; *Breaking the Wave,* ed. Kathleen A. Laughlin and Jacqueline L. Castledine; *Collected Poems of Muriel Rukeyser,* ed. Janet Kaufman and Anne Herzog and the poem "Chorus" from *The Game of Boxes* by Catherine Barnett.

Every book I write gets a soundtrack, by way of a show I re-watch for essential background noise. This one gets *The Good Wife,* team Will forever.

Thank you to my agent, Carolyn Swayze, for finding this book the home it needed. Thank you to the wonderful team at Caitlin Press, Vici Johnstone, Michael Despotovic, Demian Pettman, editor John Gould and proofreader Meg Yamamoto for their care and enthusiasm with the novel.

Thank you to my parents, Bob and Lesley MacPherson, for endless, tireless support. Honestly, I cannot thank you enough, but I will continue to try. And thank you to my late grandfather, Tom Rowbottom, who taught me the power of storytelling and humour. I will miss you deeply, and daily.

And finally, mostly, always, thank you to my daughter, Nora. You were the inspiration for this, and so much more. I will continue trying to be the best mummy you could have asked for. To the moon and back. Always. xo